Justin Cartwright

Justin Cartwright was born in South Africa and educated in the US and at Oxford University. His books include *Look At It This Way*, *Interior*, *Masai Dreaming*, *In Every Face I Meet*, which was shortlisted for the Booker Prize, *Leading the Cheers*, which won the Whitbread Book Award for 1998, *The Promise of Happiness*, which was the winner of the 2005 Hawthornden Prize and the *Sunday Times* of South Africa Prize, and most recently *The Song Before It Is Sung*. Justin Cartwright lives in north London with his wife and two sons.

Justin Cartwright

White Lightning

SCEPTRE

Copyright © 2002 by Justin Cartwright

First published in Great Britain in 2002 by Hodder & Stoughton
A division of Hodder Headline

This edition published 2007

The right of Justin Cartwright to be identified as the Author
of the Work has been asserted by him in accordance with the
Copyright, Designs and Patents Act 1988.

A Sceptre paperback

2

A CIP catalogue record for this title is available from the British Library

ISBN 978 0 340 93636 8
ISBN 0 340 93636 3

Typeset in Sabon by Palimpsest Book Production Limited,
Grangemouth, Strilingshire

Printed and bound by
Mackays of Chatham Ltd, Chatham, Kent

Hodder Headline's policy is to use papers that are natural,
renewable and recyclable products and made from wood grown
in sustainable forests. The logging and manufacturing processes
are expected to conform to the environmental regulations
of the country of origin.

Hodder & Stoughton Ltd
A division of Hodder Headline
338 Euston Road
London NW1 3BH

For my dear boys

He knew what that jubilant crowd did not, but could
have learned from books, that the plague bacillus never
dies nor disappears for ever . . .
                                        – Albert Camus, *The Plague*

I

I was waiting for my mother to die. I wasn't waiting with eagerness or curiosity or sadness – she was very old – but with a fullness of heart, as though into that tricky organ a lot of history and deception and regret had flooded. My heart was pumped full with this accumulation of feeling. It wasn't a sense of my own mortality, although you are said to feel you have shuffled up the line as your parents die, shuffled up the line towards the payout window. Or the pit. Or nothingness. A French acquaintance of mine had said to me of death, '*C'est la vide*' and I had laughed in an inappropriate manner thinking he had said, '*C'est la vie*', imagining a little Gallic *jeu de mots*, a bitter-sweet Frenchness, dark tobacco and paper tablecloths. No, I wasn't thinking of my own end, although the arum lilies by the bedside breathed the heavy musk of death. Some flowers are too nearly perfect for their own good, and arum lilies are avatars of perfection. They have veins on them like a man's penis, and this is perhaps a warning of their duplicitousness.

And as I sat by the bedside next to the small shape that barely disturbed the covers I was wondering what had happened to my mother. Once she had been a large woman, with a noble head. Now the head, reddened eyes closed, mouth moving fitfully, seemed to be attached to very little. Her body had dwindled; in the six months since I had seen her last, it had been spirited away. She was asleep so much that I wondered if there wasn't simply a semantic distinction between this state – the little sighs, the leaf tremors, the (imagined) exhalations – and the more profound sleep to come.

Earlier in the day she said to me, 'Don't kiss me, I'm

disgusting.' My heart – my volatile heart – had broken. I kissed her forehead anyway, my tears unseen, feeling the skin so dry that it seemed to me that the life-giving cells had already died, leaving her covered in parchment. She believed that her breath smelled of death, I think, but I caught nothing of that, only the rushing scents of all those forces that were accumulating, the scents of regret and deception.

'I'll be back soon,' I said. 'I'm going for a walk.'

My words fell as softly and silently as petals. I wondered, as I walked out of the wide, linoleum-lined corridors, past the clanking implements and the toothless nurses, if I had really uttered them, or merely intended to say them. The business of death makes these distinctions unimportant.

There was a freshness outside the clinic, a pleasing turbulence in the clouds and agitation among the grasses. Even the arum lilies moved stiffly, like pallbearers. A stream ran through the estate, through a dinky golf course, trimmed down for the oldies, and here in the damp hollows arums stood. The mountains above the estate are known as the Helderberg, clear mountains, but today the mountain tops were intermittently hidden by fretful clouds and then suddenly revealed, with all the pointlessness of a magic show. I hate conjurors and magicians and jugglers.

And I find mountains disturbing. I think of myself as a flat-lander, a plains person, a man for the big vista, although I grew up in the shadow of a mountain. I have contradictory ideas. Women have pointed this out to me, which I have come to understand is the role of women: to locate the magnetic pole in any relationship and steer for it.

I walked out of the gates of the estate and down a farm track that seemed to be heading for the mountains. I strode out, hoping in the turbulence of the air to harness the turbulence of feeling within me. It's a hopeless task, this obligation to try to profit from experience, to make some personal capital out of adversity. Sometimes I think, like Sartre, that I am superfluous. Sometimes I laugh bitterly at the pretensions we nurse, the idea that our lives have meaning and value. But like Sartre, like everybody else, I am trapped within this conundrum: on the one hand I know it's all meaningless, on the other I cannot avoid the consequences of being alive. Only death will dissolve the contradiction, as it is about to for my mother.

I looked back at the estate: touted to the elderly as an exclusive retirement village, it had been so oversold that from here it was higgledy-piggledy, the houses jostling each other for space around the central greensward of the miniaturised golf course.

Now as I walked down the farm road, I entered the past, without seeing the portals. The vines were nearly bare: some wrinkled-scrotum grapes still clung on among the spectacularly lurid but increasingly isolated leaves. I wondered if these were the same vine leaves that the Greeks ate. My mind, overburdened with the onrushing event, was erratic. Every detail of the landscape was familiar to me, and these details seemed to be calling to me on private frequencies although the gist of their message was unclear. I stopped by the track to look at a small colony of ants, busily fetching dried grass which they took below; other ants were excavating to make room for the grass, so producing a pyramid of sand, and I remembered the hours I had spent in the company of ants.

Although I was aware of their diligent, steady natures I sometimes threw them into the pits made by the ant-lion, a creature which operated with loathsome guile. The ants could not escape from these pits and down, just below the sand, the ant-lion waited to seize them with its outsize claws. After a brief struggle, the ant was dragged below. Goodbye ant, steady little fellow with social instincts. The science of studying ants is know as myrmecology, and the father of this science is René-Antoine Ferchault de Réaumur. And as I looked at the ants – old chums – I remembered that Eugène

Marais – a local boy – asked of ants, *What purpose have they served?* And answered himself: *What purpose do you think we have served? None*. We are ants. As a boy I read Sartre and I saw that Sartre and Eugène Marais experienced the same vibe. (Ambivalent word, *vibe*: post-modern in some mouths, embarrassing in others.)

Down this track I saw some whitewashed cottages, with outside ovens built on to the sturdy chimneys, and children – anonymous children – playing with tyres and bits of wire. A clump of canna lilies blazed orange, like a fire in an amateur dramatic production, and turtle doves burbled in their liquid, foolish-virgin, fashion. The children laughed – they jeered – the guinea fowl screamed and the crickets joined in. This pastorale was as familiar to me as the turbine sounds of London where I have lived for so long; where I have expended my essence. Standing at night in my small garden in the great city, I listened to the rumbling, the moaning, the soughing, cut by the sharp notes of police sirens and the vibrato of trains not far away, imagining myself at the centre of the great human enterprise. I saw the city as an accumulation of folly and wisdom and striving and failure; I saw it as art and squalor and nobility and venality. These noises which reached me in my garden were a hymn produced by machinery standing in for humanity. The instruments of human endeavour. I hummed along with the *Fanfare for the Common Man*. I applauded those who placed every weeping brick in place to make the city, and I extended my arms in communion like the early Christian praying figures, the Orantes, in the British Museum.

But now I realised that while I was away, the ants had been busy. This should have come as no surprise. Ants have been at it for aeons. But they have not evolved. They are found trapped in two-million-year-old Baltic amber, exactly the same ants as scuttle the earth today. Ants have a peculiar, purposeful way of walking, something like traditional Japanese women, humble and conscious of their pressing duty. My thoughts were disordered. But on that particular day I made allowances for myself because death was creating advance eddies.

I remembered as a child laying my head on the ground to hear warning of enemies approaching, as Aboriginals were able to do. Then I heard nothing, although I tried to tune up my senses so that I could detect footfalls, even from a mile or so away, and in a related exercise I tried to speak to horses. There was no manual to learn either talent, and willing it did not make it happen. But now I heard clearly the not-so-stealthy approach of death. It sounded to my over-receptive ear like the beating wings of a flock of birds – approaching, naturally.

At the end of the farm track was a gate flanked by white pillars. On one of the pillars was inscribed 'Nooitgedacht' which in my excited state I took to be more than a coincidence because it means 'unexpected' in Dutch. Old Dutch.

A smaller sign, painted on a piece of hardboard and attached to a post, read 'Children's playground and tea'. I walked up the track towards the house which was mostly hidden behind oak trees and an overgrown hedge, except for a glimpse of a tin roof and a modest gable. On the left was the children's playground, some painted seesaws and swings, and a thick knotted rope attached to a huge oak. Some ducks were confined around a small pond, which was crudely made of cement. A peacock, with a grey, colourless tail, stood listlessly near a model locomotive, made of breeze blocks. The mountains behind were suddenly clear, their slopes a green and grey and silver needlepoint, and the crags above were summery, looking like Cézanne's 'Mont Sainte-Victoire', although higher. I have been to Cézanne's house, Le Jas de Bouffan in Aix, and swum in his *bassin*, which is just as it was when he painted it. The painting hangs in the Metropolitan Museum of Art. When I saw it – I wasn't looking for it – it was so recognisable that I expected to see myself in the middle of the *bassin*, striking boldly for the far end, where a romanesque lion stood, guarding a fountain. Beside me, swimming with a sort of frantic small-boy eagerness, would have been my son Matt, seven. He was swimming like an insect, with jerky movements, aware that he was only marginally buoyant. In fact he would have sunk without my occasionally outstretched hand holding his small biceps.

I approached the house through the overgrown hedge. Just as suddenly as they had cleared, the mountains were now disappearing again behind a foaming torrent of cloud, which poured over from the far side, but vanished at a certain altitude, just below the level of the brown cliffs which moments before had set me thinking of Aix-en-Provence. The house was probably once completely thatched; now it had a makeshift tin roof flecked and faded red, the precise colour and texture of certain sea anemones. Only one slope of the roof of an outbuilding was still of thatch, wet and rotten. The steps up were cement, painted red and polished, gleaming in contrast to the mottled roof. The café was in the front room, the *voorkamer*, and two young women stood ready, wearing aprons. The cakes were laid out on a table and each cake was covered with cling film. The tea was poured from a large brown enamel pot into a green cup. Invited to choose a cake – *Wanna naas hoemade kek?* – I pointed at a coffee-coloured cake covered with hundreds and thousands – which, for all I knew, had ceased to exist about the time of the Cuban missile crisis – tiny, multi-coloured balls of something – perhaps sugar or marzipan – which were scattered on the icing.

As I picked up the teacup I dropped it and it broke, neatly into three pieces. I insisted on paying for it as they brought me some more tea, smiling, and wiped the pale, sherry-cask floorboards. They retreated behind the trestle table that held the cakes and a large urn, and whispered. The hundreds and thousands crunched alarmingly under my cosseted but fragile teeth. I wondered if the noise of minute fragmentation was reaching them. They were young, but farm girls still bearing the imprint of the lost peoples. It was a watermark, in their cheeks and eyes, as though their ancestors were giving me a timely lesson in immortality: look, nothing dies for ever.

The room was long, with two huge, floor-length windows, each with thirty-six panes. Apart from the tables and the kitchen chairs there was no furniture, but I knew that in this room there had once been a *riemepiebank*, a sort of settee made of yellow-wood with strips of untreated leather to sit on, and perhaps a large bridal chest and over there a fireplace for the chilly nights of winter, when – like today – the clouds were low and the air was turbulent. I sat there for a while, drinking my tea, crunching the little, lurid pellets, and listening to the whispers, which reached me only as a susurration without words. Above the mountains there was thunder. One of the girls giggled.

I walked back down the track away from the house. I adopted a half run and half walk in the hopes of beating the oncoming rain, but it caught me, icy cold as though it had come from far-off and indifferent regions. The clouds darkened and there was lightning above the mountains, sheet lightning, like the flash of artillery in war movies. The track, which had been so dry, was now awash. The children were huddled in the doorway of a cottage. They waved and jeered as I passed. *Whitey is wet.* I wondered if the ants had a way of stopping their nests against the water.

I showered in my mother's cottage and hurried to the clinic. She lay there, diminished in the hour or so I had been away.

'I'm here, Ma,' I said.

I held her hand which was as light as a leaf. The back of her hand and her arm which lay exposed were covered in brown and purple patches because of the Warfarin.

'I'm here.'

I felt or imagined a faint response in her hand. It was no more than a tremor. Perhaps the advancing Aboriginals would have given themselves away in this fashion, with a

7

barely perceptible vibration. It would be difficult, I could see, for the untrained ear to catch it.

Some moments later she sighed. I can't say it was a sigh of contentment. In fact it was fetched up from the void, a bucket thrown down to unknown depths and filled with an unknown substance, a portion of what was to come. She had had a preview of it, and it filled her with terror. I guessed that what she glimpsed was unknowable and utterly blank, bearing no meaning at all, and that was the horror.

I am working on a corporate film. I have aspired to make serious films about love and pain, films washed with an awareness of the humour and poignancy of existence, but my career has not worked out in the way I had hoped. So now I am listening to the marketing director of a new resort, soon to be built in the Turks and Caicos Islands. He illustrates his briefing with large cards. The first card is blue and written on it is YOU DESERVE IT. The marketing director is Dutch and he speaks English with a slangy, metallic, but only partly justified, confidence: 'We started from a very basic concept, reward. Which leads to empowerment. Take power. You have worked for it, you deserve it. Treat yourself. You are entitled to it. Don't stunt yourself.'

I wonder if he means 'stint'.

'Don't stunt yourself. Go for it. It's yours by rights.'

I smile encouragement. I would like to say 'by right', but of course I don't. Prepositions and other niceties have had to be sacrificed to global English. I don't want to look like a pedant.

He holds up another card; on it is written LIVE THE DREAM, against a blue sky with fluffy clouds, clouds that are there to off-set the dazzling cerulean of the sky. Very blue, cloudless skies are abnormal and threatening. White clouds, like sheep in a green field, add domestic scale and induce confidence.

'Live the dream. We are all dreamers.'

'Dreamers' comes out as 'treemiss' – *vee are oll treemiss* – which sounds like Middle English.

'Live the dream, because dreams can become reality. We

9

understand that everyone dreams of escape. Apart from sex, it is the number one dream. It would be a house in the country or a tropical island of your own. We say, you can live the dream. We empower you to live the dream.'

Now he holds up a card which reads SHARE THE DREAM.

'The way to make your dreams live, your dreams of a paradise that the ancients called Arcadia, way back when, is to share the dream. Only the super-rich can afford their own paradise, so our concept is paradise shared.'

It sounds to me like 'parrots' eyes sheared'. I think – I would – of the razor blade in *Le Chien Andalou*.

'I like that,' I say. 'Parrots' eyes sheared.'

He's pleased that I like it. Through everything, I have the ability – in the short term, anyway – to make people want to please me. I don't know why that is or what imagined qualities they see in me. He is wearing a light grey Italian suit of gossamer-thin material. But as I look at him I see one of Breughel's peasant faces, eyes red-rimmed, slightly puffy, his skin sensitive and his light hair slightly thinning, and not at all suited to the urgent, upstanding, haircut it has been given in some big city. This north European hair was designed to flop limply.

'Parrots' eyes sheared means a slize of parrots' eyes. You buy into the parrots' eyes cloob concept.'

Now he holds up the logo of the proposed development: PARADISE CLUB. I have been prescient, because each letter is formed by a brightly coloured macaw, beak-to-tail, tail-to-beak, against a background of deep-green palm trees.

'That's great. Great.'

I am not being ironic. It's damned clever. And anyway I believe that you adopt the appropriate demeanour for whatever form of human enterprise you engage in. When I worked at Harrods as a student there was a man in charge of the toilets who dressed in a brown suit and a brown bowler hat.

'Paradise Club. I like that,' I add.

'But before anyone will be saying "time share", we present the next stage, like so.'

Now he has abandoned the formal presentation and taken me into his confidence.

'We show them our club concept and explain what a club means and what lifestyle value a club attributes.'

He shows me a card which reads UNIQUE CLUB CONCEPT.

'We say: You own this club. It is your club. You are the part owner of this resort and you can be elected to the membership committee. Your membership entitles you automatically to four weeks a year, but you can negotiate with your fellow members. Oh wait.'

In his excitement he has got ahead of the cards.

'Wait. First we show them great cloobs. We show them the New York Racquets, the Royal Yacht Cloob, your royal yacht, famous Polo Cloobs, and such like.'

He shows me, briefly, the crests of various clubs, armorial shields and beasts interspersed with pictures of slim men and models sipping drinks. This is the international club life.

'It's aspirational. Every member who signs up for our presentation automatically gets an alligator wallet and a gold key, made in the shape of a parrot, and one thousand air miles. There are free trips to the site if you put down a refundable deposit.'

He shows me another card which reads MY PRIVATE PARADISE.

'What does this say to you?'

'Don't worry, I get it. Ownership.'

'You are right. It says ownership. The problem with time-share is you own ferry little. As my colleague Sergi in Miami says, you own diddly squat.'

I now have no idea what he is talking about, but I laugh merrily.

'That's a ferry big problem with time-share you knaauw.'

'I can see that.'

'But the cloob concept means that you own one twelfth of each block of condos – we call them ateliers – and because there are ten ateliers in each block and there are five blocks you own exactly one three-hundredth part of the whole cloob, including the cloob house and all the shared amenities.'

'Brilliant. So, let me see, you sell the three hundred shares at two hundred thousand pounds each.'

'Dollars.'

'Dollars, and that's six hundred million dollars.'

'Sixty million. And then there's a small yearly management fee on top and restaurants where you can order in or go out to eat and a golf cloob, where the cloob members have priority bookings and access to the lunch buffet.'

'Sounds good.'

I need this job. I am oppressed by money.

3

The northern fringes of London seem to me to be frayed, wet and shapeless. Here dull parks, clapped-out shops, gnawed golf courses and mean houses are clamped together in meaningless arrangements; crescent streets form the upper and lower jaws of dentures. A large early Victorian house over there is made more drab by the rigid standard roses, pink, orange and yellow, in a rectangular flowerbed. The house is devoted to the freeing of Tibet. Sometimes I see a youth in saffron robes carrying a green-plastic watering can. From here he doesn't look Tibetan. Perhaps he is neophyte, drawn from the growing ranks of the morbidly cheerful, those who take comfort from the belief that everything in the world is going to hell. In some respects, in some moods, at some times of day, this is true of me too. Between the buildings there are fields where muddy horses graze. Some of them wear blankets. Two greys are biting each other.

I turn down past a row of shops decorated with green and white tiles so that the north London rain skids off them, like water bouncing off the leaves of tulips. Two of the shops are boarded up. The other four are a pet shop, a garden equipment hire shop, a Chinese take-away, and a dairy. Now I am standing in the grounds of an abandoned hospital for the insane. Nobody knows where the criminally insane are now lodged, but in some rooms of this huge building there are traces of them. The criminally insane leave marks, like ancient cave paintings. I imagine them scratching and raking their own bodies, as if they believed there was something pure and unsullied inside. We are only using two wards where a lot of the action takes place, and a few offices, dressed as a nurses' home and operating theatres, and so on. But I have wandered the whole place with Barnaby, the art director, and seen the rows of cells with barred windows. Some of the walls still bear insane messages and demented graffiti. Many of these hieroglyphs have a religious motif. In a cupboard we found straitjackets. In what was once a day room, I noticed that there is a bracket ten feet up, which once held the television, too high for the inmates to choose their own programmes and attack the newsreaders, or try to fuck the children's presenters, or their dogs. I have no idea what the criminally insane do. Are they a homogeneous group or – more likely – are they mad in different ways?

Barnaby, the art director, said, 'Bit fucking depressing. Why don't we use a proper studio?'

'Money, Barnaby.'

Money is the reason I have been given the job. I am keen, I am young, I want to get on, and I don't have an agent. I see this – my first feature – as a big break.

'It's always money. This business gets to you.'

Barnaby has constructed two plausible wards, Matron's office, the nurses' home, a false ceiling above Matron's bedroom, an attic also above Matron's bedroom, and a laundry room, full of wicker baskets where rumpy-bumpy will take place. The director of the original hospital office had a panelled office: much of the panelling has been looted, but Barnaby has made restitution with sheets of hardboard coated with plastic sheeting that looks like oak.

'You won't be able to tell the difference when it's lit,' he says. And he is right.

I have an office myself, which has a deeply stained basin at knee height, as if a criminally insane dwarf had once been housed here. The walls are now covered with brown cork tiles. On the tiles my assistant, Paddy, has pinned charts, which show all the scenes: who is in them, what props are required, what stunts, what camera equipment and so on. We are working seven days a week for four weeks. I have a desk, a long pine table, which I've had Barnaby's painters lacquer with a deep-blue paint. On it I have placed some totemistic items, which indicate that while I may be directing a soft-porn film, I have wide interests. I have a small Roman head, an executive toy in chrome which involves shiny balls striking each other, a Philip Roth novel – *Zuckerman Unbound* (and unread) – a large sketch pad with a box of coloured pens, and a glass vase of long-stemmed arum lilies whose flowers are veined. Also on view are a director's view-finder – hired, and not yet mastered – and a Leica camera. One section of the walls is covered by a story-board, which shows day by day what we are proposing to do. The story-board artist has brought to the enterprise a strong style of his own, a sort of old-fashioned lushness, so that the scenes are pastel coloured and the actors are boldly and romantically drawn; they remind me of the cigarette ads in the newspapers of my childhood. My childhood in suburban Africa.

My father wrote about the harvester ants which cropped our lawn: 'You wake up to find a bald patch, rather like the tonsure on Friar Tuck's head. This is the danger signal. The harvesters have moved in.'

It was one of his tales in his early collection, *Animal Chatter*. Starting with our large suburban house under the mountain, with its tonsured lawn, he went on to become the repository of lost knowledge, drawn from a slight acquaintance with Bushmen, African chiefs and some forgotten writers like Maeterlinck and Eugène Marais. My father's successful work, *The Kingdom of the Ants*, proclaimed that each group of social insects is in essence one organism, developed by evolution. And of course we can learn a bit from their sober industrious habits and their understanding of the limits. Ants, it turns out, were the first Hobbesians. *The Kingdom of the Ants* made my father half a million dollars in 1972, and that was when he left to live in California with a woman he had met after a lecture at the Smithsonian on the secret life of insects. It's a truism that any man from the old Anglo-Saxon world who achieves prominence ends up with an American woman. In the nineteenth century the art and antiquities of the Old World were hoovered up by the new; now it is the cultural figures. They perform the same decorative and validatory function. They're wheeled out in Texas and California in their fustian, and they add lustre, patina and verisimilitude.

These story-boards remind me of what my parents called 'commercial art'. I don't despise it. In a sense art has always been commercial, but in the old Anglo-Saxon world which collapsed forty years ago, after staggering fatally wounded for decades (like the animals which had been darted by the Bushmen in my father's fables), there was a distinction of things done for money and things done with money. Naturally it is a distinction that favoured old money.

Yesterday we filmed the scene which involved Suzi Crispin, student nurse, being reprimanded by Matron in which Matron is in full sail, and Suzi Crispin is looking small and demure. In real life – a strange term – Matron is played by a Scottish alcoholic, Irene Ball, and the actress who plays Suzi, Terri Elms, is going out with a young south London gangster, who has twice asked me if we will be using doubles for the sex scenes. Later he called me in the middle of the night, and issued a threat: 'This is not a freat nor nuffink, don't get me wrong, but I don't see how's it's gonna be possible for us to allow Terr to do this scene in the script. I'm not tellin' yer yer business nor nuffink, but it's not gonna 'appen, know wot I'm saying?'

Later, after I had spoken to Terri about this call, he offered me a very good deal on a Rolex Prince – *bankrupt stock, not knocked off nor nuffink* – by way of an apology. Innocent times. But this conversation had consequences, because we hired a body double for the more explicit scenes and the body double – Ulla – became my mistress. As it happens Terri was carrying on with a stunt man she met on the film, a man who jumped motorcycles over London buses, and she married him. He was later to miscalculate, by two and a half, the number of buses he could jump on his Suzuki 250cc trail bike, and he is now a paraplegic. Please understand that none of the above is picaresque: this is what happened. Two years ago I sold the Rolex Prince in Burlington Arcade for £8,000, more than my fee for *Suzi Crispin, Night Nurse*. The watch expert opened it up and looked closely at it. He had very black eyebrows, which curled over the jewellers' glass: 'Pity the bezel is not original,' he said, 'I can't go more than eight.'

'I need the money. I'll take it.'

I took the initiative from him with my frankness. I guessed that he was used to people saying they were selling it for the elderly father, or that they were buying a vintage Ferrari, or that they had lost interest in collecting watches.

'A new bezel sweeps clean,' I said as I pocketed the cheque.

Today in the psychiatric hospital we are filming a difficult scene. It is our last day here although we have some scenes to shoot outside a suburban house, involving Suzi's suitor falling in a fish pond. Today, Suzi Crispin and her medical-student lover, Tom Travers, are finally making love in an attic. As she experiences the joy of orgasm, the ceiling collapses and she and Tom fall through on to Matron's bed below. We have to get it right first time as Barnaby has only enough in his budget for one take. The ceiling has been elaborately cut out and rigged to collapse on cue. It will take an hour to set up another ceiling which we don't have in the budget anyway.

This scene involves three stunt doubles and a body double. First we have to shoot the scene with Terri and Tom as they creep into the attic and Terri lies down on a mouldy mattress, much used by medical students. At the point where Tom removes her tunic, complete with upside-down nurse's watch, the body double, my lover Ulla, will substitute for Terri.

Her breasts and her very flat stomach, minutely decorated with golden hairs, which I hope will catch the light, as a small but muted tribute to my intense feelings for her, will now substitute for Terri.

In a wide shot, as the lovers begin to thrash about (the joke here, of course, is that the demure Terri proves to be insatiable), Tom and Ulla will be replaced by the stunt doubles, more robust but less attractive people, equipped with wigs and flesh-coloured patches, and on a signal from me the roof will collapse. But this must be done twice, once as they disappear through the ceiling and again as they appear above Matron's bed. My assistant Paddy and I have had a long conversation about whether or not they need to fall all the way on the first take. What he is saying is that it would be safer if they simply fell a few feet out of shot. But Barnaby says it would be cheaper if they fall right down on to the bed about ten feet below.

'Fuck it,' he says, 'they only have to land on a pile of mattresses. The last take when the double for the old boiler is in bed may kill them all, but who cares, that's the last set-up.'

He is moving on to a Jane Austen after this, with a proper budget, and he is demob happy (a phrase which has all but vanished). I have grown to love him over the weeks we have worked together. He is always complaining about the budget and the conditions we have to work under, and the location which is two hours from civilisation – he means Soho – but even as he complains he has a compulsion to do things right so that I wonder how he can live with this tension, the iconoclast and the perfectionist at war.

One day he said to me, 'This may look like a piece of soft-porn bollocks, but I believe it will be unearthed by future generations to explain to them the last years of post-war Britain. The Owl of Minerva dropping dead as dusk is falling.'

And now when I look back on those weeks in our madhouse,

I see that he was right. The date may have been 1986, but the film is unmistakably set in the nineteen fifties, with class values and sexual attitudes that had long ago been forgotten outside the worlds of film and politics which often lag behind everyday practice.

We are readying ourselves for the great collapse. Tom and Terri enter the attic crouching. Terri looks around her wide-eyed.

'This is so cosy,' she says.

Tom drags her to the mattress and then she says, 'Ooh, you don't waste much time.'

They kiss briefly. Now Tom begins to undress her.

'Cor, you're in a rush,' she says.

'Cut. Body double.'

In comes Ulla in the identical uniform. She is more beautiful than Terri with marvellous breasts, smallish but womanly and of course with her sensual down. As the director and the lover of one of the protagonists, I feel conflicting emotions. In close-up we see her breasts. I watch her face, which cannot be shown. She seems to be animated by the experience. I scan her face carefully for any signs of pleasure as Tom takes one of her nipples in his mouth.

'That tickles,' she says, laughing and unscripted, to the annoyance of the sound man, who sighs.

I take comfort from the fact that she has never said that to me. Now, as instructed, Tom's rather pink lips travel downwards over the delicate wheat field of my imagination. Before Tom can go any further we move on to the next set-up: Ulla cleverly silhouetted so that the general public – who won't of course be as familiar with her geography as I am – will not realise that she is a body double. Now she moves on top of Tom. Her love-making is athletic, even violent. We do a quick shot of Tom looking panicky and rumpled before I call, 'Cut. Stunt doubles on set. Thanks,

Ulla. That was good. Great. Perhaps too good.' She flits off in a robe, smiling.

Tom comes by and says in his friendly fashion, 'I was just beginning to enjoy myself, Governor. You saved me from embarrassing myself.'

The stunt doubles now take the place of Tom and Ulla in the artful chiaroscuro. They're called Tel and Samantha. Tel's speciality is stunt motor biking; he is a good lad and up for anything, including falling ten feet with Samantha sitting on top of him. *Piece of cake*. Samantha is now wearing Ulla's wig (which resembles, although not slavishly, Terri's hair).

'Okay, turn over.'

The camera runs. When the two stand-ins have more or less repeated the action which went before I shout, 'Action, props.'

They disappear in a cloud of fuller's earth on to the bed below which has been piled with mattresses. True professionals, they lie absolutely still, clasped together like marsupials although they are out of shot.

I shout, 'Cut.'

Now another false ceiling is put in place. Irene Ball arrives; she walks on to the set with a purposeful but at the same time vacant air, which, I have come to see over the last few weeks, means she has been drinking. But she prides herself on being a trooper. One lunchtime, drinking Riesling together out of polystyrene cups, she told me with tears in her raw eyes that the tragedy of her life was that she didn't have a man, despite her generous nature. But her generous nature is of the thespian kind, a sort of effusive and frightening sentimentality, which contains deep seams of bitterness and disappointment.

'The problem with actors,' said Barnaby, 'is that they want to be gods, but that's impossible, so they get the hump.'

Now in her nightdress with a shawl around her plump shoulders, she strides towards the bed. Make-up have covered her face with cold cream so that she looks ghostly.

'Cinders will go to the ball, darling,' she says.

With help she climbs into the bed. She has brought her Matron's cap, and asks me if I don't think it would be jolly amusing if she keeps it on in bed? No.

Her slightly distressed eyes fix on me for a moment: 'It's not Shakespeare, is it?'

Now she has to lie in bed covering her face with more cream, she has to react as though she hears some noises up above. On a signal some fuller's earth falls down towards her, released by a props man on a ladder. She looks up in horror and then tries to hide herself.

'Marvellous, Irene. Just about perfect.'

In her look up to the spot from which the stunt doubles will soon be plunging, she has packed a lifetime of theatrical experience. I find it moving, this strange ability to reproduce – even while drunk – exactly the right expression, as if there is no other conceivable way of doing it.

'Irene's last shot,' I say. 'Brilliant, we love you.'

The crew applauds, and she does a small curtsey. 'It's only acting.'

Now the stunt doubles ready themselves up above, and a third stunt double wearing Irene's wig and nightdress, her face plastered, climbs into bed. But the bed is rigged so that she is in fact kneeling, and the young lovers will not fall on her. Everything is readied. We have two cameras for this, one recording slow motion. As the cameras reach speed, I shout 'Action', but the new ceiling does not break. We stop the cameras and we hear the sound of a saw from up there. It's a sound which increases the tension.

We are ready. I call 'Action' again. This time the ceiling collapses, the young lovers fall down – clinging to each other like the pros they are – exactly as planned, but the stand-in Matron is knocked unconscious by a rogue piece of ceiling, breaking away.

*   *   *

Three weeks into the editing, I am fired. The film is later released on video. Ulla provides some comfort – actually plenty of comfort – but I see that fissures are opening in my life. I used to read *National Geographic* avidly as a boy and I think of a logger on the St Lawrence seaway, or a polar bear on an ice floe or a victim of a flood in Bangladesh, clinging to a tree. I am drifting away.

I have to collect my thoughts as I pass the mental hospital. Late summer in London is dusty, the air is oily, the plants are laden with cares of their own. In the editing room, my things, transferred from the mental hospital, look ludicrously gimcrack as I pack them up.

The editor, Gerald, is working away at the film: 'Well out of it,' he says. 'Well out of it. Good luck.' I glance over his shoulder; he is working on a scene in which Suzi Crispin is thrown into a communal bath of rugby players. But there are some extra shots of women with large breasts and unconvincingly cheery expressions, frolicking in water.

'Where did these come from?'

'Who knows? I received a can of film and I was told to cut it in.'

'Why?'

'They said the scene needed more tits.'

'Oh, Jesus.'

'Well out of it. You don't want to be involved in this kind of crap. Have a good one.'

As I leave the studio, the rows of huts, the bacon-fog bound canteen, the studio buildings which look like a nineteen-thirties model factory, the painted flats, the disused props – all fake in the weak dying light – as I carry my own pathetic props, I feel the fissure open even wider.

4

Inferring from these signs and instances
Some men have argued that the bees received
A share of divine intelligence,
A spark of heavenly fire. For God, they say,
Pervades all things, the earth and sea and sky.
From him the flocks and herds, and man and beast,
Each draws the thin-spun stream of life, and both,
To him all things return, at last dissolved:
There is no place for death, but living still
They fly to join the numbers of the stars.

After his success with ants, my father turned his attention to bees. He quoted Virgil frequently. He was drawn to the idea of the thin-spun stream of life. He made the comparison between a bee colony and a complete organism. Bees are collaborative creatures; each bee may be likened to a cell, or an atom, or something. I forget exactly. *The Soul of the Bee* didn't sell as well as his ant fable, *The Kingdom of the Ants*; he was casting around for more collaborative animals at the time of his death. The baboon had caught his eye, but for some reason the work was never finished, perhaps because he knew less about baboons than he did about ants.

From California my father wrote to me about this book. He wanted me to approve of him. This, I have found, is one of the lesser known truths of life, that parents seek their children's approval almost as fervently as children seek their parents'.

With some sections of the manuscript he sent me a note: 'Interesting fact, Virgil thought the queen bee was male. The truth was not discovered until the eighteenth century. In our time, of course, women rule unequivocally.' He wanted to be witty, urbane and rich. For a while in New York he passed for all of these while my mother entered her lonely hibernation, which is now coming to an end.

In the little cottage I am running through her books. In the clinic – *Frail Care* – she is still profoundly asleep, two days on. They asked me if they should stop feeding her intravenously: they were asking my permission to finish her off by starving her. I refused. They are now changing the nappy and will call me when she is cleaned up.

There are two shelves of leather-bound books. Leatherbound books send a message of seriousness, no longer appropriate. *The Georgics* by Publius Virgilius Maro, translated by Professor Edwin Tumaroff, Professor Emeritus, the University of Toronto, 1952, published by the Oxford University Press. The book is bound in Moroccan leather and chased with gold leaf. My father has made notes in it. He has underlined at the beginning of Book Four these words:

> *Now I will sing the celestial gift*
> *Of honey and Macenas, I beseech*
> *Thy kindly favour also for this part*
> *The wondrous pageant of a pygmy world.*

The books and the papers had once lived in less cramped circumstances in our house nestling under the mountain, where my father, on his return from the war with his tailored suits and smart naval uniforms (recorded in pictures which are scattered around the cottage), had set about his career as journalist and popular sage. At the time I was born, in 1952, he was already well known. Eight years later he set off for America and there he fell in love with Ann Kjellin, a Swedish American teaching at Berkeley. Later he wrote me a long letter explaining – I was eleven – the reasons for his desertion. He put it down to the human spirit. He had things to communicate and he had to free his spirit from the smallness – the pygmy scale – of life in Cape Town. He knew I would one day understand. A year later he sent for me and I flew all the way to San Francisco. Our two weeks passed in a daze. He had become a pleasant but unreachable stranger, always on the phone or rushing out to see things in his big car, or excitedly suggesting lobster dinners and visits to vineyards and country inns. One morning when Ann was out of the room he asked me, 'How is your mother?'

'Okay.'

'Just okay?'

'She seems fine.'

He began to cry suddenly and I sat on the overfilled lounger staring straight ahead. Just as quickly he was himself again, back on song, his new get-up-and-go persona in place in time for Ann's return. I had no way of judging then, but now I would guess that she was sexually enthralling. She had long, straight hair and wore straight skirts. She was like an item of Swedish design. The cleanness of the lines suggesting a losing battle with inner turmoil. But it is my experience that nobody can know how others carry on in the sexual realm.

As a matter of record, my father didn't leave us all at once. His lecture tours and his publicity trips and his projects simply expanded so that he was seldom here, and then he said he wouldn't be coming home again. *The Soul of the Bee* had reached, my research shows, number six on the *New York Times* best-seller list. *The Kingdom of the Ant* had held the number one spot for five plump weeks. It was around this time that Nelson Mandela went to jail. The bees – busy with their pygmy pageants – and their propagandist, my father, appeared not to have noticed.

My mother, who is now having her old mustard-and-tan flesh cleaned up, took my father's desertion in a peculiar way: she joined the Claremont and Wynberg Players, who performed outdoors in a park during the long summers, and in the Scout Hall during the winter. We never discussed my father, but I see now that he must have been quite generous, because my brother and I were still at the best private school, and we always seemed to have a maid at home and once a week a gardener would arrive to mow the lawn and water. His name was Solomon and he was an African. Watering was his speciality: he stood for hours with the hose pointed at the shrubs. The water was warm and brownish. The maids, who were Coloured, gave him his lunch at the kitchen door because he was an African.

My mother was usually out rehearsing. There was a fellow actor who looked like Robin Hood, with a red beard and active, wealth-distributing eyes, who she became close to. His name was Eric Finn, no relation. My brother explained that he thought he looked like Errol Flynn. In real life he sold swimming pool equipment. Now I remember that one of our maids – Carrie – made a jelly with honey-flavoured hanepoot grapes. The remarkable thing was that the clear filling was embedded with whole grapes which she had peeled. They were suspended mysteriously in the jelly. I haven't given them a thought for thirty years and I long to sink a spoon into the yielding, honey-coloured jelly, and retrieve a peeled grape. Also I remember that she sometimes poured sterilised cream from a tin on to the jelly. I preferred it to the real cream from dairies.

My father has also noted these lines:

> *They have, moreover, the strange character:*
> *They take no joy nor waste their lives in love,*
> *Nor labour in the pangs of giving birth.*
> *Without a mate from leaves and pleasant herbs*
> *They get their babies in their mouths, and so*
> *Produce their kings and little citizens*
> *And populate the waxen realm anew.*
> *Oft wandering through the rocks they bruise their wings*

And freely give their lives beneath the load,
Such is their love of flowers and pride in toil.
Wherefore, although the span of life is brief
And ne'er beyond the seventh summer lasts
The race abides immortal, and the house
Stands firm through generations without end.

He has twice underlined 'the race abides immortal'. And I see now that this fits well his earlier thesis that co-operative creatures are really just cells of a greater organism. From this it is a small step to the conclusion that

> *There is no place for death, but living still*
> *They fly off to join the numbers of the stars.*

We are all immortal; life is just a phase during which our little star burns bright for a while. In this scenario my mother's star is about to dim. But I hope that in some way it is true that we continue to exist on a lesser (or maybe more exalted) plane, in incomprehensible ways. Let's face it, it can only be in incomprehensible ways, and when we get there – if getting there comes into it – we won't know, just as a bee doesn't know what it's doing in its six-year life. (Can Virgil have got this right?)

I go to sit outside. There is a straggly grapevine falling over a pergola. My mother's garden furniture has rotted. It is anyway indelibly marked with grapes – like Carrie's jelly – leaving vinous stains and blotches and not very noble *pourriture* in a natural fresco. My heart crumbles: this fucking matchwood, this poor-white junk, is all she has. I step out on to the lawn and the stars, the numbered stars, pour contempt on me. As it happens I don't see loads of bees heading up there, or my old mother flying upwards transmogrified; I see instead utter loathing, mineral loathing – the worst sort – for what I am, a man of forty-seven who has let his mother die surrounded by squatter junk. A poor-white, *bywoner*, rubbish tip. I smash the furniture with my foot, and bag it up. I find a pot of paint and I paint out the number of cottage ninety-one, which she has drawn on a wall near the front door with a pen. A mute and unheeded appeal for attention.

I resolve, whether she is alive or dead in the morning, to go and buy large brass numerals and have them fixed to the wall. The other, richer, inhabitants, I have noticed, favour these big showy numbers. As I paint out her pathetic scrawls my eyes are full of tears. It is dark and I am painting by the light above the front door, which has attracted insects and prowling geckos. A nurse arrives from the clinic to tell me that the bed-bath is complete. She is missing two teeth in her nervous face, small, brown, prematurely puckered and shadowed, perhaps the effect of the light. It's nearly eleven o'clock – late for these parts – and she is disturbed by the sight of me painting. Even in this light I can see that it is a mistake to use Dulux gloss paint on a whitewashed wall.

'Thanks,' I say, 'I'm coming. Ek kom nou-nou.'

I find my Afrikaans appearing from nowhere like the lines of half-forgotten poetry which sometimes rise spontaneously. 'Nou-nou' is idiomatic, a sort of nursery talk. She tells me that my mother is still sleeping, but sister – she pronounces it 'susteh' – has reattached the drip.

I walk through the aromatic garden; the automatic watering system is on and the sandy soil and the wetted foliage are releasing a scent – actually a hundred scents blended – which resounds in the bony cavities of my face calling up deep memories. This is the memory which, my father wrote, we don't even know we have, phyletic memory. And it is this idea of the phyletic memory which opened so many doors of possibility, which made him rich and unstopped the ears of money. Money seems to be like that – it is obedient to a few, for no obvious reason.

There is not much to see in the clinic, except the small hillock that is my mother, lying still. Her face, her big strong face, moves minutely, the lips curling back as if to speak, but no words come out. Her head now appears to be lying on the pillow alone as though it has no connection to what's under the blankets.

A nurse has opened a small box containing a cameo brooch and propped it up as a kind of decoration, or perhaps a talisman, beside the bed, next to a well-stocked tray of pills. I haven't, knowingly, seen a cameo brooch for thirty years. What was the point of them and where have they all gone?

5

It's hard to imagine what the attraction of music hall could have been. People lit cigarettes and sang in silly voices and twirled canes and rushed on to stage shouting 'I say, I say, I say,' before telling some excruciating joke. I've seen music hall in revival and marvelled at it like some anthropological rite.

Irene Ball had started in music hall. Her way up from an Edinburgh tenement building to the West End stage and films was hard, and this struggle had left its marks.

She lived in a small cottage on the banks of the Thames. It was difficult to find, out somewhere near Bray. At that time a lot of actors and entertainers lived near the water. In showbiz, a view of water and waterfowl suggested success. Irene's big break came when she was fifty in a Joe Orton play, *Entertaining Mr Sloane*. She often recited her favourite line, 'Ooh, you're a heavy boy, Mr Sloane.' Malcolm Douglas had sat on her knee. The way she said the line, her mouth pursed tight in a little cupid's bow of lust, made me think she could still feel the imprint of his – then – boyish buttocks.

There is a certain tragedy in the incompatibility of old and young flesh. It is a chemical reaction. A few old men get away with juxtaposing their seasoned flesh with something more pristine, but older women, however brightly the furnace is burning within, seldom succeed. Young flesh is endangered by old flesh, which is as contagious as the mould which spreads quickly from one pear to another.

It was rainy and wet branches and tentacles bowed down by water scraped and whipped the car as I bumped along Duck Lane towards Duck's Landing. The cottage was camouflaged and strangled by roses; small stone animals, impervious to rain, lined the path to the front door. The front door was studded and armoured, as though to repel Viking raiders who might sail up the Thames.

As soon as she opened the door, I could see Irene was drunk. Her cheeks were bright, feverish. Her eyes, heavily made-up but smudged, were watery. She was attended by cats.

'My babies,' she explained. 'One for the road?'

Behind her in the Venetian-glassed, cushion-embroidered, roof-beamed, memento-laden interior, was a trolley of drinks of colours which do not exist in nature.

'Champagne cocktail?'

'Why not?'

'Why not, indeed? You look rather like Malcolm in that suit,' she said.

'I got it in Barcelona.'

'That's not much of an explanation. Malcolm likes off-white too. Very naughty boy, Malcolm. Very naughty indeed.'

She threw a sugar lump into the cocktail, where it fizzed quickly like an Alka Seltzer.

'Bottoms up!'

I drank this livid potion and looked out at the Thames, thick and murky after the rain.

'I've had a very happy life, you know,' she said.

'I can believe it.'

'A happy, happy life. But somehow, through no fault of my own, I have ended up here with my cats.'

'Beautiful view.'

'A view is not always enough. In fact it can be fucking depressing. A view is no substitute for living. Another cocktail?'

'Not at the moment.'

'I will.'

She mixed herself another. I had the feeling that she lived more fully on film sets and in theatre. Here she seemed to be confused and diminished. She gave the impression of waiting for someone to make an entrance.

We drove up the lane. She didn't know the way although there was a limited choice of turnings, and we found ourselves briefly in a boatyard, where cabin cruisers were rotting away.

The restaurant was hushed. The reverential waiters, the ruched curtains, the watery view on to the river, the songs of the Ardèche, the Gallic snobberies, had dampened the other customers. But Irene smiled cheerily and waved unsteadily as we were led to our table. Beneath us the water sped vertiginously by. Our fellow diners had cheered up, as though the tipsy old actress had been sent expressly for their amusement. She gazed around happily. *Lights. Curtain.*

'I can't read the menu,' she said. 'And it's in French of a sort that went out with Molière. Just choose the simplest thing you can find for me, darling.'

A woman came over with an Instamatic, and we posed.

'He's my toy boy,' said Irene merrily.

The famous chef-proprietor emerged. He kissed Irene's hand and spoke to her in the tones of Maurice Chevalier.

'Zis eez zee first ladee in zee 'ole of zee country. I 'ave something special for you, Irène. I 'ave zee smoked salmon with quail's eggs en croute. A light deesh, just what you are adoring, followed by zee Dover sole weeth just a touch of Bearnaise.'

He told me that over the years he had come to know that Madame Irene loved simple food; and good quality ingredients.

'Quite right, darling Michel. I don't like it mucked about,' she said.

She was delighted that dear Michel had chosen for her. Everyone was happy, and I was spared three pages of translation, a whole gallimaufry of *ballotine*, *concasse*, *velouté* and *timbale* and so on. It's not the language of Molière so much as the language of the grand hotel in the mouth of the petit bourgeois. Now the hushed, restrained, sepulchral restaurant has gone in favour of the noisy and informal, where neither French nor etiquette intrude, and the petit bourgeois have joined the inexorably dead.

Irene's cheeks were by now the colour of cranberry juice. She was so drunk that what she said was meaningless, although the sentences were complete. It was as if her life was a collection of phrases from scripts and encounters.

'Salmon swim upriver to die. I'm a salmon really. A Scottish salmon. Rabbie Burns. I would like to die in Scotland. I've had a happy, happy life. Apart from men. I have not made a success of men. No, I have not.'

A couple of Americans politely asked her to sign a menu which she did blearily.

'Where are you from?'

'Ann Arbor, Michigan.'

'Shakespeare. I've played there at the Shakespeare Festival run by my dear, dear friend Ira Levine. Professor Levine. Marvellous acoustics.'

When they had gone, bearing her signature on their Old Testament parchment menu, Irene turned to me.

'You're a clever boy, I can see that; why don't you do Shakespeare?'

'Nobody's asked me.'

'Don't throw your talent away,' she said, placing a hand over mine. The skin of the back of her hand was like lichen.

Michel saved me from further painful exploration of this line of thought by bringing two perfect small soufflés to the table. He pierced them and inserted a spoonful of Armagnac with the skill of a surgeon.

'Ooh, look. They can't stay up for long,' said Irene, prodding hers with a fork so that it collapsed, 'like the men in my life, dear, darling Michel.'

'Oh, I don't believe zat for a moment.'

'We have been making a film together, Michel, a rather saucy film.'

'And you are a wonnerfool actress. Parfect,' said Michel, moving away, glamorous in his chef's outfit and his leathery son-of-the-soil smile.

When we finally left the restaurant, Irene holding my arm and waving, I felt as though we were leaving a stage. And the drive back to her house through the moist patchwork of suburb and country was appropriately muted. Irene was slumped heavily against the side of the car. I had to support her through the armoured door of Duck's Landing and into her bedroom.

'Would you like to stay? No hanky-panky of course.'

'I must go.'

'I must go,' she repeated, and shut her eyes. 'Story of my life.'

I could not find it in my heart then to look charitably on her, as she lay in her suffocating bedroom amongst the flowery covers and framed photographs. Not even the picture of a pilot – an airman – complete with neat moustache and jaunty cap, touched me. I remembered some story, some old theatrical nonsense, about a pilot lost over Germany, her broken heart, the love of her life, and I didn't give a damn. I was also a little hurt that she had mentioned something that was already becoming clear, that I had made a terrible error in doing this film.

Now I think that I must have been wondering on the drive home, via Ulla's little flat, what I was doing in this tired and ridiculous world pretending that I was somehow above it, ironic and detached. I can say that now, but I suspect the truth is that at the time I was still sure that I could turn it to my advantage, that I could achieve some purity and clarity in my work. My work. *Mon oeuvre*.

Ulla had no hard-and-fast rules about time. It was late when I finally got there. She was in bed watching a video and we were soon making love. She had a mirror above the bed. I remember that I looked at the blonde hairs on her neck, just below the hairline proper, and for me they were unbearably sweet, in their childish innocence.

You can't trust your own memories of course. There may be memories you don't even know you have, as my father thought, a sort of biological leftover like the appendix, but it is true that the memories you preserve are not always based on actual events. Yet the memories of that night – the booming dining room, the comedy night out with Irene Ball, the short defenceless hairs on Ulla's neck – have now become in my mind true memories, fused forever.

There used to be, and for all I know there may still be, a medical procedure for cauterising the inside of the nose to prevent nosebleeds; the lining of the nose was sealed with a hot iron. I now think that something comparable happened to my life: it was sealed off that night. This understanding comes with the benefit of hindsight, but at the time and for years after, I didn't see the sudden closure that was happening as I was admiring the childish hairs on Ulla's neck, which entranced me as much as, or perhaps more than, her perfect tits.

6

After the ceiling had knocked out the Matron-double there was a nervous excitement in the air. Disloyally, I hoped that the producers hadn't paid the insurance and that the union would take them to the cleaners. But the double came round in the ambulance and she sent word back to us that she was fine, *just a few stitches in her head, nothing to worry about, all part of the job, hope she done the business, knew nothing about it, can't remember a thing, slight headache, taken a minicab home, good luck, sorry I can't be with you for the knees-up.*

The events of the day had certainly excited Ulla. After all, somebody had been nibbling her tits in full view of the crew. She wanted to celebrate her role as a body double, which was coming to an end. I, by contrast, felt the day weigh heavily on me.

It was a day when I felt my human essences thinning. In her small flat behind a supermarket I, in my turn, nibbled her tits and fell prey to morbidity. Her delayed excitement was uncontrolled. The movie business, the illusion, the self-importance, the exhibitionism, had produced a state of ecstasy in her. I was lying on top of her and underneath her and she and I were making love as if we were gods, entitled to something special. If sex came in categories we were in the top category – film people – who had a right, maybe an obligation, to experience the ineffable. And as we cavorted, I thought in my over-analytical way that sex this intense – she was shouting and gulping for air and the sweat started on her breastbone – was a lesson in mortality: unlike my father's indestructible bee spirits, this couldn't last. And finally the string of semen, lying on her belly, looked dead to me, not so much a garland for our heroic efforts, but a wreath.

When she wasn't doing body-double work, Ulla worked in a boutique. The boutique has gone the way of the cameo brooch. Even then the word had an ironic sound when spoken, suggesting otherwordliness and aimless skipping down the King's Road. Money was at last being seen in its true role as the agent of happiness and freedom. Women were wearing power suits. But not Ulla. She housed her perfect bosom casually in yellow waistcoats and cheesecloth and her earrings were the components of mobiles and wind chimes.

I didn't know, although I was soon to find out, that my film career was over. But something else happened which, I would guess, happens to everybody in some degree: I found that my sense of a destiny, of a sort of inevitable success, had taken a pasting. By success, I don't necessarily mean wealth, but a kind of confidence, a sense of being in the best of available worlds. It was a shock to me to learn the truth; it seems incredible to me now that I had never contemplated it.

These last twenty years – as the finer impulses, the betrayals, the spurts of achievement, the weaknesses, all chafed together, all out of time – have worked on my soul. There have been stretches of blankness and despair, which have taken on the appearance in my mind of roads stretching endlessly over a plain. Landscape and geography have entered my thinking, sometimes displacing ideas. Ideas were important to me. But now ideas had become lesser entities, subservient to things, to material facts.

Later on the evening when the ceiling broke and the blood spurted alarmingly on to the bedcover, Ulla said, 'Let's get married.'

It seemed to me a strange remark to make to a father and a man with a deeper inner life. I didn't want to marry her; she was beautiful with her thick blonde coconut-scented hair and

her mouth as warm and fragrant as a freshly baked brioche
– I had recently been marvelling at Poilane – and her small
and defenceless buttocks and, of course, her breasts, soon to
achieve wide exposure; all these things had worked on me
in a disturbing fashion. Here was a young woman with a
certain physical blitheness, a mayfly perfection, an uncritical
sensuality, suggesting that we get married, and I was shocked.
She could see no obstacles.

But most of all she couldn't see, and I couldn't tell her, that
someone like me, *un homme sérieux*, was not going to throw
his wife out and abandon his beloved son to marry some totty
who worked in a boutique selling fake leopard-skin thongs and
knee-high boots, as worn by Abba, and halter tops made of bits
of parachute and white belts studded with chunks of coloured
glass. To put it crudely, fucking her was one thing, marrying
her another. This is an age-old dilemma, and it has been my
experience that it applies equally to men and women.

Strangely, her remark about marriage, as casual as a suggestion that we get takeaway or watch television, had a corrosive
effect on me. Of course, I couldn't ditch her immediately. Also
she possessed something which I lacked, a straightforwardness
and a kind of innocence, despite her sexual brio. As it became
plain to me that my modest reputation ('A young talent to
watch' – *Variety*) was in ruins I began to wonder how long
it would be before Ulla withdrew her offer of marriage.
Meanwhile she tripped off to the boutique each morning
dressed on some inexplicable whim, one day in a feather
boa, another in a satin evening dress, another in shorts. At
weekends I returned home to our gloomy house and our walks
with Matt, whose little legs, once as fat as Italian sausages,
had slimmed down and were now providing him with a new
motive force to propel his bike. As I plodded around the park –
crack of cricket bats in the distance, squeak of bicycle wheels,
pant-pant-pant, slap-slap of athletes running about – women
were just beginning to jog then – I had a vision of Ulla in her

cramped flat doing ... doing who knows what? And why should I care? She wanted to marry me, she wanted to end the mayfly activity and I treated her offer lightly.

My mother is speaking. She hasn't spoken for four days. I lean close.

'Is that you, James?'

'Yes, Ma.'

'Good boy.'

I am hoping she will speak again, but she is silent. Her breathing seems to be stronger now. It has a rasping, but more regular timbre. A few days ago, when I entered her cottage for the first time, I noticed a familiar scent. The aromas of our old house had been transported here, so that cottage ninety-one contained the essences of our life. The ink-and-papyrus of books, the face-powder, the lanolin-enriched shampoo, the dried lavender bags and the naphthalene in the cupboards are all recognisable. And this harsh breathing – she was once a smoker – is familiar in the same way.

In the clinic the scents are dead and chemical, the noises off are metallic: the wheels of trolleys, the clatter of buckets, the clash of tin trays and Petri dishes.

As I am sitting here, trying to read Virgil in this medical twilight, the book itself produces a faint gust of home. My father has underlined this passage about bees:

> *Alone they bring their children up in common*
> *And share the shelter of their city's roof*
> *And live their life beneath the rule of law.*
> *Alone they have a country and a fixed home*
> *And, mindful of the winter, toil in summer*
> *And put their winnings in a common store.*

Are you there, James? Good boy.

I am here, and I feel that I must stay and be present at the moment of departure because I think that although she will not be aware of the moment, someone should be with her in the waiting room. Death is a journey, even if it is a journey which proves to have no destination. Not that we will know, of course, as we die that we have been cheated of a destination. Her face now is rather red, as though there is some struggle going on in there. But it subsides again, the flux passes. Her face is almost unbearable to look at because it is giving a preview of death, her mouth gaping, seeking the boundaries of the skull.

> *To him all things return, at last dissolved:*
> *There is no place for death, but living still*
> *They fly to join the numbers of the stars.*

I agree that life is thin-spun, but I can't believe that she, or her essence, will fly off to join the numbers of the stars, as much as I might wish it. But I have a curious notion suddenly, that I should lie next to her and die with her, to keep her company: *Yes, I'm here, Ma, and I'm coming with you.*

I think in staccato but banal images, of my grandmother's travel rug, of the old green Thermos we used to take for picnics on the beach, and of floppy sunhats and the uncomfortable sandals we wore. Looking unremarkable was an essential part of childhood.

A nurse comes by with a cup of tea. The therapeutic properties of tea are known all over the anglophone world. I don't recognise her: her face is large, quite brown, with plump liquid eyes like prunes in Armagnac.

'Thanks. Are you new here?'

'No sir, I've been on my leave.'

'Thank you for the tea.'

'No problem. How's the old lady?'

'She spoke.'

'Spook?'

She doesn't recognise the past tense of 'speak'. She thinks I said 'spook'.

'Not spook. She was speaking, she speak to me.'

'Ooh sorry, sir. I think sir is saying spook.'

'No, not that, not yet, anyway.'

'Sir must just ring the bell if he want something. Goodnight.'

Her hips are fat. Her green unform rides up. She is not a real nurse, more a helper.

The night sister, who is a far bigger cheese, also comes round to check my mother's pulse and listen to her breathing. She is a white woman with a face that is smooth and untroubled as a nun's. Her features appear to have been worn by water, so that her face is unnaturally lacking in human detail. She has an appropriately spiritual manner.

'She's doing very well. It's probably because you are here.'

'Do you think she really knows I'm here?'

'Antjie said she spoke to you.'

'Yes, she did.'

'It gives them great comfort. It's lonely dying.'

She bustles off. She's seen lots of death. I wonder if you begin to think of death not as something to fear, but as a resolution. The whole thing – the history, the hopes, the family, the curious beliefs, the inchoate longings, the slights, the minor, meaningless successes and of course the pains and infirmities – is ended in that one moment, if it is a moment, of death. Maybe if you are a nurse you come to think that this resolution is the whole point.

I myself sleep. Although I think of my sleep as having been brief and fitful, when I wake there is light outside the blinds of the window. I fear my mother will be gone, but her breathing, though faint, is regular. When the day staff arrive to change her drips and clean her up, I go out along the little golf course and up the farm track past the cottages.

It's a Monday, and in the distance are the noises of work going on: the *doof-doof* of tractors and shouts and anxious lowing as an unseen herd of cows is driven to milking. I pass the farmhouse and head up over a stile on a path with a neat sign, 'Nature Reserve'. Beside the path there are silver trees with hairy, tough leaves, and clumps of dense, aromatic bushes. The higher I go the more of the bay I can see, the deep-green-blue, the breakers falling on the endless beach, the mountains now emerging, as my perspective changes, the long lizard back on the far side of the bay and then below, a few miles away, the naval college where I won a boxing match. I remember now, and my stomach tightens, arriving for the fight to see rows of raw, tough young sailors in uniform eager for blood, my blood. Although by some miracle I won, I spent the night in hospital with concussion. I have been expecting tumours or epilepsy ever since.

From here the water below looks ordered, its surface pleasantly patterned, wrinkled with the odd white cap, but I know that it is treacherous. Sharks enter the bay after seals. Kelp lines the rock shores, thick ropes of a monstrous seaweed that swing to and fro in the swell and break loose during storms. Down there in the kelp on the way to Simon's Town, my father claimed to have almost hooked the biggest Red Steenbras, *petrus rupestris*, ever seen. This was in his story, 'The Biggest Fish I Ever Saw', which comes just before his story 'All Snakes Look Longer Than They Are' in *Animal Chatter*, his first published work. The fish, he said, was the size of a small submarine. It could not be landed. He once saw a python fifteen feet long.

I think now that he may have been looking for recognition. He didn't know it and he wouldn't have recognised the condition, but he was after celebrity.

From over there on the other side of the bay where we lived, the big publishing houses of New York, the newspapers of Fleet Street, the intellectual mills of Paris, must have had a powerful attraction. He had a sense that he was in the wrong place, by an accident of birth. People fetched up here as a result of large forces which they could not control. (In this way they are like the columns of kelp on the beach.) These forces were world-historical in nature, such as religious persecution, or more mundane, such as bankruptcy. Sometimes they were just the product of whimsicality in earlier generations. The first task was to reverse this flow, to get to where the action was. I have myself suffered from this anxiety of being in the wrong place.

Up here there are tiny birds poking their long beaks into the flowers of the shrubs. There is one they favour, a long stalk bearing trusses of small red flowers above thorny, tough leaves: I think it might be an aloe. I am always troubled by what I don't know: the floral kingdom, science, unread books. Nobody is asking me to make excuses for myself, but I think that I have lived in a rather unsettled spiritual climate, so that I have been unable to keep my mind to any one task. And maybe this is not a bad thing: success, the accumulation of money, for example, depends upon narrowing the vision. I think of how in my close inspection of ants, I used sometimes to scorch them with a magnifying glass by narrowing to an intense point the focus of the lens. My father claimed in one of his articles to have learned from the Bushmen the art of firemaking with sticks and dried dung. The big problem in everyday life was the scarcity of dried elephant dung. Still, he said he could do it from a standing start in six minutes. With a magnifying glass, you could start a bush fire in seconds.

Below me, shifting the gaze away from the bay and the pendulous mountains and the charged, dangerous sea, I can make out the old farmhouse clearly. The plan is obvious, although some of the walls have gone: a house, a stable block, a kitchen garden, enclosed against the limitless space of Africa, which started just over the mountains. The whole neat, diagrammatic outline is easily imagined from what remains, although chicken coops, a park for rusted farm implements, diseased fruit trees, the children's playground, a round, corrugated-iron reservoir and some minor but splayed building improvements have blurred the plan.

I walk up, higher into the mountains. Nature is having a powerful, but suspect, effect on me. It seems to produce a grander perspective, as though all these screaming insects and heavily scented plants and watchful lizards and jewelled birds and the ancient geological disturbances and the glimpse of small grey-green deer – all these things – are a reproach to my unsettled and petty thoughts. To my father, whose slight acquaintance with nature produced his famous theory, famous in Middle America and the Home Counties, we, like ants, like bees, are simply part of a greater whole, and so immortal. We are souls, we are part of the universe, contained in the finite. If his theory didn't quite answer the question of where we were going to end up, it did make a strong case for believing that wherever it was, it was ordained. To judge from the sales of books, this theory was reassuring in Lansing, Michigan, and Guildford, Surrey.

From up here, too, I can see another landscape, a landscape of women I have known. It is a strange landscape, a sort of collage. Without wishing to cause unnecessary offence, I must report that I see a landscape of hillocks and valleys and groves. As if a painter had carefully positioned it or created perspective that draws the eye, I see Ulla's breasts. Encouraged by birds and flowers and scuttling things, lizards and so on, I feel an intensity as though I am close to homing in on the sublime as painters and poets used to. At the same time this vision suggests to me that my idea of the sublime is not very substantial. Yet I enjoy being up here in the early morning. I have the airman's perspective, and his detachment. Down below, the topography, the animal kingdom, the vast stuttering bay, are all reduced. They have taken on the scale of the ant world I used to inspect. I see myself again in khaki shorts and sandals studying the ants and wondering how they were always able to find their way home, even after I had ploughed up their track with a twig. I was not wondering in a scientific way, nor in a poetic way. I was simply wondering what gave the little buggers their tenacity? And why did they want to run up your khaki shorts and bite your scrotum? And how did they know that it was going to hurt so much?

And now I have an idea: I will finish up my father's book on baboons before I go home. I will find a typewriter, update it, and sell it as a lost masterpiece. And then maybe some money will reach me.

7

Days have gone by – five now – and still my mother is alive, or at least just this side of the borderline between life and death. It's a border indistinctly drawn, I now see. She hasn't spoken to me again although I have said, 'I'm here, Ma,' a number of times in the hope that she will hear through whatever haze and mist and vacuum chamber surrounds her. I feel closer to her now as she is dying than at any time since I was about seven years old. She once told me that I was an excessively affectionate child. I had beseeched her, anxiously, not to die young as her own mother had. She said, 'We are angels, you and I.' And now she is dying, finally.

The pace of it is a little too sedate for the nurses. The doctor, a grave young Afrikaner with large, bony hands, is very calm. It might take a few more days but he said the vital signs were weakening. The vital signs. I didn't tell him about the noises in the night, the accumulation of sighs and groans. These were not the sort of vital signs he was interested in, these echoes and reverberations – meaningless no doubt – of a life, as if the store cupboard of human emotion was being emptied of oddments.

I don't care if the days of dying stretch onwards. When I wake I walk up the track to the mountain. While I'm out the nurses clean her up. And then I read the books in the cottage and I have employed a handyman called Johannes to fix the place up. No doubt the elderly who pass shuffling by think I am doing it to improve the resale value, but they are wrong. I am doing it as an act of atonement. I'm doing it for the past, and for the lies and the deceit.

47

There are photograph-albums which my mother has doctored. People who upset her have been cut out. My father is duck shooting, but the person next to him has gone. Luckily for the ducks, my father was very short sighted. My brother's wife has gone from her own wedding photograph, leaving a hole which demands attention, like a bomb crater in a city. There are lots of pictures of me. I am sitting on a stone, aged about eight. In another picture I am receiving my degree at Oxford (Oxford was a place of reverence for my mother, the Lourdes of Englishness). And there is a picture of my mother in an amateur dramatic production playing, as she put it, 'a young thing'. I trailed behind her, not more than six years old, as she went around Stuttaford's and then Garlick's looking for a suitable dress for 'a young thing', and even then I experienced a wave of embarrassment at the phrase. Children want their parents to behave in a conventional fashion.

And now I find a picture I have, as far as I can remember, never seen before. It too has been mutilated. I am standing next to Robert Frame at his pool. Beside him is an empty shape, almost a human shape, and to our right, beyond the shape, is the Frames' dog, Blanco. It is an albino Alsatian which looks like a wolf. Robert and I are poised in our cozzies shivering between dives to retrieve a *tiekie*, a threepenny bit, from the floor of the pool. I can't see the gooseflesh in the photograph, but I can feel it. And I remember Robert's mother, Edna, who had passing enthusiasms, photographing us with her new camera.

But I can't remember who the missing person could be, the person who my mother has excised. Judging from the cut-out the missing person is also a child as we were. Of course it's possible that it was a taller person, standing further away, but I don't think it's likely. There is a picture of my mother at a ranch in Rhodesia before the War, with her school friend Blanche. There was a small dog, and my mother has written, 'Spotty, soon after taken by crocodile'.

Those were pioneering days, though not of course for the blacks who had lived there for many thousands of years, and would have been able to predict that a fox terrier from the old country would be eaten by something or other. If they'd been consulted. Like children, they were never consulted. (As a matter of fact, children are increasingly consulted now, although the questions are usually loaded to reflect the parents' concerns.)

And now, spurred on by these thoughts of black people, the anonymous rows and legions and platoons that I have met and half known with their dusty faces and their respectful demeanours, I suddenly remember who the missing person is in the swimming pool photograph: it is Sephos, the son of the Frames' cook. And I remember now what happened to him. On the day of the photograph, he was watching us swim and we invited him to come into the water. We found him a cozzie in the dark cavern where the pool filter and some mouldy towels were housed. I noticed his long, uncircumcised penis as he changed.

He said he could swim, but he couldn't. Halfway across the pool, he stopped swimming – probably realising that what he was doing so far was an act of faith. We swam like eels and we tried to save him, but he clamped both arms around my neck and dragged me down. I dived to the bottom to escape him and he sank. How deep was the water? Perhaps six feet. He sank and lay very still on the bottom. I dived down again and almost succeeded in pulling him to the surface, but he seemed to become heavier the closer we got to the surface. Robert had run for his mother. Screaming, his mother and the cook arrived as I sat shivering and crying, looking down to the bottom, where Sephos lay in his unfamiliar Speedos, his body very brown on the blue-white floor of the pool. Edna dived in, and I remember seeing her Playtex pantie-girdle, lightly ribbed, and she hauled Sephos out, but it was too late. The ambulance arrived and the body, wrapped in a grey blanket, disappeared. There were no questions. I saw how things were ordered, and I never forgot.

I couldn't go back to the Frames' ever again, but I went to see Robert once in Courchevel where he had become a ski instructor. We didn't mention Sephos. I imagine now that I would have liked to ask him how he felt about it but his new Alpine demeanour, and his reflective sunglasses which were rimmed in chrome with Swiss-cheese holes, suggested that it wasn't the right moment. But I don't know.

And now I see that somewhere along the way, my mother has tried to excise this memory of a drowned black boy. The surprise is that she had ever had it in her album, and how she got it is equally mysterious.

The Frames' pool itself I remember very clearly. Like ants, swimming pools played a big part in my early life. The smell of them, the insects and toads that were trapped, even the occasional snake, but above all the endless diving and searching the bottom. And later there were girls and their bodies still inhabit my dreams along with the scent of water, the bubbling of the filter, the texture of the wet towels we lay on, the coarse kikuyu grass, the noise of a hand lawnmower, the wedges of chocolate cake, and the first kisses. What a magical thing, to clasp your wet, chocolatey mouth on someone else's and daringly to mix your saliva. I understand why prostitutes prefer sex to kissing: kissing is far more intimate, performed where it counts.

I have in my mind a picture of a tanned forearm, little golden hairs catching the sun, and skin still puckered, but relaxing under the sun's influence. So it seems to me incredible that I have given no thought to Sephos, who lay on the bottom of the pool splayed out. You would have thought an event like that would have been in your mind every day. But the mind is a strange thing, selective in what it remembers and subject to its own rules.

There is another picture of my mother on a horse. She is

smiling at the camera. The horse's head is blurred, caught in a sudden movement. This picture saddens me, and I compare this vigorous young woman with what lies only just alive in a clinic. Nothing has been excised from this picture. A little African girl stands off to one side smiling shyly. From the fact that she is wearing only a small leather apron, I deduce this must be in Rhodesia again.

Looking through the album, I see that what my mother wanted was to remove from her pictures anything discordant. She seemed to be trying to return to a time and a place when she had been happy. I have neglected her, caught up in my own troubles – just a life – while she has been casting her thoughts backwards to images of me sitting on a stone, and of us as a family before my father's defection, and her years of bliss as a young mother and amateur actress. I'm filled with sadness.

The phone rings and I fear the worst. For days the phone has been silent. It is not the clinic but the lawyer; he introduces himself and asks if I could come down to the little baked town in the valley below to discuss some issues.

'Of course.'

'How is your ma?'

'She's more or less asleep all the time.'

'Shame. She was, I should say is, a remarkable woman. Bloody difficult but extraordinary.'

'Can I come down tomorrow?'

'Sure, I'm not going anywhere.'

I know what it is going to be: liabilities, unpaid medical and legal bills, the arrangements for the sale of the meagre assets.

'Okay. I'll come down about eleven.'

'The coffee and Marie biscuits will be waiting.'

My heart is becoming heavy. Pascal said that great thoughts come from the heart. I am not so sure it's a question of thought so much as of feelings. It is certainly in this region that I feel more elemental things, the familiar unease which calls from lawyers and disappointed women and bank managers produce. The heart seems to yaw and heel. I think of the heart not as an organ, but as a highly sensitive, but devolved region of myself, reacting too critically or too readily to trouble. In Afrikaans a *voorloper* was a boy who walked ahead of the oxen. My heart is a sort of *voorloper*.

My mother is still breathing in that minute way, with the occasional upheaval from within her thin chest. Her chest has worked loose from the nightie. As a child I remember her with large breasts, spaced widely apart. Now the breasts have gone to be replaced by small, dry pouches, containing neither substance nor nourishment. I close the nightie.

I hold her hand and I tell her the story of Blanche's farm which she often told me. I remind her that they were out one night to scare off lions which were approaching the cattle kraal, when they suddenly saw green eyes in the beam of their flashlights. Boetie, Blanche's husband, fired and just nicked the ear of his favourite dog, Simba, which yelped.

'The dog wasn't hurt and you were happy; you loved dogs. You laughed, Ma, you and Boetie and Blanche laughed. Do you remember our old dog, Toby, which Dad said was a Russian bear-hound? It was actually a Dachshund crossed with a Labrador? Blanche's dog, Spotty, was eaten by a crocodile, which was very sad I should think. You and Blanche rode every day, and your horse was called Jupiter and hers was called Sambo. Not very PC, Ma. And you told me that the grey, greasy Limpopo was brown. In reality.'

I'm on a roll now. As I speak I remember her stories and I remember the books she read me, and I remember the way she used to hold me between her knees and towel me after a bath, and I remember that the leap from bath to towel was always a cold one. I tell her all these things, and I find myself talking in a quiet and warm voice, completely naturally, as if I have in the face of a death acquired some bardic qualities.

I hope it's getting through. Despite my own failures and transgressions against women, I have always believed that women have deeper roots in this earth and a clear connection to humanness. I think of myself delivering a modest eulogy. I repeat to her the stories she told me. They weren't stories of any great consequence, but as I relate them I see them as voluminous as Greek mythology. She doesn't wake.

Outside the gardeners have started and the watering system has sprung to life. The little jets of water attract lustrous birds that shower themselves and shake the droplets free, as if they can't bear to be wet for another moment. My mother fed the birds outside her cottage every day, and a few diehards still turn up for a handout.

I begin my walk up towards the farmhouse and the mountain beyond, which today is panting with heat as though the bare exposed rock up there is almost smouldering. What I think about my mother is that lives are never wasted; whatever she has done for nearly eighty years, not much as a matter of fact, not by the standards of pointless motion which are prevalent, is finding its way back into the geography, directly into these mountains, a process which will be laid only by memory – I'm in a fervour of memory myself – but in the end it will all come to the same thing. I don't find these thoughts depressing. On the contrary, I recognise the freedom of accepting the necessary. For the first time in months I feel liberated. My life too will fade into the geological and physical facts, and I don't give a fuck.

I bound up the mountain – I must be becoming fitter – taking a track which leads, according to a sign, to the nature reserve. As if to confirm this way lies nature, a baboon calls from the rock above. It's a hoarse, smoker's bark of alarm, but it contains a welcome, I believe.

8

Ulla had a habit of eating just before she went to sleep. It was three in the morning. The Crunchy Nut cornflakes were rowdy. I could hear their progress from box to plate; I could hear the milk splashing and the spoon clattering and then Ulla's approach, the flakes living up to their billing as she crunched them. She sat heavily on the bed, wearing just a tee shirt. I loved the way her thighs met her hips, forming a little erotic valley. She was eager to talk. All sorts of things filled her mind at these moments. They weren't necessarily very profound thoughts but for me they had great charm. She would talk about television programmes and the people who had come into the boutique, or she would relay her concern about the famine in Africa. Her hair sometimes seemed to oscillate, as though picking up the intensity of her thoughts.

That evening I was tired after my night out with Irene Ball, and I was barely listening.

'This bloke comes into the boutique and he asks me to try on a shirt, he says his girlfriend is about the same size as me. I hold it up and he wants me to –'

At that moment the phone rang. Ulla picked it up.

'It's for you,' she said.

It was Paddy, my assistant.

'You've got to get down to Chelsea Hospital. Your son's ill.'

'Jesus. Who rang you?'

'Eleanor.'

'Did you tell her?'

'No, mate, no I didn't. I just said I'd ring around. She said you were with Irene Ball, that's why she rang me.'

'I was.'

'It's Harrington Ward. I'll ring to say you're on your way. Where did I find you?'

'Sleeping at Irene's. It was raining and I was a tad pissed.'

'Okay, mate, I hope it's all right.'

Ulla was sobbing quietly; she cried in the way that rain falls in Scandinavia, softly but insistently.

'I've got to go now. You heard. My son's ill.'

'Please ring me if you can.'

'I'll try.'

But he was dead. I didn't ring Ulla. I was mute. My grief and my shame made me mute. I'd rather have spoken to stones. I held Eleanor's thin, angry body to mine, and I thought of a thousand ways to make it up to her, but even as I conjured them I knew it could not work. We found it hard to speak ever again. Once or twice we tried to talk about Matthew's death; I found myself drowning in a vile fluid so that my words and hers were distorted and inaudible.

After the funeral, Eleanor and I could not be in the same room again. She did not ask me where I was on the fatal night and I did not enquire about Matt's inhaler, but the air was full of unspoken recrimination. His asthma started four years before when I bought a kitten. It took us two years to make the connection, even though there was plenty of publicity about allergies. In fact allergies were a new thing during Mrs Thatcher's second term. Allergies and jingoism were in all the papers. By the time we'd had the tests done and given away the cat, the asthma had taken hold. There were nights, as I listened to his thin chest sucking and clawing for air, when I wished I'd taken the cat outside into the reverberating garden and knocked it on the head with a spade years earlier.

And so I lost my son and two women all on one day.

*   *   *

Down in the little town, which is baking along a wide street, wide enough so that ox wagons could turn, I walk through the rows of small houses and two-storey brick office buildings and garages that sell pick-ups – *bakkies* they call them – and past the shops selling cheap clothes and junk food. These brown people who stop or loiter or wander along eating are not attractive people. They have faces that have been knocked about by life. Of course, I know that this is a cultural judgement, but I am not here to weigh and consider or to make allowances for history and deprivation and injustice. There are plenty of people better equipped than me for that. Coming back to my fatherland this late in the day, I have no wish to add my voice to the chorus of analysis and judgement. Anyway, my own life has not qualified me to pass grand judgement. These brown people, the Coloureds, are small and ugly. I don't know how I look to them, if they care at all, I in my linen suit with its torn pocket caught on one of my mother's eight dining-room chairs, which stand as in a junk shop, against one wall. Getting rid of the chairs would have suggested the death of hope. She wrote to me sometimes saying that she was planning to have a few people round. From the letters alone I can summon the dark scent of the cupboard where the drinks were kept, and the quick aroma of juniper as the gin fell into the glass and coated it briefly before the tonic was released. I could never forget that quinine is made of bark, and I imagine something arboreal in the air. Maybe she too remembered these things.

The lawyer's office is in a side street which retains a little of the old colonial calm; a huge shady oak stands outside the whitewashed and thatched building. The turtle doves are loud, although this is a relative term: their vocal range is limited. There is no air down here in town. I feel my suit sticking to me. It is an English suit, never worn by colonials. An Englishman, particularly of the older sort, feels compelled to buy a linen suit and a Panama hat if he is going somewhere hot. My suit is a prop from the promotional film I made for the Paradise Club in the Turks and Caicos Islands. The film was never completed but it got further than the resort: only a model and a show suite – the *atelier* – were built. Some waving palm trees and an invitingly blue ocean were filmed and an actor of roughly my size, dressed in a new linen suit – in those days all its pockets were firmly stitched – explained the concept of buying a share in paradise. The Paradise Club. Deposits were taken but, alas, the proposed development was in the path of biannual hurricanes. Prospective purchasers of paradise found dead animals, uprooted palm trees, and the site office upside down fifty yards from the beach, holed by a flying palm tree. The beach, described in the film as 'dazzlingly white, each individual grain of sand polished and faceted' (I wrote the script), now resembled a gravel pit, if you can imagine a gravel pit festooned with seaweed, rotting fish and lumps of tar. The actor had offered to kick back half his fee if I gave him the job. In the event he did not receive any of his fee, and I kept the suit.

And it is this same suit which is clinging to my back as I enter the lawyer's little offices. The lawyer is evidently a sporting man. The waiting room is decorated with pictures of him in dozens of teams including, a brief survey reveals, golf, rugby, cricket and boxing. The receptionist asks me to sit down. She says, with a touch of reverence, that Mr Pennington is on the phone. She returns to her computer and types. Her face is a cinnamon colour and she wears a light-green silken suit. She might be of Malay origins. I find that I am speculating about the racial origins of everyone I meet. The lawyer's progress from the Under Tens to his university team is documented in details. I can spot him in a crowd now: his eyes are the only aspect of him which does not change; as he grows bigger and more muscular, his eyes, closely set, seem to huddle together in the middle of his face. Here he is as captain of the Under Fifteens. So good is he that he has been entrusted with sole charge of the rugby ball; he holds it on his lap. It is a heavy, leather object, impossible to catch in wet weather. Here he is in cricket clothes, wearing a blazer decorated with a badge that looks like a bishop's mitre. He has cricket colours too.

I wonder why a man would decorate his office with all these reminders of pygmy wars.

The intercom on the secretary's desk buzzes. The secretary stands up. Her shiny suit is creased around the backs of her thighs. She tugs it down. In that strange accent she says, 'Mr Pennington iss ready to see you naauw.'

She shows me to an inner office. Pennington stands up apologetic, waves dismissively at a pile of documents:

'High Court. Utter fuck-up,' he says.

I like these little provincial Julien Sorel games. Pennington's eyes are now, because of the profusion of the once sporting flesh, almost in single file. His large face is spotted with the effects of standing in the sun for so much of his life. Gingery hairs peer inquisitively out of his ears. He orders tea and Marie biscuits. These biscuits are circular and very plain; they have the same effect on me as a Madeleine had on Proust. The Five Roses tea is poured. I take a biscuit, dry but fragrantly familiar. Pennington takes four spoons of sugar in his tea. I can't wait to bite into the biscuit.

'So, I meet you at last. How is your ma today?'

'No change.'

'Shame. Look, there is something I want to tell you now. She didn't want you to know until later.'

The biscuit is sweet – not over sweet – and crunchy. As a boy, Marie biscuits were poor relations of Pyott's Lemon Creams, but you could put them in a saucer of milk and they would double in size, a childish miracle.

'She didn't want you to know.'

He thinks that I am not paying attention. Actually, I'm fearful: so many things have gone wrong that I am like the

Inuit, who have no word for hope in their language, only fear. (So I have read.)

'When he died, your father left you some money, quite a lot of money in our terms.'

'What? How much?'

'It's about one and a half million, let's say a hundred thousand pounds. Your mother had the option of using the income if she wanted to.'

'Why didn't she want me to know?'

'Because she thought it would be bad for you.'

'So why are you telling me now?'

'Because it takes weeks, even months, to get trusts and documents and wills and so on through the authorities these days. If you tell me now what you want to do with the money, I can get my ducks in a row.'

I'm not exactly sure what he is talking about. Like Proust's Auntie Léonie, I dip my biscuit in my tea. It is soft, pap.

'I want to buy a farm.'

'Where?'

'Here. Up the road from the village.'

'Are you sure? You can take the money out, you know.'

'I know.'

'And the cottage is worth some more. Probably twenty thousand in your money.'

'What was your favourite sport?'

'What?'

'You are obviously keen on sport.'

Behind him is a picture which shows him as captain of the Helderview Golf Club.

'Now it's golf, but then it was rugby. I would have given my left bollock to be a Springbok.'

'What's so special about the other one?'

He laughs. I feel a locker-room camaraderie with Pennington, who has brought me this good news. I might join his golf club soon, with a new set of clubs, each one encased in soft chamois leather. I would take golf lessons first, of course.

'Your father also left you his manuscripts. He thought you could sell them to university libraries.'

'Did you speak to him personally?'

'No, but he wanted to make sure your mother and you would be all right after he died.'

'Did he speak to my mother?'

'Yes. He came to see her in your old house before she moved here.'

'She never told me.'

'I liked your mother. Ag, I like her. Forgive me.'

His large face with the liver spots honourably gained in the service of sport is generous.

'No problemo,' I say (the golf club lingo).

'Most of them couldn't stand her. But she was so alert. She couldn't bear to pay useless compliments.'

'The usual hypocrisies.'

'Another Marie biscuit?'

'Why not? Hang the expense.'

On the drive back in my mother's old car – a sort of Ford Escort so antique that it is modish – I brushed the crumbs of Marie biscuit off my shirt. I was happy. *Por dinero baila el perro*, the dog will dance for money. If I am prudent, my dancing days are over.

Even in old age my mother is unsure of me. I have sat by her bed for days and I have tried with limited resources to remove in her mind the distinction between being alive and dead. (Which, by the way, may not be all that big.) I have tried to keep her company. I have tried to suggest that we are going somewhere together. The veil will be lifted, and we will find ourselves on the other side. Of course, I will have a right of return, but I have sat there night after night willing myself into a state of non-being. At times I wondered if it wouldn't be better on the other side, achieving solidarity with my mother and father. And Matthew.

61

Yet she didn't trust me with my father's money. Or manuscripts. Before I left him, Pennington said that he had the manuscripts in safe custody; I could have them whenever I wanted them. He had taken the liberty of finding out how you offered such items to academe. It seemed there was a demand from universities in the American South West.

I feel an unaccustomed affection for my father. The idea that twelve years ago, seriously ill, he had taken a trip here, to leave his family something, moved me. Death of course is a powerful sharpener. As Pennington said, twelve years ago the money was worth something. Still, it would perhaps buy me the farmhouse. Now that I've blurted it out, I'm coming round to the idea. It's a strange thing but until I have said something out loud it can remain in the mind unformed, like dough before rising. Like plaster of Paris or Polyfilla, ideas and enthusiasms don't set until they are exposed to the air. I can buy the house, or another, and edit my father's papers, and grow vines or keep bees. And through my bees, I may draw the thin-spun stream of life to myself. As my father discovered, there is a great appetite for this kind of stuff, DIY for the soul.

Instead of heading back up to the hills, I turn down towards the coast. This huge beach, unending, with its detritus of kelp and seagull-pecked fish and occasional lone fisherman casting deep into the water and stranded jellyfish and pieces of weathered planking and always the wind and the relentless waves, used to frighten me as a boy. It was implacable.

The wind comes ashore in its peculiar, heartless fashion. It throbs as though it has picked up sounds on its long journey from Patagonia or the Antarctic, or wherever it starts. Little birds march about where the waves have retreated, pecking hurriedly before the next arrival. I walk along their territory, barefoot. I remember now the sand is hardest just where the waves have retreated from. If I turn my back on the waves, I can see the Helderberg, throttled by cloud. Behind the first range is the farm which I have foolishly told the former athlete, Anton Pennington, that I am going to buy.

I see some women with whitened faces collecting firewood which they are stacking in huge bundles. Why are their faces whitened in this fashion? I watch them as they hack the leaves off the brushwood and then as they tie the bundles together. Seagulls are screaming. The wind is tearing at their clothes.

The women hoist the bundles of wood on to their heads and begin to walk over the sand dunes. I follow them up on a parallel track. From the tip of the dune I see down below, where they are headed, a collection of shacks made of scraps of wood and wire and plastic sheeting. Children are sitting in the sand, their backs turned to the wind. The white-faced women greet them and throw down the bundles. From a higher sand dune stripped of vegetation, I see valley after valley of shacks, shot-blasted by the wind.

The waves are thundering on the beach. They create a low booming noise and a whistling as the spray from the breakers hustles away on the wind.

9

A small semi-detached house near Ealing. It is in a row of identical houses with bow fronts, red tiles, and tidy front gardens. Each garden has a path leading up to the front door, and most have, like this one, Number 28, standard roses lining the path. The front porch of Number 28 has two windows beside the door of stained glass, divided into leaded panels. Just to the right of the path is a fish pond. To be honest, the fish pond seems out of place.

A young man is walking up the path. He has a chubby face, unfashionable glasses, and he is carrying some flowers. He walks in a peculiar, diffident fashion, as though the crazy paving is hot, or perhaps noisome. He arrives at the front door, straightens his tie (he is wearing a suit) and reaches for the bell.

'Cut.'

The chubby young man looks round.

'Go again, Andrew, don't overdo it. You look like, I don't know, fuck, you look like – as though – you have a corncob up your arse.'

'I wish.'

'Okay, once more, Andrew. Go.'

The garden and the front of the house and the improbable fish pond and the porch are lit by huge lights and the cables run to a generator truck, standing, throbbing, in the road. This time Andrew – the actor – walks with more purpose, although he conveys nervousness by fiddling with his tie. The director is happy. Now the camera crew move in for a close shot. The big lights are wheeled in, and from inside the house a smaller light plays on the stained glass which has patterns of colour in the shape, perhaps, of a tulip on each side. Above the door is a leaded panel also with the tulip pattern.

'Okay, Andrew. Action. In you go.'

Andrew approaches the front door, holding his flowers. He rings the bell, and stands nervously waiting. The door opens eventually, and a young girl dressed in a short nightie, her hair tied up in bunches, looks out.

'Oh. It's you. She's getting ready.'

The girl slams the door, decapitating the flowers.

'Perfect, well done, Linsay. That worked.'

The door opens and the young actress peers out, smiling.

'Going again?'

'No, that was perfect,' says the director.

'Am I in the next one?'

'Yes, you are, darling. You're behind Terri when she comes out. Everybody ready. Stand by.'

It is evident that this film is being made at speed.

'Andrew, stand there looking at the flowers.'

'How?'

'Puzzled. Bemused. Pondering the meaning of the universe. Good. Okay. Action. Come out, Suzi.'

Suzi Crispin, played by Terri Elms (whose tits are played by Ulla), now comes to the door. Her sister stands behind her.

'Nice flowers,' she says.

'Yes, sorry they got caught in the door.'

''Ere. Take these.'

Andrew, who plays her boyfriend, Lionel, is burdened with her suitcases and bags.

'Okay, exit frame. Good. Do we need a close-up of Andrew? No? Okay. Let's move back down the path.'

This next scene works very well. As Lionel staggers down the path with Suzi's luggage – they are bound for the nurses' home – he treads on a garden rake, made of balsa wood, which springs up and hits him in the face. He falls over backwards clutching his eye, right into the pond which now can be seen in a new light: it is perfectly positioned for this gag.

'Cut. Cut. Well done, Andrew.'

A true professional, Andrew is lying on his back semi-submerged.

'Stay there, Andrew. I've got an idea. Let's do one close-up as his head comes out of the water. Put some weed on his head. You'll have to hold your breath for a moment. Oh, Andrew, say "Sorry, Suzi, I am a clot" as you come up.'

'As quick as you like. The fucking water's freezing.'

'You are here to suffer for your art.'

'How will I know when to come up? I didn't study sub-aqua acting at RADA.'

'Ah, I didn't know you had studied acting at all. We'll run the camera, submerge yourself, and then count to three before you come up. Don't forget the new line, will you? Ready. Tuck a bit of weed behind his ears. What about a goldfish in his mouth? Are there any plastic goldfish? No. Okay, no we haven't got any, it seems. There's never a goldfish or a halibut available when you need one. Okay, turn over, and action, down you go, Andrew, one, two, three.'

Right on cue his head pops up, draped with pond weed.

'Oh, sorry, Suzi, I am a cunt,' he says.

'Go again. Quite funny, Andrew, but not in the script.'

'What script would that be, duckie? Can we go again before my bollocks drop off?'

The house we rented for the filming, Number 28, is lodged in my mind as the quintessential English house. Between the two bay windows, red tiles were hung, and the gable above the upper-floor window was half timbered. The rest of the walls were covered in pebble-dash. The roof tiles too were red except where mosses and lichens and bird shit had darkened them. Every nuance of Englishness was contained here: the minor snobberies and antipathies, the cosiness, the bucolic pretensions, the skinny roses, the dinky garage for a dinky car, the clipped privet hedges. It was the sort of house where murder was a form of recreation, like Scrabble. It was the sort of house where bank clerks masturbated looking at *Titbits*. It was the sort of house that had one fading electric bar in each pale-green tiled fireplace. It was the sort of house where the washing was hung out on a spindly plastic carousel. It was the sort of house where women went quietly mad. It was a sort of dreadful hymn to England.

So I thought.

I was young and full of scorn. I was, after all, a director to watch. I hadn't appreciated then the full range of human qualities; I hadn't seen then that we are all participants in a human drama whose purpose is unclear, but which is unstoppable. I hadn't realised that people make accommodations with life. I hadn't read Lévi-Strauss, so I didn't know that all forms of belief are perfectly good explanations – none of them necessarily true – for the human predicament. I thought then that there were two forms of reality, at the very least – the higher one, which I inhabited, and the lesser one, where people lived behind privet hedges feeding roses. And I had many other, earthbound, delusions.

The actor, Andrew Devenish, who fell into the fish pond is the same actor whose suit I wear for sub-tropical encounters.

These houses are called by architectural historians 'debilitated Queen Anne'. They contain elements of 'speculative Tudor': to achieve the Tudor look, creosoted planks are nailed to the gables. How I hated them. I saw behind the curtains people with the skin texture of mushrooms. I imagined a race of quiet perverts, who kept budgies. For all these reasons I sited Suzi Crispin's family there: the slob of a father; the minor snob of a mother; the nymphomaniac daughters. Probably, I thought that I was making a disguised state-of-the-nation film. But one day the producers, having seen some rushes, decided that the film was too arty. It needed more sex. I was forced to cast naked women in the film soaping each other in the showers without purpose. Something in my human essence went down the gurgling plug-hole with the suds.

A strange thing: these naked bodies, pretending to be nurses after hours, aroused in me a deep fellow feeling, which I have never quite lost, for the peculiarities, the strange topography and burdens, of female bodies. Breasts which are widely spaced and filled with heavy liquid; small breasts which are empty of substance. Legs that seem ill-assorted; buttocks that carry anachronistic substance. All sorts of variations. No surprise that women were so different, but gathered together here, naked, they were defenceless and sexless. Their eyes were red after the third and fourth take. For me this scene, designed to bring sex to our film, was deeply dispiriting: we are all just bodies subsiding gently. The naked women soaping each other with extreme artificiality also produced in me uninvited thoughts of death. And I see now that death and futility are linked.

Of course it's easy as you look back to assign significance to moments or episodes in your life. Up until then, film had seemed to me to re-order and add a new lustre to life, to events, to stories; film was the finest art form ever. But I began to realise that art could not be graded in this way. Film hadn't saved me from producing a third-rate sex film. Film itself had no power; film had no special advantage. With Ulla I was living a harum-scarum life, a film person taking a share – to quote my father, quoting Virgil – in the divine spark. What a delusion! I had mistaken the self-congratulatory complicity of the film world for something more magical, even something numinous. And now I see that all over the world, young people share this delusion as they clamour to be admitted to film school and media studies. Good luck.

Standing over the camera, watching Andrew get out of the fish pond, do I have these feelings that I have attributed to myself? Probably not. Despite the dreary surroundings and the tawdry nature of our enterprise, I still believed. I thought that I was practising at some higher level. I was in a sort of fervour, with the work and Ulla, and family guilt. We ate at expensive places late at night, far from the debilitated Queen Anne and the fog-bound canteen of the studio. We took drugs, we ran up a huge bill for the chauffeur service. Late at night, early in the morning, Ed Wilmott was there in his grey suit and chauffeur's cap with a thistle on it, waiting our pleasure. (Why do chauffeurs have a thistle on their hats?) Ed had the pallor of security guards and night-shift workers. In film fashion, I began to think of him as my creature, a kind of pasty Caliban. Sometimes I would go home to see little Matthew and weep at my own duplicity.

It was a time of change. (All times are times of change, it's just a question of degree.) Mrs Thatcher and her curious collection of ministers, men with expensive suits and self-regarding haircuts, pantomime characters, were mounting a revolution. They were promoting self-interest. They were dealing firmly with foreigners. (The Argentines threw in the towel.) Whether they intended it or not, they disturbed the temper of the high streets and the sleepy suburbs. The country became loud.

Our film was doomed. It belonged to the folk art of a previous time, of smutty jokes and pompous figures of authority, which included the hospital consultants. It belonged to a time of seaside postcards and jellied eels, of men in flat caps and women in curlers, of old maids on bicycles. It dealt with sex as though it were a corny joke which had been played on us, and which we must accept with stoicism and humour. In this reading, women were the acknowledged experts in sexual duplicity. God gave them tits to make men compliant. Such was the folklore. It didn't matter that I thought in my heart that the film was subversive.

After the roof came down and the stunt doubles spouted blood, and Matthew died, I saw myself as deluded and ridiculous. I was removed from the film because I was unable to work. It was done in a spirit of compassion, but in truth they were glad to get rid of me with my silly and inappropriate ideas.

You have to suffer for your art.

A year later I saw Ulla in the street. We went into a bar where we had once fed our important needs. We had sat down there in the gloom against the exposed brickwork in a tumult. Now, on the same spot, I was thinking of her removing her clothes. It was unbearably erotic. But she seemed already to have half forgotten our affair. At least what she remembered was all pleasant and trivial. She had no recollection of asking me to marry her.

'You don't remember?'

'It's not that I don't remember. It never happened. I would never have asked.'

'Oh well. Are you still working in a boutique?'

'No, it more or less closed. It sells cards and knick-knacks. No, I'm married now. I'm studying make-up and psycho-therapy.'

'You're married? Who is he?'

'He's a film technician.'

'Anybody I would know?'

'You would. He was the focus-puller on our film.'

'Oh. Billy Cox.'

'Yes. After your tragedy William was very friendly. It just went on from there. It's lovely to see you.'

'Are you happy with William, né Billy?'

'Very happy. I'm going to have a baby. Here. Feel.'

She takes my hand, my hand with its stubby fingers which have explored every centimetre of her careless body, and places it on her stomach, which is rounded and hard although not big. I wonder how long I am expected to leave it there. Am I supposed to carry out an amateur obstetric examination, feeling for human life and movement?

'Congratulations.'

'I don't know why people say congratulations. You don't have to do anything different.'

I remove my hand. This aperçu, which I take to mean that our love-making was nothing special either, stabs me. I look closely at her face for clues, but impending motherhood, the secrets of psychotherapy, the passage of a year or so, have made no impression on her. Her face is blank and, I now think, Scandinavian. Her mother is Norwegian.

It was dark down there as I groped to detect any deeper understanding or regret. Her mouth was small, a sort of sexual culvert. Her eyes – slightly too rounded – were bright with the wonder of maternity.

'My tits are becoming huge,' she said.

'Would you like me to feel them too?'

'No thanks.'

'Your tits which a few million have seen.'

'Without knowing it. William gets upset about that. They're out on video.'

And me? I seem to have been written out of the tits story.

In fact, I had been removed from the picture as effectively, and mysteriously, as my mother had doctored her family photographs. Maybe like the little black boy, Sephos, I had drowned too. Drowned in my own troubles. But then why should you want to stay firmly lodged in other people's affections? Particularly ex-lovers'? But to me the intimacies carried out with mutual gusto were a marvellous thing, almost a sacrament. Though of course it was me who had broken off contact, I somehow expected Ulla to have waited, knowing my reasons. Instead she had taken up – how quickly? – with a member of the crew: the oily rags, the suburbanites, and little Billy – William as we must now call him – was jealous because millions of people had seen her anonymous tits. Or perhaps – I draw a little retrospective comfort – it was really jealousy that I had seen them first. But the truth cannot be hidden: I have been forgotten. Like Sephos there is a gap in the landscape that once I had inhabited.

My chance meeting with Ulla lost all erotic momentum. She talked brightly about the flat they were buying – property was booming – she told me how the baby's room would be done up. I was thinking of my own Matt, who had died when he was at that delicate beautiful stage of boyhood – legs like pale tapers – while I was lying with this Nordic airhead, who was now talking about pink or blue curtains. She didn't believe in knowing the sex of a baby beforehand. It took all the natural mystery away. She felt that one of the problems of modern life was that we don't any longer open ourselves to mystery. I could have told her that my father believed much the same thing decades before. Instead, I listened to her recalling history – my history – so blithely with growing despair.

'I've got to go, Ulla.'

'My gynie says I can have two glasses a day. I was just about ready for the second.'

'No. I've got to go. Let's get together one day, you, Billy, the baby and so on. I'll ring you. I've got Billy's number somewhere.'

I left her down there in the gloom – brown was fashionable then – and I rushed out on to the street. All around the city was grinding away, heedless. This city has a kind of heartlessness. The bricks, the countless bricks, the pavements, the river itself, are washed with indifference.

And now I'm walking on a wild beach at the other end of the world, a beach made more wild by the fact that I can smell wood fires and see on the sands those tireless women with their bundles of driftwood. Some are picking up fish. I walk closer. They are dogfish, a kind of shark. Africa has arrived from up country. The people are practising ancient tricks to survive. And they are going to need them in their shacks: a cold wind is coming down from the mountains.

I wonder how long my mother can last. It seems obvious that the elemental is proposing to reclaim her.

10

I met the owner of the farm. He was a butcher in a nearby town. His sausages, particularly the dried sausages, were famous, so Pennington told me. We talked in the butcher's shop. He was a small, thin man, belying preconceived ideas about butchers. His skin was not good. His face was a mass of old lesions and recent eruptions that looked like nascent boils. Fruit should have been prescribed. But actually the whole effect was of a natural event, a rugged moon landscape. He stopped chopping the leg of what I guessed was a sheep. The farm, he said, was not strictly speaking his. It belonged to his wife. There were two women working in the shop, one mopping up and one packaging cheap cuts of meat. This woman blasted the packages with a kind of gun, leaving a label. I read one: *Bredievleis, 90c.*

The butcher, whose name was Roos, spoke to the women sharply and led me to his office at the back. Bloodstained bits of paper were impaled on spikes. His wife had inherited the farm. The house was falling down, but some Germans wanted to buy the place and plant vines. We were coming to the question of money. They made no money out of the teas and cakes. How much did he and his wife want for the place? There were ninety-six hectares, he said.

'How many acres is that?'

'Ag, shit, man, I don't remember acres. Maybe two and a half to a hectare, so that's two hundred and fifty, more or less. That's a lot of grapes. And a lot of vines.'

'And a huge expense,' I countered.

'Those Germans are rich. They've got Deutschmarks. Anyway, I'll have to ask my wife.'

'Have you heard from the Germans? I only ask because I read on the plane that the German government said that this is the most lawless place on earth. Actually, number two, after Colombia. And the German economy is in decline.'

Outside his window I could see some sheep penned. They had an anxious look. In London the trade of butchery has been separated from its etymological roots. Butchers' shops disguise the reality with Astroturf displays and paper coronets on the lamb chops and organic fairytales. Here the reality – that something has to be butchered – was not disguised. Banging the sheep on the head and chopping them up was old-style work.

Money. I could sense that it was listening to me. Roos wanted my money. I gave Roos my number: I'll have cash. No bond. Money, even trivial amounts like this, gives you a moral grip. Roos promised to talk to his wife, Tienie.

'Auf Wiedersehen,' I said.

He went back to chopping. One of the girls was slopping up the pink-stained water. I don't have the money yet. I'm in no hurry.

I spend a good part of each day sitting with my mother. Nine days have gone by now, I think. She hasn't spoken to me again, although she makes noises which are close to speech. I go in to see her now, after my trip to the butcher.

'I'm here, Ma.'

She sighs.

'I didn't tell you, Ma. Yesterday I walked on the beach. It was a wild day. Just away from the beach are shacks in all the dunes. There were small dogfish on the beach and driftwood. Xhosa women were collecting the wood and the fish, then they struggled back over the sand dunes. They have fires going. I watched them. They seemed to have moved away from their cattle and their huts up country to live here on the sand dunes.

I wondered what it was. Maybe it's because they think they are closer to the action. I have suffered from this anxiety myself, Ma, the idea that there are more interesting things, more interesting people, somewhere else. *Il faut cultiver son jardin*. You were pleased when I learned French. You wanted me to be a *boulevardier*. You wanted me to be able to converse with the sophisticated, about Malraux and Mallarmé. I didn't tell you that last year I met Charlie Chaplin's granddaughter, did I? I was at a minor French film festival – the French love this sort of thing. They invited me, unaware that my film career is over. She's a beautiful girl, and she asked me to the family home in Switzerland for Christmas. I said no. I would love to come another time. I said I was working on a script, but in fact I couldn't afford the airfare. I spent two whole dinners discussing Breton seafood with the mayor. That's because I was placed next to him. We talked about *coquillages* including *huîtres* and all sorts of bivalves, not forgetting *langoustines* and *bêches-de-mer*. Sea urchins to you and me. He was very knowledgeable and almost lyrical. This is how I use my French, Ma. Oh yes, the students at the local catering college made a display: the whole wall was covered with a fishing net and lobsters and sea bass, and beautiful piles of fish were underneath and there were mountains of ice. You wouldn't have liked it: the fish had their heads on, whiskers, button eyes, spines. The women on the beach yesterday were picking up the dogfish nervously. Some were still alive, their tails flapping quite slowly the same way they swim. The French have no qualms: they will eat almost anything. Do you think that's more or less civilised?'

I talk on. There is no hope of her hearing me, but I feel easier. I tell her again about Paris and New York and the places I have been. She sees them, I know, as impossibly remote and glamorous. I imagine that my voice has become a familiar but meaningless accompaniment, like birdsong or the rhythm of train wheels. I hope that it is reassuring. I don't tell her about the farm, or the legacy or the butcher's shop. She won't eat anything that appears to have some recognisable element of an animal in it. Her cupboards are pathetically bare: they contain a few tins of peach halves, and bottles of fish paste and spaghetti hoops, white asparagus, and an almost empty jar of The Gentleman's Relish. Nor do I tell her that there are no more gentlemen. They are a forgotten category. A lost race. The relish – the list of ingredients reveals that it is made of anchovies and butter – has lost any little snobbish appeal it might have had. Eating The Gentleman's Relish will not convince the world that you have distinction. The Gentleman's Relish is in a stoneware jar from Fortnum's. I remember that I sent it ten or twelve years ago as a Christmas present. I sent her butter and anchovies mushed up and placed in a fake Edwardian jar. And she has kept it as something priceless.

Welsh rarebit, and vintage port, and devils-on-horseback, and soda siphons, all gone.

Her face is hot today, scalded. One eye opens for a moment, but it closes quickly, as though she has seen all she needs. Perhaps she will find the Turks and Caicos Islands interesting: the sea that laps the coast is clear; the waters are full of bright fish – we are on a fishy theme – the central highlands are clad in jungle. Hurricanes batter the place every other year. When they had battered the Paradise Club and the developer vanished, I had to sell my small basement flat in Marylebone to pay off Eleanor, who proved to have the stamina for a long personal struggle. I was bankrupt. All I had was my modest wardrobe, bolstered slightly by the suit which Andrew Devenish had worn as I filmed him beside a mangrove swamp: *Paradise Club. A new concept in shared ownership.*

At times I had imagined that without possessions, without money, I might achieve some monkish happiness. This proved to be a delusion. I took work as a motorcycle messenger, flashing around London. I fell off the motorcycle four times that first winter. I broke my collarbone in the

Gray's Inn Road. I made a pornographic film in three days. Anonymously.

Then one day I had a phone call from my agent, the first for many months, who said that an industrialist called Simon Chiswick wanted to make some films: 'Would you be interested?'

'What are they about?'

'They're political: he doesn't like the Europeans. He started a political party to oppose links with Europe. He approached us to find a director.'

'And you said I know just the man.'

'Exactly.'

'No, you said there is only one person who will take them.'

'To be honest that's more or less true, although I didn't put it like that. I said, I know just the man. I've got to tell you the whole thing is rotten. The only reason I didn't tell him to get stuffed was because I knew you needed the work. We won't, by the way, be asking for a commission.'

Simon Chiswick had made his money in Hong Kong, where apparently it was easy for implausible Englishmen to become rich. And while they were becoming rich they could live in a little corner of the past, with a steward and a few ayahs and a boat-boy. Now, back in England, he was shocked by the laxity, the lack of rigour, of his countryman. His political party, Britain First, was going to put up candidates in fifty seats.

We met at his house in Eaton Terrace. The Filipino man-servant let me in; I walked over a carpet of tremendous geometric opulence, and was shown into his library, impressively full of important-looking books and panelled in lustrous walnut. He was sitting at a vast table in the middle of the room. It all looked unhappy, bought by the yard. He stood up and offered me his hand, small, white and delicate, from beneath a lustrous shirt. It had a shimmering quality, not unlike the fish which nose about in the coral off the Turks and Caicos. His face was soft and unformed, and his hair was carefully brushed over and fixed to cover his skull. He seemed to have difficulty holding me in his vision, his eyes refocusing constantly as though he was looking for something underwater. He introduced himself and we sat down.

'Don't get me wrong, I'm not anti-French.'

'Nor am I.'

'Marvellous culture. Long history. Fine food, et cetera, et cetera. Do you agree?'

'Absolutely.'

'But different. They have their history, we have ours. They have their culture and we have ours. We don't want to dilute our history in Europe. We want to keep it. We don't want them to lose their history or culture. Follow me?'

'So far so good.'

'So our party, Britain First, shouldn't be seen as a negative force. Far from it. We are for diversity, we've got to put that across. We're not talking here about cheese production, but about core values. What is a culture, in your opinion?'

'A culture, I would guess, is, as its name suggests, something which a nation has grown up with over millennia.' I added, seeing which way the wind was blowing, 'Something which they have nurtured and cultivated and which is uniquely their own.'

'Exactly. I have been out in the East for twenty-five years, and during that time I remained essentially English. What a long absence from your own country achieves is that you lose your cynicism. You see what the other chap values, and you contrast and compare. I hope I am not blowing my own trumpet when I say I have achieved a certain clarity.'

'I'm sure you're not.'

'Anyway, my main aim is to remind our countrymen what made them what they are. And this is where you come in.'

Simon Chiswick agreed a generous fee. He gave me some of his thoughts and speeches to study, and asked me to produce ideas for a series of short films which he would be sending to his candidates, who were being sought even now in all walks of life. I agreed to come back to him in two weeks with scripts.

The enterprise was doomed. Simon Chiswick had bribed a minister in government in South-East Asia. He had also written about de Gobineau in the *Straits Times* reminding the Singapore Chinese of their racial purity. Just after I had made the first film, a newspaper exposed him. Plans for a regeneration of British values – the core values – were shelved. It was the last film I made, apart from an unseen pilot on marmosets which lived in the hair of Amazonian Indians. I ate boiled spider monkey on that trip. I had to: the tribes stole our rations.

Sitting with my mute mother, I have plenty of time to go over this – and other – mistakes that I have made. It became known that I had worked for a neo-Nazi. I seemed to be the only person who didn't know that Chiswick was backing forced repatriation and eugenic studies. Even the Conservative Party had rejected his money. Everyone knew his true nature, except me. In those four or five weeks when we discussed history in very crude terms, I had realised that his grip on reality was loose, but I took it that great wealth removed the need to take journalists and academics and politicians seriously. What did they know? They were poor. The poor have, necessarily, a very jaundiced view of the world.

The film I did make for Simon Chiswick was one of my best. In propaganda I had found my métier. Chiswick walked in the Lake District and in the Highlands and along the Thames and in Cambridge and on the White Cliffs and I filmed him from a helicopter and from high vantage points and reflected in water, and I overlaid these visuals with Churchill's words read by an actor, and clips from Olivier's *Henry V* and John of Gaunt's speech from Richard II: *This royal throne of kings, this scepter'd isle.*

I staged a scene in which Chiswick and his family – in reality rather cowed – prepared for Christmas: they all sat around a rustic kitchen table (hired) making a Christmas pudding. Chiswick believed in a traditional Christmas, the whiter the better. The table was laid with piles of raisins and sultanas, dried fruit and nuts. A good stylist was standing by as the enervated children of his second marriage stirred the pudding and smiled wanly.

Later I took on the design of town gardens, without success. I also wrote treatments for films, and a few scripts which were never made. Women helped me from time to time.

In the cottage I have my father's papers from Pennington. My father wrote in exercise books, neatly and legibly. Pennington has written to an agent in Austin, Texas who takes a small commission for selling manuscripts to universities. Disloyal, I wonder if my father's books have sufficient weight for academe. The manuscript of *Animal Chatter* is so slight, it looks as though it's a child's school work. It is subtitled 'Tales from the Living Veld'. What does this mean? In the introduction he says that these are more sophisticated versions of stories that he used to tell his children. I don't remember the stories. Apparently we liked the story about how he tried to photograph a python. It ended up on top of him. He was in Bechuanaland, he said, and the snake was pulled from a hole by three men. I read all the stories again in about an hour. Their jauntiness – motiveless cheer – drags me down.

I walk up towards my farm. (I know that Roos is aching to sell. Money has given me this magical power over him.) These barefoot and ragged children, who are throwing stones at a large can, may become my responsibility. I don't want retainers. I had better look at the situation carefully before I lay out my money. Pennington will know the score.

In my father's book black people play no part, except as amusing onlookers or helpers or servants. I can cope with trees, a piece of mountain, thick walls, mouldy thatch, a stream, some clapped-out farm machinery, but black people, children, are too much. They may be protected now. There are laws. I'm sure there must be. I remember Virgil: *praise large estates, but farm a small one*. I mustn't get carried away by money.

I have some hopes of my father's manuscript provisionally entitled *The Soul of the Baboon*. I am sure that I can update it, or annotate it, and find a publisher. My heart, my blood, is racing with possibilities. In the house I have a piece of lemon cake with my tea. I look on the two girls as my staff now. Perhaps I can keep them on. I must find out about salaries and so on. There is a German couple sitting in a corner near the window. They are dressed for hiking; at the moment they are eating scones. Then I wonder if they are casing the place wondering how many vines could be planted. I smile at them.

After tea I walk around to the back of the house to see what's there. There is a chicken run. The chickens see me and rush naively to the wire mesh. I like the idea of chickens. I can see myself – although my cholesterol is quite high – eating a fresh boiled egg each morning. I can see myself, even earlier in the day, raiding the laying boxes. Hens give up their eggs without much of a fight. Some will even let you put your hand under their warm, soft bodies to feel for fresh eggs. The food for the hens must be organic, for flavour rather than in the cause of ideology. They must be allowed to run into the orchard – as soon as I have got rid of the moth-eaten peacock, the dirty clamorous ducks and the breeze-block fire engine. I realise that there is going to be a lot to do.

Now I see a cage against the wall of an outbuilding. Inside it, sitting hunched and morose, is a large baboon. It reaches through the bars towards me. Its hands are a dark blue, almost black, and delicately creased and folded, the joints of its fingers round and inflated. I have nothing to give it. It slumps and looks away, its reddish-yellow eyes like bumble bees under the high, sloping and distracted philosopher's forehead.

I learn that its name is Piet.

11

In a remote part of the Transvaal (my father writes), soon after the Anglo-Boer war of 1899–1902, a reliable witness, a local doctor, reported that a farmer, Mr Willem van Staden, and his family were involved in an extraordinary incident involving a large male chacma baboon. The baboon, named Tjol, was tied to a pole in the yard of their farm, Doornhoek, which means Place of the Thorn Trees. When Mrs van Staden, a strong Boer lady, gave birth to a baby, Mr van Staden took it out into the yard to show it to Tjol. Tjol was very interested in the baby. He made the characteristic baboon begging noise, a low whimpering cry, as if he wished to hold the baby. But Mr van Staden decided not to risk bringing the baby any closer.

The baby was not yet christened but she was soon known as Antjie. Tjol, the baboon, discovered that by climbing up the pole to his sleeping quarters (an old tea chest covered in tar paper) and climbing on to the sleeping box, he could see Antjie's cot in the open window of the nursery, which Mrs van Staden, with frontier ingenuity, had decorated with calico trimmed with a generous border of flowers. Tjol climbed every few minutes on to his sleeping box to spy on the sleeping child.

The farmer and his wife regarded this obsessive interest as quite endearing. They often pointed out to visitors, including the local doctor, Dr O'Leary, the baboon's fascination with the baby. Dr O'Leary wrote that the baboon had probably been deprived of social life. He was probably correct: as we now know, baboons display a great deal of reinforcement activity, including mutual grooming between age groups, and this may be significant in what was to follow. On the day in question, there were no men in the house. Suddenly Mrs van Staden and a servant heard the baby crying violently. They rushed to the nursery. To their horror they saw that the baboon, had broken the chain that held it to the pole. It was sitting on the window ledge holding the six-weeks-old Antjie. As the mother approached, the baboon bared its huge canine teeth threateningly. The mother bravely rushed at the baboon, which easily could have held her off. But the baboon retreated.

Outside the window was a thick creeper, the water vine, and the baboon, with the baby held upside down under one arm, climbed up the creeper to the roof of the house, where it sat on the pitch of the thatch. The panic-stricken mother decided that she must distract the baboon. She placed plates of biscuits and preserves, the fig jam of the area, on the ground. She called for dried peaches and nuts.

'Kom, Tjol, kom my booitjie,' she cried.

But the baboon was not tempted by these sweetmeats. Far from climbing down, the baboon now appeared to find its position on the gable end dangerously exposed and climbed up into a huge wild fig tree, *ficus capensis*, which shadowed one side of the house. Holding the screaming baby negligently (and still upside down), by one arm, Tjol climbed to the highest branches that were strong enough to support his weight. Adult male chacmas weigh, as we have seen, as much as one hundred and thirty pounds. Now the baboon held the baby to its hairy chest. Soon Antjie calmed down and appeared to have fallen asleep. The distraught mother sent for a neighbour. Still the baboon was unmoved. The mother and the servants held a large blanket – Dr O'Leary, a Fenian, reports that it was a grey army blanket, and adds that it had come from the Waterberg Concentration Camp where Boer women were held – under the tree in case the baboon dropped the baby.

Eventually the neighbour arrived on horseback. His only

suggestion was to shoot the baboon and try to catch the baby. But Mrs van Staden pointed out that this was a greater risk than simply waiting to see if Tjol released the baby. For half an hour or more, holding the blanket and adjusting their position each time the baboon made a move, five people stood beneath the tree. Way up above them the baby was silent, perhaps even content, rocked by the motion of the tree and warm against the baboon's hairy chest.

Another hour later, one of the servants appeared with a Bushman called Dabe, who had once worked at Doornhoek and was a friend to the baboon. Bushmen, it was widely believed, have a natural rapport with wild animals. Their hunting skills are based on a close understanding of the prey. Like the Indian of North America before the arrival of the white man (that despoiler of natural understanding), the Bushman sees the natural world in terms of friendship and dependency. We have lost this ability: we have failed to listen to the music of the natural world. We are denying our kinship with the animal kingdom, and depriving ourselves of understanding.

The Bushman, Dabe, asked the women and servants to go inside and he told them to take with them the biscuits and conserves and stay out of sight. Dr O'Leary does not repeat what Dabe said to Tjol, or in what language, but it is probable that he spoke in onomatopoeia, imitating the noises that baboons make. Soon the baboon climbed deliberately down from the tree to where the Bushman crouched on the ground. It showed no sign of fear. Dabe held the baboon by the collar and talked to it. He was then able to reattach the collar to the chain. As soon as it was back in captivity the baboon allowed Dabe to take the baby. In fact it seemed to be delighted to relinquish responsibility.

Dr O'Leary was summoned. The baby had a few scratches from the tree that needed some iodine.

The saddest aspect of the story is that the neighbour then

shot the baboon. We don't know if Dabe protested, we don't know what he thought about the incident, but for me this story speaks of the tragic abuse that we have visited on our close relatives, the apes and the primates. I like to believe that Tjol, the lonely chacma baboon, was trying to be true to his own instincts, the social and nurturing impulses which are not so different from our own.

O tempora, O mores.

As I read my father's typescript, I remember Bellow's *Herzog*, 'A man could do worse than love his monkey.'

It seems that the baboon at the farm was orphaned when Roos's father-in-law shot its mother which had ventured into the barren orchard. It was thought that a baby baboon would attract children to the tea garden. For a few months this marketing strategy worked well: children came to see the baboon and to play with it. But then two things happened: firstly Roos's father-in-law died and secondly the baboon grew bigger and less loveable. It was put in the cage, where it has now lived for two years, deracinated and depressed, and seldom visited. Roos tells me all this when he calls to say that he has discussed the sale of the farm with his wife, Tienie. Tienie is, in principle, prepared to sell but she wants to retain the mineral rights. Pennington tells me that all Afrikaners are obsessed with mineral rights; they don't want to be duped like their ancestors who sold out cheaply to Jews who knew that diamonds and gold lay beneath their dry pastures. This loss of their birthright lies deep in the race memory. Roos is sending through particulars of the farm, and when we receive them we should submit a 'tender' to his lawyers.

'All bullshit,' says Pennington cheerfully. 'He's desperate. I know his lawyers.'

I am down on the beach, which once I feared. I collect a few shells. I look at their delicate symmetry and pale intricacy. I wonder, without hope of an answer, if our sense of proportion comes from observation of natural things or from an innate sense of order. And then I run for a few hundred yards, propelled by the wind. I am drawn to these women who clamber up the dunes and hack at the scrub for firewood. I think of the beach as common land, and I don't leave it, although I would like to see how they live in their shacks. I wonder where the men are. Have they gone to the city to look for work? Two women, working in the scrub, hacking with small axes, are carrying on a conversation although they are fifty or sixty yards apart. They laugh. One stops and looks at me. I wave cheerily and trot away. Their voices float after me. I could say, as I did to my mother, that Africa has arrived here. But I know that it is not that simple; I would guess that the women don't see themselves as reclaiming their country. For a start the white people haven't gone away. White people always have more. Somehow it is their birthright, along with the mineral rights. Black people will always be knocking at the door; that's how they see it, I think.

The Penguin Club, Lourenco Marques, Mozambique. With my friend Mark, a fellow member of the junior athletics team, I am sitting close to the small dance floor. It is our second night here. We are drunk on Portuguese wine. But more than that, we are drunk on sex, or the anticipation of it. A black stripper is lying on the floor writhing. Even as we look at her, I am aware of certain inescapable ironies. The greatest of these is that this woman, abasing herself, is the first black woman who treats me without deference. She has agreed, after her show, to take me and Mark to her home for sex. For money. But she is fully aware that I am a seventeen-year-old white boy, and she knows that for me to have sex with her has profound meaning. Because I think – I can't speak for Mark – that I must have sex with her to experience Africa even in a small way. When she comes near us on the dance floor, I can feel the heat and fragrance and taboo of Africa.

'Jesus,' says Mark as the drums beat, 'my cock is bursting.'

There are some things people say which sound high-minded and well-intentioned, but which nevertheless lack all truth. And there are other things which sound crude and unpleasant, that contain a certain honest poetry.

The stripper's name was Lydia. She and her friend, Queenie, took us in a sweating taxi to a ramshackle Portuguese apartment building and there I lost my virginity. The women made love with a vigour that I guessed – I had no means of comparison – was wholly African. Lydia told me that once she worked as a servant in South Africa.

As we drove back to the pension where we were staying – tired, drunk, subdued – Mark said, 'Jesus, I thought my balls were going to explode.'

'At least your cock didn't explode.'

'No fuck, no that would have been a disaster. I've realised that decadence is for me. I am devoting my life to following my cock wherever it may lead.'

He was in deadly earnest. We laughed ourselves into exhaustion. Sometimes I think I don't laugh enough any more.

So many events in my life have faded like fabrics in the sun, but Lydia and the Penguin Club and the small apartment with a large bed hung with kikois and lit by candles have remained distinct. And I remember her warm, pink musky mouth. Prostitutes habitually don't kiss, but Lydia was profligate with her mouth.

Back in Johannesburg we presented ourselves nervously at the General Hospital. A young doctor, to whom we confessed our fears, examined us.

'Ag, sies,' he said, 'fucking a black woman. Hell man.'

I guessed he was intrigued and wanted to ask how it was. Anyway we were fine. I was glad. I have retained a loyalty to Lydia's memory, and it's the memory of a warm and kind woman, not a pox-ridden whore.

At first Mark talked about our adventure, but then he began to go silent. For myself, I wondered often if Lydia remembered me. I doubted it. Why should she? She had seen white boys before with all their contradictory impulses. And nothing, I knew, was more ridiculous than believing that losing your virginity (itself a ridiculous term) to a stripper in Portuguese East Africa bestowed some special insight.

The next day, in tropical heat, on three hours of sleep, I won the hundred metres in the fastest time ever recorded by a boy under eighteen years of age.

'All bullshit,' said Pennington, 'he's desperate, I know his lawyers.'

The loudest noise in the aromatic garden as I walk to the clinic is the desperate shrieking of the crickets. Far away the burble of turtle doves and still further away the cry of a guinea fowl, a paranoid, panicky, shriek. Above the mountain the sky is a deep indifferent blue, although there are some grape-shot banners of cloud handing down its front. There is a deep, tangible, elemental calm. I can hardly recall the hum, the deep-mined juddering of London which never goes away. Landscape is always compared from one country to another as though countries are in competition or as though the inhabitants of one place have some special advantage over another as a result of topography. I wonder, if I buy this farm, whether landscape will be enough. And I wonder about the dark people. In the end they are probably unknowable (despite my secret cache of knowledge). Also I am not sure I want to play golf with Pennington for ever.

As I confessed to my mute mother, I suffer from an anxiety about being far from the eye of the storm. There are certain people – I am one – for whom the news means nothing and has no purpose until we have read it. Politicians can only go about their business with our blessing or caution. Sportsmen require our acute evaluation. For some reason we also need to know what's happening in big cities. We are reassured by the urban thrum, and we compliment ourselves on our savvy and we congratulate ourselves each time we hear of a new urban outrage. Recently a friend told me that some boys he had reprimanded for dropping litter in his street (a foolhardy move, if he had asked me) had filled his front hall with dog turds. And the papers reported a gang of young girls and boys throwing two students off a bridge into the Thames for a laugh. One had died. In some way we believe it is to our credit.

But here? Mineral facts, insects, crashing waves, and over the sand dunes in their shacks or even on my farm, legions of anonymous black people

Living in another country which just happens to inhabit the same borders.

I ask a nurse how my mother has been.

'Shame. She never wakes up.'

Is this a metaphor? I hurry to her room and gratefully detect the minute breathing and then a whispered sigh.

The Afrikaans doctor – thin, serious, careful in his diction – comes by. His Adam's apple sits prominently above his tie and his collar, which gape from his neck.

'She's very weak,' he says.

I don't ask him to guess how long she can live. I have come to see that this question means nothing.

'Ma, I saw a baboon yesterday. It's pathetic. It's in a cage. Its eyes are the colour of cider.'

Her face is no longer livid. I hold her hand and squeeze the flesh, as thin as rice paper, very gently but there is no response.

12

This morning on the beach there is a whale. It seems to be dead but two whites, a man and a woman, are rushing back and forth to the water dousing it from a plastic bucket. It's about fourteen feet long, with what look like barnacles attached to its snout, a sort of wreath of crustacea. The woman asks me if I want to help and hands me a child's bucket; I find myself carrying water up to the whale corpse and throwing water on to its huge, tadpole head. Close up its blue-black flesh looks to me fibrous, as though the inert tail is attached to the body by enormous, closely fitting rubber bands. A faint gurgling comes from the blowhole.

'Is it dead?' I ask.

'It's weak. The vet is on his way,' she says.

'What's it got on its nose?'

'They are normal. We call them collosities.'

She is panting and her face is rapt. Up in the sand dunes I see two women – perhaps the same Xhosa women – watching our efforts. And now I see the four-wheel drive approaching fast down the water's edge. The jeep stops and three men get out. I pause, but the woman tells me to keep fetching water. So I'm jogging down the few yards to the waves and filling my bucket. One of the men is the vet, and he says the whale is sick with a virus. There is no point in re-launching it. The woman who enlisted me weeps. One of the men is wearing a Whale Watch tee shirt. He puts his arm around her. They thank me for helping.

'Very sad,' I say primly.

'Ja, it's sad, but we don't really know why they are dying,' says the vet. 'We know bugger-all about whales, really. But we do our best. It gets the juveniles, like this one.'

They offer me a lift back to the town up the coast, but I explain that I am walking.

'Don't go too far up that way by yourself.'

He points in the direction of the shacks.

They can see that I am a stranger – a stranger in my own land – by my clothes. I am wearing a pair of very old shorts which read 'Paradise Club' on the front. On the back, ambiguously I now fear, the shorts read 'A slice of paradise'. My shirt is long sleeved, which marks me out as a foreigner.

As soon as they leave, the two Xhosa women come cautiously down the beach. They are followed by the children. They all gather round the juvenile whale. I say hello to the children. They smile and hide behind their mothers. Suddenly the whale exhales; it's a loud despairing bellow of air and water, perhaps some of the water I was pouring on it a few minutes before.

One of the women comes back when she sees I am not afraid. A little girl follows her but hangs back.

'Hello,' I say to the woman.

'Molo, umnumzana,' she says.

'This is good meat,' I say.

She laughs. This is whitey's little joke. Anyway the meat comes protected by about a foot of impenetrable hide and another few feet of blubber. I give her this unsolicited fact because I have unused stores of knowledge, and must share my cultural capital with her. In Tokyo I have seen the Japanese bidding excitedly for whale meat.

'Goodbye.'

I walk on down the beach. Half an hour or so later when I pass by, five or six children are climbing on the whale. The little girl comes up to me. 'Goodbye,' she says. She is about seven, I guess, and her hair is neatly plaited in corn-rows. She laughs at her own boldness and runs back to her friends.

Can you know other people? Even those I have been closest to have been mysteries to me, except Matt who was my own flesh. These children, who live on the sand dunes in shacks, don't see me as the same species. I am as unknowable to them as the whale and I have similarly mysterious origins. I give the children a few coins. They handle them with caution and inspect them for flaws before running up the first range of sand dunes. A loose association of seagulls is looking at the dead whale speculatively.

And now that my mother is dying, I find that I didn't know her either: why has she exorcised those pictures? Why has she hidden from me the fact that my father visited her for two weeks and gave her money, some of it intended for me? If I can't even answer these questions, how can I ever answer the big questions which we used to think were so important? For instance the question of human progress away from the swamps of irrationality and hatred?

I never stopped thinking about these things. But I began to believe that it was not within my powers (admittedly rather limited) to make any difference. And if this was so, why expend my mental energy uselessly? Also I began to find – apparently I was one of the last to notice this – that people active in changing or nudging history are often not pleasant, and act from suspect motives. It began to seem to me – in relation to my native land – that I could never fully share, even if I could understand, the suffering of the black and brown people. I have heard one or two white people say, in a boastful fashion, 'I'm an African,' but I think the brown people know that this cannot be true and that it is an affectation. And because I could never be party to their desperate thoughts and feelings and desires, it was presumptuous of me, and futile, to line up with them. I could never know them.

The little girl appears at the top of the sand dunes and waves to me before disappearing again. Maybe she is semaphoring some message on the deeper issues. But now I am looking down, not up or into the distance. I'm looking at the minute life, the little volcanic air vents that erupt in the sand as the waves roll back, the small white crabs and the mussel shells and the broken kelp cables and the corpses of the yellow blow-up fish that not even the gulls will eat. And I feel the awful aloneness of childhood faced by this natural indifference. I wonder if that little girl ever has cosmic fears, living in a shack on the blasted sand dunes.

The air is rich. My father used to say sea air was full of ions and iodine and perhaps fish oil. It was a tonic. Seawater was good too, because it cleared out the sinuses. I've always believed as a consequence in the healing power of seawater, and so (in my Slice of Paradise shorts) I enter the waves and feel their thrilling power. My God, they are huge when you are standing there contemplating them as they rush in all the way from Patagonia. I try to surf. I remember how it is done: you have to catch the wave just before it breaks and swim hard. The first wave throws me down on to an abrasive shingle of small stones and carapaces, but I catch the second and for a few triumphant moments I rush towards the shore. Now I can't stop. I catch wave after wave, flailing my arms for a few seconds and then speeding in, one arm outstretched, body rigid. I exult in that moment when the wave is breaking and there I am, my head poking out of the wall of water, just before it folds and crumbles and crashes down towards the beach. An immense wave, a dumper, throws me directly down under a mountain of water; I roll into a ball and wait until it has passed. Above me are ten feet of turbulent, sandy, effervescent green water, but I don't panic. It passes. *Tout passe.*

After an hour or so of surfing I'm exhausted. I dry myself with my shirt and lie on the hot sand. The shrieking of gulls and the roaring of the sea drive out any awareness of the world beyond the tide mark. I sleep.

When I wake I feel my back and the backs of my legs burning. But I have slept the sleep of the just. I am crusted with sand. I think of those fish in Spain that are cooked in salt. I feel calm. My failures, my failings, my fatal lack of judgement, all seem far away, beyond the swaddling sound of the waves. It's laughable but I feel some order in my thoughts which was lacking before I went to sleep. My father was right about seawater; the restorative powers he believed in seem, however briefly, to have worked on my soul too. I am full of optimism for the life to come – the farm, the chickens, the old thick-walled house, the vines and the garden (only indigenous plants). And the baboon. I will improve his life, maybe find a home for him somewhere. And I don't see warnings in this giddy upwell of feeling. Far from it. At my best, before Suzi Crispin and its awful coda, I was prone to these swings of happiness, even euphoria.

Away down on the beach is the dark shape of the whale, deserted now by the children.

My mother would be horrified by the sight of a huge dead whale; it would confirm strongly what she already fears, that randomness and disorder are everywhere. Still I tell her about the whale. I describe its metallic sheen (dulling fast) and its small innocent eyes and its curious barnacle beard. And I tell her about the children who play on it, using it as a slide, and I tell her about the bleached people who were trying to save it. There are dead dogs and donkeys and cats and cattle on all the main roads, but this giant creature obviously merits special treatment.

'Do you think the reason is that whales seem to be innocent, Ma? And mysterious? From another more innocent world?'

I imagine that if she's listening or able to hear she will enjoy this harmless kind of speculation. But, if she is listening, she gives no sign of it. I am happy to sit with her, even though what is left seems to be only a fraction of what was there before.

Even though she is thinning to nothing, I see myself embracing the stuff of life, fattening up with human qualities.

13

Standing on the practice range, driving balls on a slewed parabola into some gum trees, I see ants busy beneath me. Even as I hit, or mostly scuff, the balls, the ants keep on. So much to do, so little time to do it. Eager little citizens of the pygmy world. Now I have Virgil and my father conflated.

When by chance I hit a ball properly, it seems to fly away under its own power. Pennington recommended a few buckets of balls and he has set me up at the club. The last time I stepped on to a golf course was in the Turks and Caicos. In fact it was not yet a golf course but the swampy land where a golf course was proposed. Andrew the actor stood on the hillock between some palm trees. Behind him we had placed a flag and a local dressed as a caddie. The rest of the landscape was alluringly out of focus. My script claimed that this was the new Paradise Glades Club, a championship eighteen-hole course, designed by Robert Trent Jones Jr himself. The course, I said, was soon to have its own golf academy and would be hosting international PGA tournaments. The Paradise Club could organise corporate golfing events with luxurious accommodations (I had opted for the word 'accommodation', but was overruled by the marketing director, who pointed out, in kindly fashion, that there would be more than one).

It was all a lie. As far as I know the alligators, or perhaps they were caymans, still doze there in deep untroubled peace.

Andrew had become querulous. The food was poor. Supplies were flown in from Miami every fortnight, when planes could be spared from the drug run.

'I am used to better than this,' he said.

'Aren't we all?'

'The last time I worked with you, I had to fall in a fish pond in Ealing. A golden age of thespianism, by comparison. Something is biting me.'

Something was biting all of us. Mosquitoes congregated over the alligator habitat. Perhaps they couldn't believe their luck that a pale, soft collection of film people was standing there waiting for the light. I hadn't realised that there are ferocious mosquitoes which come out by day and attack in swarms. We sprayed ourselves and the surrounding atmosphere with Jungle Spray, trying to create a no-fly zone, but to no effect. The light now gave the alligator swamp a pewter sheen.

'Okay. Run the autocue. Ready, Andrew?'

'Ready.'

But the autocue wouldn't work: moisture and mosquito zealotry had jammed it.

'Don't worry, I can do this. I'm a trained fucking actor. Give me the script. Robert Trent Jones Jr – eighteen holes – golf academy – ouch, fucking mosquitoes – spray, spray – Tiger Woods, PGA – no problem. Let's go. Ready?'

And he did it, watched by the unimpressionable eyes of half a dozen alligators. Out of this morass he conjured an Arcadia of rolling fairways peopled by shepherds in plaid Bermudas. In truth I think you can see a desire for Arcadia in all the resorts that have sprung up, excluding the awkward natives, subduing the unruly climate, and sanitising the local food.

Pennington takes Wednesday afternoons off. We are going to have 'a gentle nine holes' later. He is pretty sure that Roos will accept our 'tender', a word which suggests that there is competition. There is none. He has checked with the other attorneys.

'Is that legal?'

'Word gets around. It's a small place.'

He's not, of course, talking about the dark people. Although

I get the impression when I go into town on a Saturday that there are lots of them, they haven't yet stormed the legal heights, or the golf club. Nobody knows what they are talking about. Nobody is interested, it seems.

The balls that I do manage to hit are scuttling weakly off to the right, each stroke jarring my wrists. I sit down on a bench and watch the ants at work. The blue gum trees lend the scene an aromatic character. Their leaves are thin and dry. As a boy I used to dislike them. How, I wondered, did Australians live with these untidy, peeling, intractable trees? My mother told the gardener, Solomon, that on no account were gum leaves to be used in compost. Gums were from such a low form of tree life, in the same way that Australians came from a criminal stratum, that they contain no nourishment. White people were always nourishing the soil. Darwin had shown that worms were the basis of life, and worms ate compost, and in some way the process enriched the soil. The ants were doing important work too, chomping up blades of grass, dragging them underground, aerating the soil, excreting terrific fertiliser without knowing it. And out of these low-level (in every sense) activities, my father had made a reputation.

I had tried to make my reputation in art. I would sit in the cinema and be filled with the most violent and uplifting urges to create. I believed that it was the only thing. To sit there in the dark and to be completely overcome not just by what was on the screen, but by the desire to produce something myself – out of nothing – that was the only meaning life could offer. Now my ambitions are more modest: to create a simple garden, and restore the house, and live in a whole fashion. I don't know what this could mean exactly, but I hope that in some way I can align myself with the land and the mountain and the sea. In fact, typically, I am becoming expansive: I see myself, in Virgilian fashion, as having been touched by the sorrow of dispossession. Surely there is a proper way to live, and a proper place to do it?

But now there are more pressing problems. Pennington has arrived. I arise from my ant reveries. Pennington is a panjandrum of sport and comes burdened with important symbols of office. As a sportsman – his true self – he is pushing an immense bag of clubs. Behind him he drags a slimmer bag, a poor relation to the first, magnificent, chariot.

'Roos rang. He says he can't accept our offer, but that's bullshit. He will. How did it go?'

He indicates my bucket of balls and the far-flung mushrooms that litter the middle distance and – more numerous – the foreground.

'I haven't quite got the hang of it.'

'Never mind. Let's go. I've brought you these clubs. The main thing is to understand that you are hitting the ball. The swing is secondary. Just look at the ball and give it a sweet little tap.'

At the first tee, he gives the ball a pasting. It flies off into the distance, cleverly turning left past some trees.

'Good shot,' I say.

'Bit of a draw. Not bad for the first shot of the day. Nice and easy now.'

I hit the ball about halfway up and it bounds along the fairway.

'A worker,' he says encouragingly. 'Promising swing.'

And so we proceed. He gives me genial advice, and gradually I find myself relaxing and hitting the ball more sweetly. Sweetness is the essence of ballgames, and ballgames have a sort of internal harmony. To Pennington this attunement to the music of sport is a manly, noble thing – philosophical, even religious.

'Just a few more holes. Take it nice and easy. That's it. Jesus, look at it go. Don't get too good.'

His big sun-ravaged face is happy. It firms up with ferocious concentration as he prepares to hit the ball. He wiggles the club twice, and then with unexpected grace lets the ball have it. We talk about handicaps and the state of the golf club. He's pleased to tell me – he probably imagines I'm going to ask – that they have some new Coloured members. Not bad golfers, some of them. There are encouraging signs all over the country. But the truth is, I don't want to know.

Eleanor used to accuse me of a certain impatience with detail, but it was not strictly true. I was impatient of the arguments and evaluations that proceeded from facts, or from what were thought of to be facts. They seemed to me to have a bogus authority. I have been in Israel and heard from both sides the tedious logic of facts. Which facts? That's the question.

Simon Chiswick claimed to possess a suppressed government report that showed that immigrants were deliberately breeding fifteen times more quickly than the native British. Sometimes he held it in his hand at party meetings. I only discovered this much later. What Eleanor could have accused me of, with more justification, was a reluctance to be shackled to any set of facts and beliefs. They seem to come in bundles. And people with deep beliefs, people like Simon Chiswick, have strange rigid deportment, as if they are conscious of needing to align themselves to receive the messages of history. Awkward aerials. The spin-off of my fastidiousness was what Eleanor called self-exculpation. It drove her mad with anger that I saw my detachment as a form of higher consciousness. She had been reading books which explained human motives in terms of identity and commitment.

'You don't need a manual. It's all in the classics,' I said.

'Now you claim to have read the classics. For example?'

'You are trivialising the argument.'

'Is it trivial to ask why you were half an hour late at the school? Perhaps you just had to finish *The Brothers Karamasov*.'

'In Russian we emphasise the second vowel. It's not Karamàsov. It's Karàmasov.'

'In English, we say fuck you. If you can't get to the school, just say so, but don't let Matt down again.'

Of course I did. I found him there white faced, alone, only the next week. Now, as Pennington and I walk up the fairway, which has been scarred by golf clubs and reaped by busy harvester ants, and as the damn turtle doves warble in deep ignorance, I feel my face flushed with regret.

'You look like you caught a bit of sun,' says Pennington.

'It's getting hot.'

I look with loathing at my ball, lying just off the fairway. I select a club at random and thrash the ball, which flies towards the green leaving the chest-rub odour of eucalyptus where I've dug a small trench.

'Sweet. Sweet as a nut. Pro-shot.'

Poor Matt, abandoned in the classroom, holding a coloured pencil, trying disconsolately to draw an owl, waiting for his delinquent father whose body was warm and pungent as if Ulla's human pigments and secretions had coated him, like the wash painters put down on a sheet of paper. And I remember exactly what he said: 'Hello, Daddy. You've been busy, haven't you?'

In my misery I putt my ball straight into the hole from the 'fringe' as Pennington calls the grassy verge.

'That's a birdie four. That's overdoing it. I preferred it when you were shit.'

But he is a genial man. In the clubhouse he is king, a majestic, gracious figure. He buys me a drink at the bar and scoops up a handful of nuts to fuel his largeness of spirit, and body.

In 1884, the *Cape Argus* reported that Jack, the baboon, had become a railway signalman near the town of Uitenhage (my father writes). His owner, James Edwin Wide, who had lost both legs in a railway accident, was a signalman and trained Jack to pull the levers or to bring the key to the coal bin, depending on the number of whistles from the approaching train. Passengers were uneasy about a baboon at the controls, but the railway board tested him and found that he was perfectly competent and put him on the payroll. His salary was two shillings a day. On Saturdays he was given half a bottle of beer. His usefulness extended to domestic work. He pumped water from the well, worked in the garden and pushed his master to work each morning on a trolley. For nine years Jack, the faithful chacma baboon, carried out his tasks without an accident. He died in 1890, and to this day his grave may be seen near the signal box.

My father writes about another baboon, Jackie, who accompanied his master, Albert Marr, to join his South African regiment at the front during the First World War. Marr was struck by a bullet in 1916 and Jackie licked the wound until the medics came. In 1918 both Jackie and his master were wounded by shrapnel, and Jackie's right leg was amputated. But the baboon made a full recovery and took part in the Lord Mayor of London's Victory Parade sitting on a gun carriage. He had been promoted to corporal. He returned to honourable retirement in South Africa and died on Marr's farm in 1921.

My father writes that there is something extraordinary about these friendships across species, which defy conventional understanding. I think that different species must recognise that which is common; the baboon, after all, is one of our closest relatives in the animal kingdom. My father says that there were touching, although unconfirmed, reports of native children of the Venda tribe playing quite happily and naturally with young wild baboons, watched over by benevolent elders in a scene from *The Jungle Book*.

Reading my father's stories, I see that I should abandon the idea of republishing them, but instead I should write a film about the friendship of a man and a baboon. It is that one remark of my father's, that there is something extraordinary about friendships across the species, which appeals to me. I think now that money is in a receptive mood towards me and that this could be successful. For the first time since Matt died I am eager to write a script. I feel a surge of confidence and the rush of elation.

Down on the beach the wind is strong and the waves have been beaten backwards into the bay so that when I strip off to my Slice of Paradise shorts, I can't achieve anything like the wild rides of yesterday. But still I am tumbled and thrown about, and I rinse my sinuses and I continue to sluice my soul in some mysterious way.

As I run down the beach to dry off – I must get a towel – there is no sign of the women and children, but from the sand dunes, flayed by the wind, come fast-flying streams of smoke and the scent of burning wood. I run as far as I can, and then walk and jog back. The sun is already behind the mountains to the west, and anxious strings of dark birds are flying fast, low over the water.

The sea is troubled and uncertain, the puckered electro-plate now tarnished. I start to run again in that childish way, pursued by the imagination. Only now do I realise that the whale has gone. Some authority has decided that it must be dragged away. It's hard to imagine why.

My mother's little car's been vandalised, the headlights smashed and two windows broken. I brush the glass off the seat and start it up. The fact that the engine responds, with a sort of dogged clunkiness, is very welcome. After all, it's growing dark and who knows what desperation lives in the sand dunes? There is an awful human smell in the car, but I don't stop to investigate. My soul, so settled a few minutes ago, is heaving with foreboding. Fifteen minutes later, safely back on the retirement estate, I find human turds on the back seat. I remove them with plastic bags and I spray the tattered car with toilet cleaner. Vim with lemon.

I wash myself with a little hand shower and grow calmer.

The lawn-sprinklers are on. The crickets are tuning up. The air is fragrant with flowers and wet lavender. In the morning I'll have the car fixed and steam cleaned. My mother loves this car which she will never drive again; I feel under an obligation to restore it. A sacrilege has been committed and I must atone. I see the car as a household shrine rather than what it is, a twenty-four-year-old Ford Escort.

I am relieved to find that my mother is still alive. It is sometimes difficult not to believe that all forebodings are portents of death. The nurse with no teeth – she looks like a kind of troll – tells me that my mother has had some soup. Pea soup and ham, she says, trying to add verisimilitude:

'Ertjiesop met ham.'

I don't believe her. After the nurse has gone, I sit down near my mother to give her an edited account of my day: I describe the golf, the conviviality of the clubhouse, the nineteenth hole et cetera, because I think it will please her that we talked golf and made jokes in the clubhouse. I tell her, too, that I've been running and swimming. In fact I can see that my ribs are already beginning to rise to the surface of my northern flesh again. I tell her about the turbulent sunset and explain without evidence that the civic authorities have removed the whale.

I see now on her clean nightie a small green stain, and when I put my face close I can smell pea soup. Is it possible that she has been drinking soup? I sniff deeply, and I imagine I can detect a little whiff of ham.

14

I have located a repair shop on the edge of the small town. I have scrubbed the car with Lemon Vim, and removed the jagged glass so that as I drive towards town it is possible that anybody looking would not realise that there is much wrong with the car, and that the headlights are naked. The odour is heavily masked by lemon, although this is a lemon made in a factory, not in a tree. I feel ashamed, not of the car but of the fact I have let it be attacked by unknown people. I haven't entirely wasted the last decade; in my own mind I have been making a study of what it means to be human. I hardly need say that I have come to no firm conclusions, but I have added this event to the catalogue. Today, with the sun warm, the car expunged and vividly scented, it is easier to take the broad view.

My father wrote that baboons are omnivorous. In some parts of Africa they killed lambs and small antelope, but elsewhere they were known to eat lizards, worms and insects. The bulk of their diet – eighty-seven per cent on average, he said with authority – consisted of fruits, nuts and roots. There is a store by the side of the road and I stocked up there with lychees, peanuts, some apples and an avocado pear. I was up early; I walked along the farm track, past the two cottages, carrying my supplies. Pennington said that Roos was only holding out for a few days for the sake of appearance, so I walked with proprietorial confidence. It was time to buy some land-owning clothes, and I wanted to expand my rather limited choice of one pair of shorts (Paradise Club, which doubled as a swimming costume), one pair of grey trousers, two striped shirts and the linen suit.

The farm was quiet. In the house I could hear the girls vacuuming the tea room. I walked round to the back and looked briefly at the hens with their prim faces. I guess that you have to treat them with sympathy, because they are very passive, dependent creatures. Piet saw me and came forward grimacing, pulling back the skin above his eyes so that I could see white patches. I hoped this was a friendly greeting. His arm, which was black and grey and dark underneath, stretched out and he whimpered.

'You're in luck, Piet, my boy.'

I stroked the palm of his hand briefly and placed a few peanuts in it. The pads of his hand were black, and lumpy, as if inflated. He shelled the nuts and swallowed them quickly, before sticking out his delicate hand again. Now I gave him some lychees. He scampered off and sat on a box in the corner to eat them, first finding out how to peel them. I could say his eyes were sad or contemplative, but it might not be true. I told my mother they were the colour of cider, but in fact they are the colour of the diluted Ribena that Matt favoured.

Piet came close to the wire, his eyes bared again, whimpering, and I took a chance sticking three fingers through the mesh to scratch the back of his head. He bent his head downwards, and then begged for more food. I pushed the whole lot through the mesh, paring the apple and the avocado on the wire. Piet gathered up this hoard carefully and returned to sit on his box, perhaps fearing I had made a mistake and would want it all back. He had obviously never seen an avocado before; he inspected and rotated in his hands before biting it carefully. Then he twisted it open and scooped out all the green and brown flesh and squashed it into his mouth.

The repair men told me that it was not really worth spending the money on the car. I asked them to go ahead anyway. They listened without interest to my story about wanting the car to be perfect for my mother when she came out of hospital. I couldn't explain to them that the old car must be restored for reasons that are not fully clear, even to me. They agreed but I could see that they think I am a fool. This is one of the advantages practical people have over us: they have daily opportunities for condescension. They were able to lend me a small Toyota pick-up, a *bakkie*, for the day and I set off to find our old home in the suburbs of the city, which is forty miles away.

From the highway I can see thousands of shacks on the sandy, windy plains. The place where I swim, where the whale landed, I can see now is the very outer edge of this great shack metropolis. Near the highway a wall has been built, probably to keep stray animals off the road. But even here women are carrying bundles of firewood through gaps in the wall, small animals are grazing and children are playing football beside the highway.

Up ahead Table Mountain, a liner beached on the flat sands, comes ever closer. We lived in its shadow. Nearly thirty years on it still enfilades my dreams. Although the city and its suburbs are now linked by new highways, it is easy to navigate by the mountain. The mountain is the main thing, lending a Lilliputian scale to everything around. Like us, at Number 17 Cheltenham Road, where we lived on after my father left for America; the mountain, rising upwards in woody flutes, diminished us too.

I park the pick-up outside in the leafy road and approach the gate. Why do I feel so anxious? I notice first that despite all the years of composting, the garden is still sandy. I don't know what I'm looking for, if anything. I walk up the path, slates of granite from the mountain, and approach the front door, which is still shielded by a small roof supported on two artfully carved beams. Directly above is the dormer window of my mother's bedroom. The doorbell makes a new sound, more urgent and electronic. Hibiscus and banana trees cluster around the house: these are new. Nobody comes to the door. I walk around the house and peer in the windows. The interiors are cool and dark, and I can make out the square teak posts of the heavy staircase through the hallway, and now I see the fireplace, edged in red tiles, where we burned pine cones collected on the slopes of the mountain. Just beyond that is the kitchen where my mother arranged flowers, great scented bundles of freesias and arum lilies. I want to see the bathroom where my mother snatched me up and towelled me. Without climbing one of the loquat trees at the back of the house, this is impossible.

It is difficult to believe that the woman who chafed my shivering body – Matt also had goose bumps at bath-time – is the same woman now waiting at a faint borderline to be admitted to another country.

As I leave the house, eating a loquat, two men in uniform step out of a car that is luridly got up to look like a police car. They are carrying guns at their hips and bar my way.

'Can we help you, sir?'

'No. It's my old house, where I lived as a boy.'

'That's okay, sir. We just got a call to say there was an intruder.'

'No, I'm not an intruder.'

I am in fact an intruder, intruding on the half-remembered past.

'We have to be very careful, sir.'

'I can understand. Sorry to put you out. Where is the owner?'

'They left the country, sir. We just security, we don't know nothing really.'

They speak in the Cape way, a sort of auctioneer's rise and fall which we used to think was comic. In London there are still elderly people who think, in the same way, that Cockney is amusing, as though the speaker is putting on a turn. Sometimes these people do imitations: *Cor Blimey, love a duck. How's yer father*, and so on.

'Goodbye, sir.'

I give them money.

'We can't take that.'

'Course you can. Thanks.'

I drive down the main road in my pick-up. Our house is still slumbering as I leave it. I must buy some clothes. Where I remember a cobbler and a fruit stall, there is a huge mall. I find a shop selling outdoor equipment – sleeping bags, rucksacks, boots, waterproof matches, gas stoves, and so on. They also sell khaki, green or blue bush shirts, trousers and shorts. I stock up with these clothes, and treat myself to a pair of *velskoen, made the traditional way*, comfortable boots. Disloyally, I ask the assistant to throw away my Turnbull & Asser shirt. But I hang on to the Paradise Club shorts. I also buy lurid new swimming trunks, some rough towels, a bush hat and sandals. Nearby is a sports shop and there I buy some running shorts and some highly engineered running shoes. The assistant offers a waterproof CD player specially made for runners, but I resist. I do, however, fall for a pair of turtle flippers for my hands, apparently the latest thing in body surfing.

It occurs to me in my expansive mood to establish contact with Eleanor again, and help her in any way I can, although I can't imagine what help she needs from me.

I leave the shadow of the mountain gratefully. The highway is smothered by the smoke rising from the shacks and the townships, and in the smoke plastic bags and anonymous bits of detritus fly across the road propelled by a strong wind off the bay. Surf's up.

The waves are huge and I spend an hour at least flying down precipices of water aided by the new hand flippers. Also I am able to dry myself on my own towel. I wish now that I had bought a camping stove so that I could brew up here in this moot, restless landscape, this Gaza Strip, between the highway and the sea. I hollow out the sand, because the wind is fierce, and lie in the shallow grave wearing my bush hat, and catching the sun. My skin has gone from tourist's pink to a pleasant cinnamon colour.

I sleep and remember the hairy roughness of the loquat tree and its strange enticing globules of fruit. Although I can see no use for these thoughts or good reason for my visit to the old house, I find this unpicking of memory soothing. But do we unpick memory? I don't really think so. Nor do I think there is necessarily anything instructive in memory.

When I wake, the children are watching me. The little girl lays particular claim to me as though she is some sort of go-between. The children run off when I get up; only she stands a few yards away. Perhaps she is waiting for money. One of the two little boys has a sore on his upper lip, and his lips are cracked and full of mucus which runs from his nose. His arms are pathetically thin. I decide that if I do give them money, they will expect it every day, and I would soon have to move along the beach, towards the town. Although at the same time, I feel oppressed by a quandary: with my money (according to Pennington the wheels are turning) I could buy a few camping stoves and gas cylinders, so freeing them from the need to find wood every day, and then what? Build them a house? Arrange scholarships to Harvard? And introduce them to my tailor? My former tailor. And why should three children be picked by me from the thousands, probably hundreds of thousands, who live in this sand? And how would their sociable wanderings be affected if they no longer had to spend long hours in the scrub? But I do have some fruit which I give to the little girl. She holds out her hands, one hand resting politely on the other forearm, and bows her head as if receiving communion. I get a strangely touching view of her rows of hair, their symmetry representing hours of patient work. Even as I give her the fruit which she accepts with a smile that hides any possible disappointment, I see that I am making a moral judgement: fruit is healthy, money is corrupting. I am not qualified to play God in this way. Of course, playing God was the great attraction of the colonies.

I jog back to the pick-up, vowing that I will learn Xhosa or Zulu because – I have no proof – it is through language that you can enter the mind of another people. Although I am troubled by the big questions, I am soothed by the minor facts, happy to be running on a beach, to be toasting myself brown, to have mastered surfing, with hand flippers, and to have my own towels. The wheels are turning on my behalf. I know, of course, that the landscape around me, and much further inland – in fact all the way to the Sahara – has been a graveyard of good intentions and a charnel-house of fellow feeling, but I am prepared to take my chances. In a way I am a pioneer. Sartre's failure was, some said, the failure to embrace the stuff of life. What would be closer to the stuff of life than an old farm, a few hens and a baboon? With plans for bees and vines?

They've done a good job on the car. They've given it a service too so that it hums sweetly. On the way back, I sing a song about a baboon climbing the mountain which comes back to me: *Bobbejaan klim die berg, bobbejaan klim die berg.*

I sit with my mother and tell her about the house. What I am telling her is really a kind of apology, having left her all these years ago to make her own way. So I remind her – I remind myself – of family matters. I tell her of her beloved garden (still sandy) and the loquat-scented happiness we had there. She is not listening, but just in case she is, I am trying to send her away into the next world with her ears stuffed with my thanks. Also, like a small boy, I am a little resentful that she has kept secrets from me, and I want to flush them out with my evident goodwill. Did she always think I was unreliable? Or suffered from poor judgement?

She opens her eyes and looks at me.

'Oh dear,' she says, and falls asleep immediately.

My ears have sand in them. It's clean sand, lodged there as I was surfing, and a small trickle falls out on to the bed as I kiss her.

Later, back in the cottage, I start to write my treatment of a film about a man and his baboon. I am thinking of titles: *Surfing with Baboons* is my favourite so far.

15

There's a delay. In my affairs, there's often a hitch. Pennington says that it is nothing, just the fact that the new masters are always drunk or out of the office. Welcome to Africa, he says. The mineral rights to the farm Nooitgedacht, which I have happily forgone, have not yet been registered. Without that there can be no progress. But my deposit, which Pennington is holding in his client account, ensures that Roos's lawyers – Pennington suggests that they are backwoodsmen of the profoundest ignorance – are moving as fast as they can.

One of the maids at the farm, Lena, says that Piet the baboon used to be taken out for walks and a chain was attached to the collar round his neck. I have discovered that baboons are mature at the age of seven so Piet, who is about three, is still young. I take him more fruit, some cashew nuts and some dried and sugared peaches, which can be bought in a sticky roll. I spend much of the morning with Piet; he seems pleased with my company, though what he likes most is the dried fruit. When I leave, he whimpers and turns his back to huddle miserably, as though expecting the world to end at any minute. I wonder – my mind has been worked free by the solvent of money at the same time as my body has been loosening up in the surf – exactly what a baboon's cosmology might consist of.

My father speculated about the possibility of friendship across the species. I seem to be Piet's only friend at the moment. This morning I saw the farm worker who feeds him on Roos's instructions; he simply throws into the cage a handful of corncobs and some poultry food without pausing.

This man says that he will find the chain and fix it to the collar so that we can get Piet out. He tells me that baboons bite. He points to his own creased mouth and bares his canines, which are somewhat isolated, and laughs harshly. I have the feeling that these farm people – who may soon be my retainers – with their wary, worn faces, their defensive eyes, and their slurred, metallic voices, are more familiar with pain than I have ever been. Not to mention the existential pain.

He returns with a chain and a thick whip and unlocks the cage. He doesn't talk to the baboon, but holds the whip high with one hand as a warning. I am reminded of Boswell's Circus all those years ago, and the exciting possibility that a lion might get out of the jerry-built enclosure and rush amongst us, scattering our candyfloss.

Piet crouches nervously and the man, whose name is Witbooi, brings him out of the cage. He used to do a few tricks, says the man. Like what? Like walking on his hind legs. Do I want to see? No, I don't. I want to take him for a promenade. So we set off up the path leading from the farm – my farm – to the mountains. The man regards the baboon as he might a violent lunatic. He is ready with the whip. Piet walks on all fours, warily, but covering the ground easily. His back feet are very human in shape. I take the chain from Witbooi and offer Piet some nuts, but he is too nervous to take them, so I throw them to him underhand. We walk up the path. Piet looks frequently at Witbooi, as if he is expecting to be struck.

Where the path emerges from the line of the stream, we pause and sit on some rocks, looking down to the distant bay. I am aware that, sitting in a line like this, baboon, Witbooi, and me, we look like some Victorian illustration of evolution apparently in ascending order. What a delusion! Piet sits carefully – alert, nervous. His watchful orange-yellow eyes have a certain haughtiness.

Witbooi tells me – we speak Afrikaans – that his family has

lived and worked on farms around here for ever. The young people now work in towns, if they can. None of them wants the black people. The Xhosas. He points downwards to the shack city which from here is glinting, like a huge rubbish dump. If you look more closely through the haze of smoke and fast-flying sand, you can detect the individual shacks, neatly spaced. Yesterday I watched the women remove some large bits of intestine from a plastic bag and begin to clean the remains of its contents out. This looked like the grass that used to stick to the underside of my lawnmower, when Eleanor and I and Matt had a house and garden in London. The tripe was chopped into short lengths, presumably for cooking with the onions which were in another bag.

I ask Witbooi if there were any baboons in the mountains above the farm. There are, but they have become very shy and nervous, and don't come down to the lands very often. I am thinking, of course, that it would be good to reunite Piet with his fellows, although I have seen enough television documentaries to know that rehabilitation of wild animals in this way is not easy. It may even be impossible.

Piet tucks his chin in and pulls back his eyelids. I reach out to stroke his head. For a moment he seems pleased, his eyes staring into vacant space, then he withdraws to the end of his chain, out of reach. Perhaps he, like my mother, is agoraphobic after his years of captivity.

Witbooi rolls himself a cigarette. His mouth has deep creases; his skin is like a dried tobacco leaf itself, as though there is a vegetable connection between him and the cigarette. He smokes parsimoniously and puts the cigarette out after a few puffs. He keeps the remains behind his ear for later use.

'Come, Piet, let's go.'

Piet is ready. We walk back down the hill, through the aromatic and leathery bushes – I will learn the botanical names – and then through the tree ferns by the stream and back to the farm. Witbooi returns Piet to his cage, and he climbs on to his box. In the penumbra of the cage his coat acquires a dull sullenness; the greens and browns are tweedy without any sheen. I leave him some nuts, but for the moment he crouches, his warrior-scholar face turned away. I wonder how happy he is. Can he miss what he does not know? Does he have – to use my father's term – a phyletic memory? If there is such a thing, why couldn't baboons retain some memory of a more human state?

Witbooi lives in one of the cottages along the farm track where the children play. Arum lilies grow in clumps around a small dam nearby, lending the squalor a deceptive charm. He has seven surviving children and maybe thirty or so grandchildren. He winks, congratulating himself, as he tells me. Tomorrow, I tell him, I will take the baboon out myself. He smiles, and his parchment face fragments. I almost expect it to become dust.

These people, these lands, those arum lilies, the distant screeching guinea fowl, the oak trees and the thick-walled house, in fact everything all around that can be seen (mineral deposits are unseen) are all waiting for me to take possession, yet it seems unlikely. I have owned a small terraced house with a patch of garden, a hover mower, and a few tired plants, but now I am about to take possession of all this. And a baboon. When I ask Pennington if I would acquire the baboon, he said I was buying the place as I find it. In a way my horizons, like Piet's, have shrunk, so that I am still coming to terms with the immediate geology and botany which will be mine.

Also there is the effect of talking to my mother, who doesn't respond while waiting for this natural event, delayed nearly two weeks now, when the little that is left of her will depart. Late last night I was addressing her mute, increasingly outsize head, 'If I could, I would come with you, Ma,' but now I see that death as a metaphor for a journey as completely false. Nobody's going anywhere. There is no train, no station, no flight, no destination. Just what James Thurber called the soft darkness, the dreamless sleep.

At the same time I feel washed clean. Strange that the prospects of death and money should have done this to me. I am, in a small way, born again, full of enthusiasm and ideas. I have been jotting down notes for the film, *Surfing with Baboons*, and I see the way ahead, a buddy movie which explains the notion of friendship (I will dedicate it gratefully to my father) across the species. It's the sort of thing people are interested in.

As a matter of fact, I am interested in it. I find myself worrying about Piet's state of mind and his whole welfare. In my film, first tentative ideas, a man wrongly accused hides near a beach in Africa where he befriends a baboon. He has no way of proving his innocence, but then he realises that if he can train the baboon to retrieve his file from a vault in the CIA, where a corrupt operative has hidden it . . . There are still plenty of problems here, but I think I am on to something. For example baboons can be taught to perform important tasks – viz Jack the signalling baboon – and baboons can be loyal friends – viz Jackie the regimental mascot. And of course baboons can climb anything.

I am full of the possibilities. I feel ashamed to be in such good spirits, because I see that death is the narrowing down of possibilities until nullity is achieved. My mother and I are like the figures in that clock at Liberty's, in the old-baroque style, where, for one figure to come out, the other must disappear. I have the feeling that I will never go back to London. It's not a premonition, simply a sense that the London where I lived, and against whose indifferent weeping bricks I have made my accommodations with life, was a place – I can barely understand this – that I dreamed.

When Simon Chiswick came back from Hong Kong, he looked at the piles of bricks, at the mean suburbs and the wet streets and the pinched faces and the polyglot peoples, and he saw a downward evolutionary spiral. Everything he had clung to out in the sweating tropics seemed to have been thrown overboard. In his mind – like all obsessives – he rehearsed and nurtured completely mad ideas and simple solutions. Religious ideas and remedies. At the time I thought he was just a rich man trying to buy his way into public recognition. People who have made their money in business or banking believe that they are in tune with something elemental: that is why they despise journalists and commentators who have never had to understand the laws of money, which are not *radix malorum* after all, but the wellspring of human life.

Now, sitting here in this small room, still redolent of my own distant past, I understand that we all make our own landscapes to conform to our inner desires.

When I first came to London I saw the ads on the underground escalators – the underwear, the puns, the innuendos, the class allusions, the air of sexual promise – as a not-too-difficult code revealing what sort of city this was. The streets had not yet undergone their convulsions of new building and refurbishment, but still the city was semaphoring a new understanding of the meaning of existence: gratification. It has been explained that the Hindu religious classes, which lost the impulse to work, turned idleness and the consequent poverty into a philosophy. In London I saw the last bands of restraint being thrown off. And it has been those who were squashed to the bottom by the weight of deference who have thrown them off with least inhibition. They are gadding and growing fat and fucking and screaming and fighting and pissing in the street, and they are larding themselves with an inchoate philosophy of self-expression and individualism.

While down on the sand dunes not far from here they are chopping up cows' intestines and removing gastric grass clippings and sheltering their children against the spume-laden wind with plastic sheets.

You could go mad trying to reconcile the disparate landscapes of the mind. But I am losing sight, alarmingly quickly, of London. It seems to me to be retreating back into literature and films and myths. In fact to where I first encountered it.

One evening after filming we are sitting in The Zanzibar. There are mirrors and tables, an invitation to cut cocaine. (I have never fully understood the reasons.) We have drunk two bottles of champagne. We have forgotten that we are to be up at five-thirty to shoot a scene which involves Nurse Suzi Crispin seducing a patient in traction. (Ulla will stand by with her impeccable tits.) Ed is outside with the limo. I like to imagine the limo purring, wasting carbon fuels. I feel the whole of London gathering outside the door, stretching out from Covent Garden to the flatlands of Essex, and down the river all the way to Joseph Conrad's infinite darkness. Like a pop-up map, I see Cambridge and Oxford, and not much else, way off on the edges. Next to me Ulla is leaning forward to light a cigarette and I can see her flimsy bra, as can a waiter, who envies me my luck, and despite all the apparent jollity, I feel deep unease. At this moment Terri is telling Paddy, whose eyes are misted over, about the house she and Daryl have bought. Now the manager comes to see me.

'There's a bloke trying to get in. He says he knows you.'

'What's his name?'

'Daryl Tong.'

'It's me fiancé,' says Terri.

'Okay. Let him in.'

'I don't fink that's a good idea. He's not usually violent nor nuffink, but 'e's finding this 'ard to take.'

'Let him in. Give him a drink.'

Daryl Tong comes stiffly towards us; his gleaming mohair suit has cuffs which are rolled up his forearms and his hair is tousled and tinted in what – if I remember – was called a lion cut.

'Hello, Daryl.'

'Fuck off. Get your things, gel, you're comin' 'ome.'

To me this is a Dickensian scene despite the haircut, the suit of lights and the affirmative language.

'Sit down, Daryl, have a drink.'

'Why don't you fuck off you ponce?'

'Come on, Daryl, we were just relaxing after work.'

'Work my fucking arse. You wouldn't know the meaning of the fucking word.'

Terri, I notice, is standing very quiet if a little unsteadily. Ulla is smiling.

'If you do somefink like this again' – Daryl waves his hands around at the admen and the expensive casual clothing, and the umbrella-decorated drinks and the bored pianist and the supercilious waiters – 'If you do somefink like this again, you'll regret it.'

I look at Terri with a concerned expression. I may even have stretched out my hand.

'I'm talking to you, you dozy cunt,' Daryl says.

'Me?' I ask, genuinely surprised.

'Yes, you.'

He takes Terri's arm just above the elbow and leads her out. There is something about the purposefulness of his movements, in stark contrast to the wooziness of the other customers, which parts the way to the door. What a treat! What a marvellous visit from the pantomime world!

'He had a gun,' says Paddy.

'A gun. Fantastic. Brilliant,' says Ulla.

'I'll reschedule the traction scene. Just in case,' says Paddy.

'Just in case what?'

'Just in case he does her over.'

Even this seems to me to be picaresque. This is a *domestic*, a time-honoured Cockney rite. *Her indoors is going to get a bit of a slapping*.

I might have prevented it by telling Daryl that, even as he brought his message from the rude mechanical world, Terri was talking about en-suite bathrooms to Paddy.

Terri was lightly bruised. She didn't complain. But we had to film the traction scene with the other girl, Fiona. Fiona was supposed to be very upper class. The joke, it seems pallid with the passage of the years, was that Suzi Crispin (Terri) was working class and prudish, while Fiona Twistleton was upper class and a raging nymphomaniac.

Fiona is on night duty. She approaches the patient, his torso is covered in plaster and bandages. She talks to him. He can only reply with eye movements. She undresses and mounts the patient. The bed and the traction have been rigged by the harassed props department, so that the effect is of an old-fashioned threshing machine; the plan is to speed up the film for comic purposes. The whole contraption and the bed will collapse on the floor. It's tricky and the stand-ins are understandably nervous. They want to be assured of what will happen when the bed collapses. We have to lie to them, saying it has all been tested.

I have a brilliant idea. We will place the scene later in the film and intercut it with Suzi Crispin and her boyfriend, Tom, falling on to Matron's bed, which we are scheduled to film next Tuesday.

The point of memory is to free yourself from the tyranny of the present. But I am enjoying a different process, freeing myself from the tyranny of the past which has constrained me unfairly: the forgotten pea-souper is falling on London (ham flavoured, who knows?) and London's outlines are becoming unclear. I hope for this fog to spread gradually over all my past, obliterating my sins.

It occurs to me that in this way, without intending it, I will have joined my countrymen, for whom amnesia is a necessary condition.

16

Some thoughts: the stolen identity is a popular theme. The hero, let's call him John Kutz, has worked for the CIA – or some other clandestine agency – and one day he comes into work to find that he has been set up to take the blame for what happened in Kabul or Baghdad. He no longer has an office. He has a hurt, but attractive, ex-wife and a child he loves. His wife is distraught; the car has been repossessed, the child has been refused a place at nursery school, the dog has been poisoned, his computer has been stripped, his credit cards have been cancelled. He is arrested, to appear on a charge of aiding the enemy. These are some of the best scenes, the Dickensian thrill of seeing ruin and degradation. The hugely embarrassing debacle – details later – has to be blamed on treachery. The director's career, the general in charge of special forces – all the high ups – must be exonerated. And Kutz, of course, is a difficult bastard, known to have questioned the wisdom of the whole operation. He is able to escape, and ends up in a hut on the coast of Kenya, where he befriends a baboon. Now the soul of the story: the baboon and he develop a friendship. This is not some domestic animal/master relationship, but a genuine friendship. Kutz needs to retrieve the missing computer data – research required – that will exonerate him. To do this he must teach the baboon to read a few words or codes. (I will need to speak to a computer buff.) The baboon will be sacrificed, perhaps it will sacrifice itself willingly.

My father writes that there are many examples of two male baboons tackling a leopard; the one which grabs the leopard's throat invariably dies. This is probably nonsense but it's the sort of nonsense that cinema-goers like.

Taking Piet for a walk can be seen as research. I need Witbooi to attach him to the chain, but I accompany Witbooi into the cage. I have with me a large supply of nuts and fruit.

'Come, Piet, let's go.'

Witbooi thinks he should come with me, but I refuse his offer. I don't want an enforcer standing between me and Piet. Piet is more relaxed today. He stops to roll over a large stone to see what's underneath it. I take this interest in his surroundings as a good sign. When I extend my hand to him with a few nuts, he reaches for them delicately with his inflated black fingers.

'Poor Piet, you need fresh air. Come. Let's go.'

All morning we climb until we are on the very top of the mountain. There are other peaks stretching way into the distance and on one side of the bay where they tail off into the sea. Piet and I share a Ratty and Mole picnic, sitting gravely side by side. He drinks from a hollow in the rock, his baboon quarters raised and his dog muzzle gently siphoning up the water without any of a dog's urgent lapping. He extends his creased hand to me and whimpers, but I say, 'No, Piet, not now.' (Eleanor and I had many discussions about feeding on demand. She was against it.) He looks away. He smacks his lips together, a sort of blubbery sound. I'm not sure if this means submission or if it's sulking.

Matt loved the scene in *The Wind in the Willows* where Ratty is complimented on the lavishness of his picnic: 'There's cold chicken inside it,' replied the Rat briefly: 'coldtongue coldhamcoldbeefpickledgherkinssaladfrenchrollscressandwidges pottedmeatgingerbeerlemonadesodawater –'

'O stop, stop,' cried the Mole in ecstasies: 'This is too much!'

'Do you really think so?' inquired the Rat seriously. 'It's only what I always take on these little excursions; and the other animals are always telling me that I am a mean beast and cut it *very* fine!'

And this was the England I knew before I ever arrived. I particularly loved *The Water-Babies* and believed that our own house (the one I visited so recently) had wainscotting and secret entrances like Harthover and which I was determined to find. This England was a place of darkness, but also it seemed that life in the chiaroscuro was richer than life out here under the relentless blue skies.

I am sitting with a baboon under the same sky. Eleanor, and any number of other people, would find it hard to understand, but I am happy. I wonder if Piet is happy; I wonder if leaving his cage to frolic out here in all this natural abundance, among the scented plants – they smell of lemon and cinnamon and wine mulling – makes him dread going back. His face is ferociously calm, his mineral-drink eyes move slowly but watchfully. I stroke his head and he bends it downwards, so that his chin, his dog's muzzle, is resting on his chest.

After the divorce Eleanor's lawyer, in pursuit of regular payments, had urged me to get a regular job. Who, he asked, as we sat in his leather-gilt phoney-panelled smug family-portraited room, had exempted me from the usual rules? By this he meant, why didn't I come down and live amongst the wage slaves. What exactly was I waiting for?

Good question because it was one I couldn't publicly answer. I wasn't against a wage. It was just that I thought I had to be ready. Even when I was a motorcycle courier, flying around London, I had the sense that I was keeping myself in training. A real job – for example, sitting here surrounded by lawyerly books and tedious eighteenth-century prints of Oxford – would be an acknowledgement of the loss of hope. Even when I was standing by the alligator haven pretending it was a PGA golf resort, I was playing for high – if undisclosed – stakes. I was keeping myself available, resting lightly on the earth. Like a nomad I was ready to up sticks.

I didn't explain this to the lawyer. Instead I said that there were irons in the fire: 'Projects. I can't throw them away.'

'Couldn't you just get a job, and work on these big projects at the same time?'

He seemed to like me, although it was his business to get me into harness if he could. Lawyers long for confirmation that their work is important, so they take comfort from the fact that people out there, people like me, who try to live on flim-flam, don't succeed very often. Money doesn't seek us out whereas it is strangely attracted to lawyers. This particular lawyer is now married to Eleanor, and they have two children of six and eight, who are attending what the English call good schools. Eleanor is Mrs Richard Filkin-Halbert – her notepaper advertises it – and she drives a red BMW with the registration ELıNR. Her bohemian days are safely behind her. Once I drew up next to the BMW on my motorbike and gazed in at the two children strapped against the sumptuously pale and pimpled Bavarian leather. Pale coloured leather denotes luxury in some places. I knew that the children's clothes were from a self-congratulatory shop called Daisy & Tom: children emerged colourfully kitted out for the folkloric but prosperous life of Chelsea. While wishing the young Filkin-Halberts no harm, I couldn't help seeing them as usurpers.

'No,' I said to my wife's future husband, 'I can't get what you call a job. It would be like asking Alfred Brendel to work as a piano tuner.' (I'd just heard the great goggle-eyed one play at Smith Square.)

I have heard that he has repeated this story at staid dinner parties – which lawyers specialise in – and I have imagined the sniggers at my presumption. Especially when I took up motorcycle work. I could have told his and Eleanor's guests about the dangers, the exhilaration, the bacon sandwiches, the

diesel spills, the contemptuous policemen, the haughty receptionists and the simple Dickensian camaraderie of motorcycle
messenger work. Particularly I could have described the life
of the mind which went on undisturbed as London unrolled
behind me. But I would have trouble now remembering the
details of what it was I was thinking about; our thoughts are
like a mad form of back projection, a poorly timed but parallel
world, related, but not too closely, to our daily lives.

In the company of a baboon I am formulating interesting
questions about the meaning of this consciousness.

Piet's confidence is growing. He doesn't yet twitch the chain
to tell me he wants to move on, but it won't be long now.
Instead he makes a noise I haven't heard before, a small
peremptory bark, and I stand up.

At the farm Witbooi is waiting anxiously, scanning the
mountain to see how many of us return. I am obviously cast
in the role of Mallory. Piet is exhausted. It's not surprising:
he has been confined to his cage, ten feet by six, for two years.
He lies down in his box and hides his eyes with one of his
hairy, dark hands, but I feel fit. In my new clothes and with
my body taking on more purposeful, useful lines, I think that
I am regaining some of my lost essences.

Back at the cottage I take stock: I see that I am still dealing
in flim-flam, with these animal stories of my father and
my ideas for films and the crumbling manuscripts. In the
computer age, the manuscripts already have a parchment
quaintness, each letter on the paper typed by hand and many
corrected by hand, the surface unevenly struck. My father's
handwritten papers, written with a pen he dipped in ink,
are antediluvian. But I do have money, the promise of it
anyway, and I am on my way to owning a farm, however
ramshackle. The money is mine, undeserved and unexpected,
nooitgedacht, although the arbitrariness of changes of fortune is a familiar theme to me from my close reading of
Dickens back in the house under the mountain. From the

same source, I am also familiar with the disappearance of fathers.

I chug in the old car to the beach and run along the hard strip at the point where the waves die. Cheered on by gulls, I jump over the blowfish and the great mussel shells and the slippery kelp. The air today is richly nutritious. I feel as though I could run all the way to the end of the bay, where the mountains, broken backed, begin a slow collapse to the sea.

On my way back, now walking and blowing, I see the little girl and two of her friends appear from the sand dunes where they must have been waiting for my return. The girl takes my hand, and urges me to follow. Over the sand dunes we arrive at the first of the shacks. The girl gestures for me to go inside. I have to stoop. After the bright sunlight it is dark in there although the bits of corrugated iron and plywood and plastic sheeting let in shafts of light. On a blanket on the floor, which is grey sand packed down, is the small boy with the split lip. He is shivering. Two women, a darker woman I have never seen before, and the little girl's mother are fanning the boy with smoke from a few coals placed in a section of a jam tin. I can read *IXL, Appelkoos Konfyt, Apricot Jam*. The script of the logo is Roman, as if it has been lifted from the Colosseum or Constantine's arch.

'Siek,' says the woman.

The boy is pathetically small, his shorts ragged, his eyes dull.

'Doctor. Come. Come.'

I gather up the boy, and take the woman by her arm. She tells the children to stay. They cower, resigned miserably to the gloom. We walk and run to the old car.

The Afrikaans doctor is at the clinic doing his rounds. He picks the boy's skin between his fingers and listens to his chest. 'He's dehydrated. He has pneumonia. Can you take him to the hospital? I will ring to warn them. He should be admitted.'

The mother stands respectfully to one side. No one speaks to her. The doctor gives the boy an injection and he sends one of the nurses to get a drip. When it comes he attaches it expertly to the thin, dusty arm.

'It's a helluva tragedy what's happening out there,' says the doctor.

We leave again, the boy's mother carrying the drip, and me bearing the light body.

At the hospital nobody seems surprised. With a sort of weariness, I see what has happened: I have been enlisted. The child lies in a clean bed, perhaps for the first time in his life. The mother sits awkwardly on a hospital chair. She smells of wood smoke. A black nurse comes to talk to her in Xhosa. The ward is full of silent children.

'The mother is worried for heh chill-ren,' the nurse tells me.

'I'll take them some food,' I say.

'She must go home to them. I told her we will look after the boy.'

'Okay. I will take her home. I'll get some food on the way home.'

The nurse explains to the woman that I will take her home. Then the nurse speaks to the listless boy, whose upper lip is a clogged mess. The child accepts her words quietly; of course I am thinking of Matt.

So we stop at a small supermarket and I ask her what she needs. She indicates bread, milk, porridge. I also buy, unasked, some meat. A large piece of silverside and some carrots. I don't know what silverside is, but it looks substantial. Then I add matches, tea, a pack of candles, a gas canister lamp and two blankets. It turns out that she speaks a few words of English. She says, 'Tank jou seh.' Her face is weary and lightly scarred on the cheeks. I think she might be twenty-five. It's nearly dark, but I walk along the beach with her purchases. The other children are huddled in the shack. A baby lies asleep on a bed made of an orange box. The mother picks the baby up. I show them how the gas canister and lamp work and leave them dazzled in unnatural brightness.

'Goodbye,' says the little girl. She is smiling.

From over the sand dunes smoke drifts. An army is encamped there. Looking back I see their shack radiating light like a religious painting.

I run along the beach; the water is warm on my toes. The waves first roar and then sigh as they rush up the sand, so that I am running at times up to my knees in the susurrating white foam. Up on the mountain ahead is a flashing beacon. In the dark I tread on something yielding, perhaps a jellyfish, and fall briefly, face first, before I am off again, racing away in a childish state of pleasurable fear, my tee shirt, shorts and legs wet and sandy. I take great satisfaction from the speed, this feeling of legs pumping. For one month I was the fastest white boy in the world. The local paper, where my father had started his career, printed a picture of me under the caption, 'White Lightning'. Thirty years later I'm running for my white life. In my rational mind I know they aren't going to come out of the sand dunes to murder a speeding, middle-aged man in inappropriate shorts. But I willingly yield up to the dark and the pounding waves and the tearing wind and the deepening darkness. As I arrive panting at the car, there are some young Coloured boys standing idly; they greet me derisively rather than menacingly.

'Where's the fire, Oom?' one asks me.

'Lekker ou tjorrie,' they say about my car and, as I get in, 'Nice and clean today, nê? No kak today.' No shit today.

My mother has a photograph of herself with a friend in Berlin in 1937. She and the friend, a dark girl called Adèle, are visiting Adèle's relatives in Germany. In this photograph there is a shop with a large yellow star painted in what is left of the window. It is my mother's only brush with history. Nothing that happened around here (the release of Mandela for example) is comparable. She told me how appalling it was to see that the remaining Jews were being hounded. I look at this photograph again – the two pretty girls, Adèle with some sort of fur stole around her neck, my mother with a stylish knit suit (her hips by today's standards are rather full). Her dark hair has a small hat attached to it. If I look closely I can actually see the nacreous top of the hatpin. Despite the intimations of a world-historical event immediately behind them, they are smiling at the camera. The picture is embossed in a sort of Braille with the name of the photographer, Wolfgang Obermann. It occurs to me that Jewish shops must have been a popular Berlin background for street photographers, rather like pigeons in Trafalgar Square.

As I walk over to the clinic, freshly showered in the invalid's bath, my skin is glowing, my thighs are aching. Here the flowering scented shrubs and trees are ordered and benign. There is no wind and even the crickets are less hysterical.

She is lying there, her mouth twitching, her eyes making minute, matching movements, as though a current is passing from one to the other. The nurse with no teeth comes in to tell me that my mother ate some stew. This is so improbable that I just smile indulgently, but still when she has gone I look for gravy stains. I compare this devastation with the smiling girl of Berlin in the photograph that I have just been looking at. Her eyes in that picture are bold and confident; now of course they are closed most of the time, but they are closed against the world. My own eyes by contrast seemed to me to be more confident and happier when I glanced in her mirror which stood next to the Sèvres-style thermometer I had sent her. What was I thinking with all this junk and hick stuff I gave her? The Fortnum's Gentleman's Relish, the Sèvres thermometer, the Wedgwood pillbox (bought at a shop in Piccadilly which also sold teddy-bears and shortbread), and a sort of art deco picture frame, in which she kept a picture of me receiving the Golden Bear at the Festival (defunct) of Jackson Hole, Wyoming. Eleanor is standing beside me, spectral. My mother's cottage is laid out to incriminate me. While I was trying to become a cultural big shot, an ambition that foundered with Suzi Crispin, my country was burning. Children were being shot. But I thought then that I had my own direct line to what was true. I thought it was routed through art, but sadly art let me down.

But now I have renewed hopes of my baboon-thriller. Although I am immune to religious feeling, I understand what the born again claim to experience: I have a sense of well-being and purpose, although I do have a nagging worry that this is a colonial condition. My life is being given new meaning by the familiar strangeness around me. Maybe this explained my mother's excisions in her photographs: she sees a sort of fatal weakness, as displayed by my father, in these feelings of distinction. She told me once that in her mother's family (they were from the deep country) servants were not allowed to touch the crockery for fear that they had venereal disease. I think that she must have come to the conclusion, as she started her excisions, that there are other forms of contagion, for example the contagion of false and self-serving emotions.

I tell her of my day, beginning with my walk up the mountain. But I make my own excisions: she won't want to hear that I went walking with a baboon called Piet, and that he inspected the roots of my thinning hair affectionately. I describe the plants I have seen (she was training as a florist at Constance Spry at the time of her trip to Germany). I try to describe the scents of these plants. And I talk of my run on the beach without mentioning the slippery kelp and the blubbery jellyfish. What I am doing is describing a sort of heaven.

I have a geranium leaf in my pocket, which I rub between my fingers and hold up to her face. It smells of baked apples.

17

The sea has suffered convulsions in the night, although now at first light it is quiet. It is so still that the waves are barely beating, just collapsing as inoffensively as honeysuckle over a fence. But the turbulence of the night has produced a harvest of kelp, sand sharks, jellyfish, puffer fish, crab carapaces, mussel shells and bleached bits of marine wood. Further down the beach some women are already picking through this bounty. A hundred small cheerful birds run in and out of the water. The smoke from cooking fires rises straight up from the sand dunes although at a certain altitude it coagulates and moves slowly inland.

The woman and her daughter are in their best clothes. She is wearing a headscarf, loose shirt and a pleated skirt; the little girl is in a pair of jeans and a faded tee shirt which reads 'The greatest cycle race in the world. Pick 'n Pay.' They had been ready for some time I guess. I establish – it seems a little late for formalities – their names. The mother is Daisy, and the little girl is Thandi. The baby is being cared for by the older woman. Thandi skips as we make our way through the wet and alien stuff the sea has produced. In the car the two sit upright on the back seat as though it would be an impertinence to lounge. After a few minutes, I notice that Thandi is whispering to her mother as we approach the town.

The little boy, Zwelakhe, is sitting up in bed. When she picks him up he clings to his mother: perhaps he thought he would never see her again. The large nurse talks to Daisy. Their conversation is punctuated by a low, bleating sound –

eeh-eeh-eeh. It sounds stoical, but I have no idea. The nurse speaks to me in English.

'This chill-ren must stay here for two days.'

'Is he better?'

'He's better but she has pneumonia.'

'Can I speak to the doctor.'

'She is too busy but maybe later you can see him by-and-by.'

'Does she understand, the mother?' I ask.

The nurse speaks to Daisy again, whose eyes are now on the floor.

'She understands. She can stay here with the children today.'

The nurse's English takes no account of tense, number or gender, I see, but she is a massive reassurance. She says something to the little boy, who smiles weakly in his mother's arms. I give Daisy some money for food and I tell the nurse that I will pick her up later after golf.

Pennington advises me not to get involved. There is no fucking end. I'll become a taxi, lawyer, bank and adviser. Soon I will have to deal with drunken boyfriends, deluded job seekers, and schizophrenic relatives. And there's plenty more of them where they came from. Plus, it's not our problem any more. They elected their own government to sort things out. It's not our fault their fucking government is concerned only with how to get BMWs at a discount.

He lets fly at his golf ball. It takes off into the sky with a purpose that so far I have not been able to achieve.

We are not people any more, he says, we are the tax base. Actually this is our best hope, because without our taxes the whole fucking thing would come tumbling down. And they know it.

Pennington has arranged for me to take possession of the farm next week. The final title and the mineral rights will be resolved in due course, but he recommends this interim arrangement. It's normal in Roman Dutch law, a qualified possession. I ask him about the people living in the cottages. Roos apparently pays only three of them now, the girls who sell the teas and Witbooi who is a sort of factotum. The rest of them he employs casually when he needs them, which is seldom.

'Between you and me, he and his wife Tienie have been trying to sell for years. Would you like to chop meat when you could live the high life? No you wouldn't. There's your ball, not too far in the shit. Try not to cock the wrists. Good. Somebody told me you used to be called White Lightning.'

'For about a week.'

'Witblits. The fastest white man in the world; I'm impressed. And you look better too since you came to live among us. They've got a sale of golf clubs and shirts in the pro-shop.'

He doesn't care for my bush shirt, which catches under my armpits as I swing the club.

'Can you come for supper tonight? I want to fix you up with a lovely little lady. A few beers, some sausages on the braai and Bob's your uncle.'

His ball is resting on the fairway. He says it's sitting up nicely. He smashes it towards the green, but it begins to veer off to the left on a trajectory of its own deciding. The face closed, he says. From this I take it a third force has intervened; nothing you can do. I manage to chop my ball up the fairway and then I hit the next one perfectly; it stops near the hole. Pennington is behind a tree.

This is, of course, how it goes in sport: if you take the tiger line you are bound occasionally to land in the shit. Bumping up the fairway is – it seems – not too manly. I win the hole. It's the only one, as it turns out, but I am gratified. Sport has a finality denied to life. On the tropical night when I ran the hundred metres in 10.37 seconds – briefly the fastest time in the world for someone under eighteen years of age – I found an ecstatic surging power. It was like catching a wave at exactly the right moment. And that is the attraction of sport: it may be meaningless, but it corresponds to an idea of perfection, a presentiment of immortality. Out here where so many avenues for spiritual advancement were closed, sport acquired a religious significance; it was an epiphany.

Piet and Witbooi are waiting for me. Piet comes out of his cage calmly. He walks in a deliberate, fluid, muscular fashion like a bodyguard. He greets me with his old harridan's face, a face stretched by agony. And I give him some nuts and some dried peach. I stroke his head briefly. I wonder if I should tell Witbooi that I will soon be the owner of this ramshackle place. Perhaps it is too soon. Perhaps I should let Roos give him the news in his own way, the way sanctioned by custom. Witbooi believes I am from overseas; there is something odd about me. He asks me now if I'm going to go back overseas. He pronounces this unknown universe 'ohferseez' as though it might be a little too exotic. He regards overseas as the great wen, but he is intrigued, even repelled, by what he has heard. I am guessing.

'No, I'm going to stay here.'

'That's nice,' he says. 'Is Master going to fix up this house?'

Now I realise that 'stay' means something different: to live at a specific place.

'No, no, I am staying by my mother's house, down there,' I say, adding to the linguistic confusion.

Also, I don't like the archaic term Master. I try to change the subject.

'Do you know anything about bees?'

'Bees?'

'Bzzz-bzzz – bees. *Bye.*'

'*Bye?*'

'Ja. I want to speak to someone. About bees.'

'Honey bees?'

'Ja. Honey bees.'

'No, I don't know nothing, sir. Only I know they can bite you.'

'Thanks.'

'That's okay, Master.'

Honey bees and a thin-spun thread of life. Piet and I walk along the path towards the stream. The stream flows down from the rock face high above, where it has probably been filtered by the mountains. I can see myself bottling it – *Nooitgedacht Mountain Spring* – and selling it to supermarkets. Or perhaps as clear mountain spring water, *a purity as old as the hills*. I am full of plans and projects: bees, mineral water, perhaps a small vineyard, and a garden planted entirely with indigenous plants, the proteas and other scented and hairy plants whose names I will be learning.

'Piet, my boy, I am going to release you now, but you must come with me, okay?'

I hand him the chain, and sit down by the stream. He sits with me until I stand up and then he follows. His glances in my direction are suspicious as though he is wondering what my motives are. He lags behind for a moment, but I walk steadily on. The new boots are well suited to this endeavour. I wonder if he is going to make a run for it, but soon he is gliding along beside me. Perhaps he is like an old con, with a fear of the outside world.

'Come, Piet, come.'

He ambles over and I give him a few nuts. He eats them and reaches out for more. His blood-orange eyes are sad, but who knows what they indicate? I give him more nuts, which he eats thoughtfully, and then we are off again, his chain dragging behind him. It snags on a bush and he retrieves it carefully. I remember now seeing a monkey – perhaps it was a macaque – in Malaysia travelling to work on the back of a small motor scooter behind its master. This man, his face deeply lined and furnished with a wispy little beard, was a coconut gatherer. The monkey was his servant. It climbed up the palms at the end of a long rope to pick the coconuts. The method was extraordinary: it twisted the coconuts rapidly with its hind legs until they broke free. But also when it worked its way through the semaphoring foliage of the palm, the monkey had to take the same route back, so as not to be garrotted by the collar around its neck. This collar had caused open sores on its neck. But still it sat on the back of the scooter gravely, apparently content, incurious about the willow-pattern panorama of paddy fields and huts and buffalo passing by.

I am full of plans and optimism. My mute companion is himself cheering up; I detect a certain liveliness in his walk now, as if he is reclaiming his place in nature. I think of myself as doing that too. Maybe I was never suited to life in the city, although I fancied myself a connoisseur of city life, knowing where the best coffee was to be had, the best views of the river, the streets, even the pavements, which gave the most pleasure. I was an insider dealer in these intangibles. What a lot of time and energy I have wasted on this endless evaluation. I also spent a lot of time reading newspapers and keeping up with films and television. But what, I now wonder, was the point? In my new self-congratulatory mood, I am leaning towards Virgil's idea of *otium*: peace, tranquillity and a sort of primal and barbaric mystery. There is plenty of that on offer here. I think, as I watch Piet pull up a small flowering plant and taste the bulb, that my film should hinge on whether or not the ape – an orang-utan could be more commercial – is willing to sacrifice itself. More plausibly, the hero can strap a bomb to the ape and detonate it from a distance. But then, perhaps he will suffer a crisis of doubt, and spare his primate chum.

We hurry down the hill. The sun sets quickly around here, and I must get back to the hospital. Piet suddenly approaches me from behind and puts his arms around me. I stand still, not sure if he has ambushed me in order to bite me. His teeth are large and yellow. Nothing happens, so I put my arms around him and we stand for a moment. We are like the relatives consoling each other after a tragedy; we are hugging in a very contemporary way, up here on the hill, just before the stile which marks the beginning of my property. Piet's fur is soft. His face has now a dreamy, abstracted appearance, like someone who has smoked too much dope. I scratch the back of his neck briefly, and he lets go. Maybe Piet and I are consoling each other.

At the hospital, Daisy and Thandi are still sitting on one chair by the bedside of the little boy, who is asleep, small and defenceless. The large nurse comes into the ward just as we are leaving. She says the doctor wants to speak to me. She tells Daisy to wait. She leads me away from the ward to a corridor where equipment is parked, trolleys and metal dishes and oxygen tubes. A young white doctor appears. He introduces himself, and asks me what my relationship is to the little boy: I explain that the family asked me for help.

'Ja, look, the little boy is HIV positive.' Before I can make the connection, he says, 'That probably means the mother has AIDS and possibly the little girl too.'

The doctor is blond and rugby-solid. His eyes have lines around them, from shutting out the sun.

'What can we do? There's also a baby at home.'

'To be honest, not much. We don't have money for the drugs. It's a helluva shame. Anyway I think we should tell them. Do you agree?'

I agree, but I'm not exactly sure why my agreement is required. I hardly know these people.

Her name is Valerie. I tell her about the Patisserie Valerie in Soho, where I have passed so many idle hours. She pretends to be interested. She and I have met before over the corpse of the whale. What a coincidence! Whales have become a bit of an obsession with her. You just fall under their spell! Pennington handled her divorce. He has his old sportman's eye on her, but the next best thing is to introduce her to me.

Pennington's wife is called Peggy, and there are two other couples at the barbecue. The men are large, knocked about by sport, and the women are bleached and covered in a fine down. They have brought immense bowls of salads of potatoes and avocado pears and feta. The men are in charge of the meat. We stand around watching Pennington turn over sausages, and lamb chops done in his special marinade. It would be easy to mock, but I don't. I am grateful for this artless camaraderie, and I welcome the familiar rituals. The sausages are heavily scented with coriander seed. The beer sends up a fine mist into the warm night sky as I pull the ring tab. Behind the mountains there is a deep darkness. One of the men says it is going to rain, but above us the air is clear; still I have the sense of the presence of a swirling gas all the way to the Southern Cross, which both Nick and Craig have pointed out to me.

'Where you come from,' says Nick, 'you have the Great Bear.'

'Ja,' I say, 'but you can never see it: the sky is so full of pollution or clouds.'

'I couldn't live there. No I'm an African,' says Nick. 'It's in my bones.'

The smoke from our small fire is now very thin. We compliment Pennington on his fire: 'Nice fire. It's a good one. I prefer gum wood, but those new Namibian briquettes from Pick 'n Pay are good too. For cooking.'

Pennington gives the sausages a final turn.

'Okay, ladies, bring out the rabbit food, the meat is ready.'

We sit at a garden table under the sign of the Southern Cross. Valerie and I are next to each other. Pennington throws a few logs on the fire, to revive it. Soon the wood is crackling sharply. We don't need the warmth, but we need, I think, the light.

Valerie turns to me: 'So why haven't you got a wife with?'

'Like a rat up a drain,' says Pennington.

'No,' says Peggy, 'no man, that's a horrible expression. Don't listen to him. Take no notice.'

We are all a little drunk. Valerie's lips are wet with white wine, and her grape breath carries to me. The scent reminds me of the leaves of the plants in the mountain where Piet and I have taken to wandering.

She asks me, 'So what exactly are you doing here?'

The burning wood is releasing eucalyptus vapour into the air.

It is very late when I finally get to my mother's bedside. Pennington's barbecue has left me smoky, and I also have the tinctures of Pennington's lovely little lady, Valerie, on me. Time has no importance here; it has no meaning to my mother, but also very little to me. As the bonds loosen which hold my mother to this place, to this bed, time's implacable but imaginary constraints have no force. There is a sort of primal anarchy going on.

'Ma, I'm sorry I've been so long. It's been a helluva day.' (I've adopted the vernacular.)

In the dissolution of time, I sit with my mother most of the night. Sometimes I sleep. Sometimes I talk to her. I tell her about walking on the mountainside with Matt. Under the circumstances, I see no reason to be scrupulous with times and dates and characters.

When I wake just before dawn, rain is striking the window, and my mother is dead, although it takes me some time to understand that she has slipped across the border without her papers.

18

A few weeks after Eleanor and I parted, turned from animal to mineral objects, someone told her that I had been 'running around' with Ulla for a few months. She rang me on a pretext of discussing our assets and their division, but in fact she wanted to hit back. I couldn't blame her. There was a violence in her that needed an outlet. If she'd had a gun she would have shot me. Instead she said something which, to this day, makes my skin clammy. She said: while our son was dying you were fucking a bimbo.

I could quibble with the word 'bimbo', but her charge was literally and temporally accurate. Worse – if anything could be worse – she said that my continued absences had made Matt's asthma more severe. She hadn't wanted to worry me because I said that we were working late, that the film was running into trouble, et cetera et cetera, and that I was stressed out. (In my pedantic way, I noted that I would never have said 'stressed out'.)

As she spoke, as she pronounced a curse, she acquired a sort of righteous dignity, as though she had plumbed the depths of human wickedness and had thankfully rid herself of any lingering illusions. She wept, but she resisted my pathetic and inappropriate attempts to comfort her. After all, I was the one who needed pity, as a sub-human. She hoped never to see me again and she hoped that I would rot in hell. She would never forgive me. And in the meanwhile her lawyer (and future husband) went to work and I gave her everything. I believed that I deserved to have it taken away. Our small house, just behind the Royal Hospital, is now the town house of the

Filkin-Halberts. Their country residence is in Gloucestershire, where the sun setting over the low hills causes the stone of the village, including The Old Rectory, to turn to honey. The clear stream, the old climbing roses, the gravelled drive, the simple flowers in the church, the sleek horses with their expensive saddlery, the village shop which sells fish fingers, the Indian Runner ducks picturesquely housed on an island, the distant cavalry of the hunt, the locals with their thread-worm cheeks, the pile of neatly chopped logs covered in verdigris, the polo sticks in a china vase, the deep mulch under the beech trees, the fat oil-fired Aga, the screech of doomed pheasants, the knotted tassels on the door handles, the Moroccan-leather visitors' book in the hall, the racks of Berry Bros. House Claret, the Spy cartoons in the downstairs loo, which has a green bamboo lattice wallpaper, the guest room with its bottle of Malvern water and Floris soap, the oil painting of a racehorse with a curious tyrannosaurus neck above the fireplace (there are three), the children's bedrooms, hand painted by a friend's cousin (or a cousin's friend), the lined curtains decorated with bunnies and airborne teddy-bears, the recovered flagstones in the hall, the black Labrador asleep, the flopsy rabbits menacing the herb garden, and the old gardener who comes twice a week. This is an English slice of Paradise. A slize of parrots' eyes.

I can picture it all, although I have never been inside The Old Rectory, Middle Turkdean. Still, I have passed by the gates once on my motorcycle, a greasy legate from a more volatile and less tractable world.

Now on the beach the sand is stinging my legs as I run. The waves are tumultuous. The sea is cloudy, the colour of old bathwater. As I run, I feel my ribs, each one is distinct. I sprint a final hundred yards until my lungs are hurting. I lay my new golf shirt down (crest: two golf clubs and a guinea fowl), and I remove my lurid running shorts and sprint into the water. The waves are coming from two directions, meeting in angry confrontation, wrestling briefly, then retreating in huge valleys and eruptions of water. It would be mad to try to swim in this but I rush in. Fuck the Cotswolds, fuck the Filkin-Halberts, fuck the fucking Labrador. I am about to be baptised. I am about to be baptised on the same day my mother has been cremated. I am about to be baptised in my native sea.

The waves are cold. This water has come from far away; it has rushed here at the first sign of trouble. It is dirty-white and foam-laden. I swim frantically, but a huge wave breaks before I can reach it; I dive under the onrushing torrent, but it picks me up and throws me back and then rolls me over. As I emerge another wave breaks on me. I only just have time for half a breath before it throws me sideways into a wall of water coming from another direction, which hurls me back. Something, I hope it is kelp, brushes across my chest. I surface and see a huge wave bearing down on me. Just before it breaks I dive under it, but still its passing turbulence spins me round. Now I am in a new landscape, the water rising so high that I can't see the shore. Another enormous, grey wave comes towards me. It is heaving upwards as it advances to form an unstable crest. I swim towards it and then turn and thrash furiously as it lifts me upwards. Just as I think I've missed it, it begins to break. It starts with a small collapse that slings me down and then it crashes in earnest. The whole cliff of water collapses. Submerged most of the way, I rush towards the shore until finally I am turned over and over in a harshly abrasive trough about fifty yards from the beach. As the water begins to pull backwards, I stand, ecstatic and exhausted. I fall and stand again, and stagger to the beach. I take refuge from the stinging sand behind the first range of dunes and sleep.

The funeral took place in a bleak church of brick. Four old ladies and the nurse with no teeth joined me in the congregation. The priest deputed the task of a eulogy to me. I tried to recall, without being specific, the happy moments of her life. I was thinking of how she had laughed when a dog's ear was shot, I was thinking of when she seized me as I leapt, goose-bumped, from the edge of the bath. Of her years of loneliness I said nothing. Nor could I explain to strangers why she had excised her photographs.

The cremation took place at another location, and I will receive the ashes this afternoon, on the same day as I receive the deeds of the farm, Nooitgedacht. The bee man is coming to set up two beehives in the orchard. I see this as a symbolic act, the start of a life of pleasantness, Virgil's *amoenitas*.

Valerie wanted to come to my mother's funeral, but I said that I'd find it too difficult. What I meant was that she was upping the emotional stakes. She is directing to me, I fear, the intensity she lavishes on whales. She leads, by her own admission, a busy life, as manager of a vineyard shop nearby, and honorary secretary of Whale Watch. She was always busy, even before her marriage broke up. Never able to sit down. She has a child of ten, a girl called Shawn, who is very sensitive. For this reason I have not yet seen the inside of her flat down in the little town on the bay. It has a nice view, she says, suggesting to me that the rest of it is not up to snuff. Whales, I can see, have a disinterested innocence. In fact they may have philosophical qualities we are sadly lacking. Because I have lived overseas, I may have untapped reserves of these qualities myself, which had been exhausted here, that's for sure. Valerie is thirty-eight and makes love in my mother's old car in an intense distracted fashion. It is curious, I think, that the mechanics of sex cannot be predicted before the event. Pennington is keen to know how this is going. I am his proxy.

I have had difficulty sleeping in my mother's little cottage since she died. I feel the weight of her possessions all around. They have lost their purpose which was to be an adjunct of her life. Now some of these things look like junk. It's a shocking transformation, containing a message that I can't quite decipher about the nature of matter. In the bottom of the drinks cupboard, which smells of mahogany and juniper berries, are her flower-arranging things. There are spiky domes on which flowers can be impaled and green sponges into which twigs can be pressed. And there is special wire which can be bent to hold the flowers just where you want them. None of this stuff has been used for years, but it recalls the freesias and camellias and arum lilies and ferns that she liked to use, and the way she cut and pounded and boiled the stems, and the way she covered the kitchen table with colour, bought from a Malay who had a stall down on the corner. Even then I had discerned that her flower arrangements were a trifle provincial: it seems I'd sprung, a fully formed know-all from the provinces. Now I long to recapture my mother's kitchen, full of these scents, and my fervent wish is that she never took my sneers seriously.

Valerie is excited by what she has heard of my farm. Already she has started to make helpful suggestions. Despite her chipper demeanour, I think she is struggling to maintain her equilibrium: pretty, youngish, cheerful, but also a little desperate. I told her about the baboon and she said she had a good vet who could put it down. This is the same vet, it seems, who'd diagnosed the whale's viral condition. I see that Valerie makes value judgements about animals. Baboons can be a nuisance. And anyway they should not be in captivity. Whales are noble and free spirits, despite a tendency to run aground.

When I wake, I jog along the beach to the car. The tide doesn't go out far, but it has left a small lagoon in which I splash. The waves have lost some of their intensity, but the sand still whips up the beach, so I stick close to the water.

Pennington has both the ashes and the deeds for me. He has also received a letter from New Mexico, asking to read the whole manuscript of my father's baboon book. They are very interested in acquiring it for clients at New Mexico State University, Albuquerque.

'There was a jockey called the Duke of Albuquerque, who rode in the Grand National at the age of sixty-two,' I tell him.

'You don't say. Could you sign here please?'

'He fell off, and broke a leg.'

I sign the papers. Pennington stands up and he shakes my hand.

'Congratulations.'

'Thanks.'

'When are you going to move in?'

'As soon as possible. Maybe next week. Do I own the baboon?'

'Voetstoots.'

'What does that mean?'

'It means you buy everything as it stands and at your own risk.'

'Except the mineral rights.'

'Except the mineral rights. Believe me there is nothing there. How is the lovely Valerie?'

'She's fine.'

'Making any progress?'

'Are you a lawyer or a pimp?'

'No, it's just that Peggy seems to think it's going well. Women. You know what I'm saying?'

'It's not a good moment.'

I hold up the cardboard box that holds the Adam urn that holds the ashes, which I am required to believe are my mother's.

I leave him, surrounded by the evidence of his prowess as a sportsman. It is also unintended evidence of the progress of mortality.

I take Piet out of the cage. He reaches for my pocket to find the treats. We walk through my farmyard and along the path to the stream. (Is it my stream? Can you own water?) At the stile I release him and unlock the chain. We walk up through the glade and then follow a faintly drawn path. Birds, sun birds and so on, are sticking their beaks into the flowers. I have the place marked: a little grove of silver trees under a pile of gigantic rocks which had fallen there aeons ago in geological time (which is largely meaningless). Piet walks slightly ahead of me most of the way. Once he comes up behind me and puts his powerful soft arms around me. He seems to want to express his affection or gratitude, I think.

When we reach the trees, we have a view on one side down to the bay; the water is regularly slashed and striped with white so that from up here you can see a kind of symmetry. On the other side are the bruised blue mountains, rising above valleys of green cultivation. I can see the white gables of my farmhouse. Piet sits on one of the large rocks as I remove the Sellotape and sealing wax from the box holding the urn. As I get the urn out, Piet suddenly leaps down and seizes it. He climbs quickly back up on to the rocks and prises it open. He sniffs it and lets it drop. Belying its appearance, the urn is plastic, painted a flat grey. It bounces on the rocks and a thin stream of ash is released.

'Goodbye, Ma. Wherever you have gone.'

I would have thrown the ashes to be caught by the wind, but the result is probably the same. Eddies are already spreading them into the surrounding foliage. Piet sits on his rock, his back turned to me.

I see now the evidence, as Valerie warned me, that baboons have delinquent tendencies.

'Goodbye, Ma.'

In this way are my mother's ashes scattered, by a baboon.

I'd like to say a prayer, but prayers extemporised turn out like the messages in Hallmark cards. I love the old prayers; I approve of liturgy because I regard it as cultural, like Shakespeare. But I can't utter one of those prayers because they seem to be addressing problems that religion itself has created. Like the problem of evil. Instead I want to speak directly, but without expectation of being heard, to my mother.

'Goodbye, Ma. I would have come with you if I could.'

Short of killing myself, I mean it.

Piet has caught my mood. He walks next to me, glancing solicitously at me. He doesn't whimper for food.

From some way above the house, I see a pick-up, which must belong to Roos, parked by the duck pond and swings. As we descend I can read on the door, *P. Roos, Vleisbehandelaar, Master Butcher*. Now I am able to read that he is a specialist in dried sausage. I already know from Pennington that he has a fine reputation for his dried sausage. Pennington served it at his barbecue as an appetiser. I am not sure if the baboon belongs to me, whatever Pennington says, so I approach the house from the back where Witbooi takes him to the cage. Witbooi tells me that Baas and Mevrou Roos are here. Sometimes when I was talking to financiers and producers I had the feeling that they were only telling me part of the story. I see that Witbooi is in the same situation: he must glean from scraps of information what is really going on.

'Witbooi, I have bought the place from Mr and Mrs Roos.'

'You stay here, by this house?'

'As soon as it's fixed up. I want you to stay too.'

'I am staying here. I'm very sorry about the old lady, sir.'

'Thank you.'

Piet climbs on top of his box and sits there hunkered like a Bedouin. I can't, of course, tell Witbooi that Piet had a hand in the old lady's obsequies.

It would be easy to see Roos and his wife Tienie as out of time, strangers in their own land. They have the faces of pioneers. She has shiny, small, suspicious eyes like a blackbird's. They're both wearing their good clothes, and this adds to the sense of dislocation, as though they have come from another place, in the way that, soon after the Berlin Wall came down, refugees from Eastern Europe first appeared with their poor

clothes and strange haircuts. I, by contrast, am in my bush shirt
and hat. It occurs to me that we would look to an outsider as
if we had got the wrong clothes out of the prop box, or that
we were extras from different film sets. I am thinking here of
those scenes of extras milling around at the big Hollywood
studios. One thing is for sure, we have bit parts; we are hardly
footnotes in history's annals.

We sit in the tea room and the two maids, Lena and
Bessie, bring out the tea and home-made cakes in a nervous
procession of bright colours. We each have a copy of the
inventory. I haven't studied mine thoroughly, but after the
formalities we are supposed to go around together and check
that everything is there. The baboon, Piet, does not appear
on the list of livestock. Tienie asks me if I want the peacock.
No, no, please, you have it. She asks Witbooi to capture it. I
see that I have acquired the rusty farm machinery, medieval
ploughs and harrows, and a Ferguson tractor. Roos tells me
that the tractor is completely fucked. He's prepared to take it
off my hands. It's buggered. Tienie lowers her avian eyes at this
man's talk. She may be looking downwards for her minerals.
Suddenly she starts to speak. Her English is hesitant but she
carries on gamely, like a child reciting in class.

'Finally I would like to say that this farm belong by my
family since four generations, since a time long before the
Boer War. It spates me – (Roos interrupts: 'It sorrows me.') –
it sorrows me to sell it. But the meat business is not so good no
more. Many farmers is leaving and the coloured people doesn't
buy good meat. I want to ask God to bless you and the farm,
Nooitgedacht. Also I want to say how my man and I are very
sorry that your mother has passed away. Thank you.'

'Thank you. I will try to look after the farm, and I want to
assure you that you will always be welcome here.'

We proceed on our tour. As we pass the buggered tractor
and approach Piet's cage, Roos offers to shoot the baboon for
me. He has a gun in the pick-up. A bolt-gun, for cattle.

'No, I think I'll keep him for a while.'

'You can't never trust a baboon.'

'I'll remember that.'

'They fine when they young. But later they mad.'

Piet comes forward and stretches his hand through the mesh towards me. I am uneasy about this evidence of my laxity.

'Before we had thirty hens but these people steals them,' says Mrs Roos, indicating Witbooi, who is following us, holding his hat in one hand. I picture the vanished flock of hens.

After the tour of inspection we exchange signed copies of the inventory, and they get into their pick-up. As I move round to say goodbye to Tienie, I see that there are subdued sheep in the back, unaware of what is coming their way.

After they've gone I tell Lena and Bessie to close up. I ask to see the day's takings. A few notes and coins lie in a biscuit tin. I count the money carefully, and write down the day's total on a sheet of paper. It is my money after all. I've forgotten to ask Roos important questions about the accounts and supplying the tea room. Later, I light a candle and sit on my verandah, drinking tea. The sun has caught the back of the low hills which I can see through the oak trees, so that their tonsures are radiant, like the heads of saints. From their cottages I can hear some children shouting and laughing, but far away, subsumed into the landscape. The guinea fowl, which during the day hang around the chickens on the scrounge, are roosting noisily in some large trees beyond the orchard.

Witbooi comes, hat in hand again, to see me. He says he will lock up after I have gone. I sit for an hour on the verandah trying to make myself one with the warm, scented night. The baboon has scattered my mother's ashes without being asked. It could be seen as comic, but I am trying to see it as a natural event. On a more prosaic level, I am also delaying going to meet Valerie at a steak house. On Fridays they have a special, peri-peri prawns, and she knows I will love them. With rice or a baked potato or chips. Shawn will be staying with her granny this weekend.

Finally I go round the back to see Piet. He is huddled in his crudely made box and his orange eyes are frightened as he peers at me.

'Goodnight, Piet, my boy.'

I am aware that I am speaking to him as a friend, or as a relative.

19

I'm too tired to run on the beach. I have a short, bracing swim. I am the only person in the world.

A night spent with Valerie has exhausted me. It isn't the sexual business which has done it, so much as lying awake next to a stranger for hours. She slept with a naturalness which reminded me of Ulla. I had the impression that she – and Ulla – had a conventional sense of these occasions: dinner, wine, sex, sleep, deserved contentment. No matter what that sex consisted of – all the great range of human-animal options – it leads to this outcome. For me it raises the deepest, unanswerable, ontological questions. To lie next to someone who is soundly, unquestioningly asleep – as happy as a Labrador by an Aga – is only to sharpen this disquiet.

Early, just as the first light was bouncing off the unpredictable sea, turning it a sort of parakeet green, and on to the second-floor window of Oahu Court, I was up.

'Where are you going?' she breathed.

'I forgot, the man with the bees is coming early.'

I was eager to be away. I was already hoping that Shawn would not make a habit of staying with her granny. I suspected that she had been levered out. Children are often used in this way.

So now I am waiting in the car park in the sand dunes, our Checkpoint Charlie, for Daisy and her children. At the right moment I see them coming along the beach having exited from the shack freshly dressed somehow. Daisy is carrying the baby.

'Goodbye,' says Thandi.

'Good morning, good morning, Daisy.'

'Molo, umnumzana,' she says.

'Doctor's waiting.'

'Thank you.'

The three of them get in the back and off we go. At the hospital it is clear that within the limitations of an overcrowded ward with harassed staff, young Zwelakhe has become a favourite. He's walking around the ward with a stethoscope, following a nurse. Other children laugh. His shins beneath the hospital shift are thin. As soon as he sees her, he runs to Daisy, who hands the baby to Thandi. Soon the young rugby-playing doctor arrives. He asks us to come with him. The nurse explains to Daisy that she can leave the children while we talk. She comes with us to a room near a Coke machine in the corridor. Towels and cleaning equipment are kept here.

'Right. Some good news. The other children and the mother are clear. Only the little boy has HIV. This nurse here, Elizabeth, discovered when we were taking blood that the little boy is the son of the mother's sister, who has died. So this woman is looking after Zwelakhe. Zwelakhe's pneumonia is much better, but he has HIV as I said.'

'I'll pay for treatment.'

'I'm just an intern; I don't make any decisions about treatment. But I am sure that it would help.'

'It's okay, I will pay.'

The nurse explains all this to Daisy. It doesn't sound like a direct translation to me, more a sort of narrative.

'Thank you, sir,' says the doctor.

The nurse says that Daisy's heart is crying: 'She is happy.'

'Okay, folks,' says the doctor, 'I have to get my skates on, but Elizabeth here will take you to the admin to arrange private treatment. Okay, Elizabeth?'

He moves off smartly through the human traffic, as though he is carrying the ball in broken play.

I have a vision of olive trees and vines and melons growing around the house, as well as my garden of indigenous plants. I explain to Witbooi, as we wait for the bee man, that the ducks can be removed to the dam near his house, and their muddy cement pond must be filled in and grassed over, and the bulging fence removed. The signs and so on can go too. He probably thinks that this is commercial suicide. Also the painted benches must go. In fact, I am proposing to hire some landscape contractors, but I want Witbooi to be privy to all decisions.

I have ordered two hives, each equipped with a small colony of bees. The bee man has recommended the Italian bee. It is a short-distance forager, he says. I am not sure if that is a good thing. Witbooi and I greet him as he drives up in a battered van. *Luigi's Bees*. He is himself of Italian origin; his father was a prisoner-of-war who kept bees. He looks around.

'Nice place, perfect for bees.'

'I'm going to be planting a garden.'

'There's plenty for the little guys on the hills.'

He is a small, middle-aged man in shorts. Some of the stunted, gnarled Mediterranean knottiness is in his legs and thick arms. His face is a motile terracotta, as though the clay is not yet finally sculpted. You would guess that he sings in the shower.

He unpacks all the necessary equipment, two white hives of clapboard, a centrifuge, a bee suit, a smoker, and some trays of honeycomb. The bees are still in the van, humming uneasily. We choose a site for the hives on the slope of the old orchard, about fifty yards apart. The stream is close at this point. Apparently bees bring gallons of water into the hive.

'One rule I have, is place the bees where they get early sun.

Then they get up early and start working. Lazy bastards, just like us Italians.'

In my mind as we carry the beehives with the movable sections into the orchard, I see that being Luigi, of *Luigi's Bees* – now my bees, my Italian bees – has a connection with antiquity: 29 BC to be precise. Strangely, it doesn't seem so long ago to me. Luigi explains that some honey is needed to keep the bees going while they reconnoitre and get settled. He says that at the end of the summer he will come back and help me extract the honey. Now we go to get the bees. Each package contains ten thousand bees in a kind of netted bag. The bees are black and yellow, milling around in the bags. Luigi swiftly places the bees in the hive. He has given me two new queens, of good stock. The queens come in a little box which is plugged with something that looks like marzipan. The queens will eat the marzipan from within and the other bees will eat it from the outside, so that by the time they have burrowed through they will have settled in. A few bees venture out to take a nervous look. It's truly a miracle: the wondrous pageant of the pygmy world is up and running in my clapped-out orchard.

'Don't worry,' says Luigi. 'They'll be out to work at sparrow fart. That's what they live for. Six weeks only.'

> *Bravery, loyalty, toil, lack of sex.*
> *Inferring from these signs and instances*
> *Some men have argued that the bees received*
> *A share of divine intelligence,*
> *A spark of heavenly fire. For God, they say,*
> *Pervades all things, the earth and sea and sky.*
> *From him the flocks and herds, and man and beast,*
> *Each draws the thin-spun stream of life, and both,*
> *To him all things return, at last dissolved:*
> *There is no place for death, but living still*
> *They fly to join the numbers of the stars.*

When Luigi has gone, after enjoying tea and Lena's hundreds

and thousands, I walk down to my hives and listen out for the bee music. The bees are just beginning the overture of the symphony to come, a faint and harmonious murmur, the sort of music you hear coming from the orchestra pit, just before you realise that the musicians have started in earnest. My eyes, treacherously, fill. I hope as I listen to this murmur that my mother has returned, in some way I can't imagine, to a peaceful realm.

If there is no place for death – if there is some form of after-life – it can only be in this bee sense, of being part of a never-ending impulse to life. And it was this sense of all the parts belonging to one greater whole that appealed to my father when he had his idea that ants and bees, and maybe baboons, are in a way just organs of one body. Of course, if they are, perhaps we are too. Our consciousness, just like theirs, may have a ceiling. Just as a baboon will never be able to read Shakespeare, we will never be able to read the laws which ultimately govern us.

The bees tuning up are encouraging expansive thought: maybe the reason we feel for monkeys and primates is that we see ourselves in them, but without the full consciousness. We see children, we see Calibans.

A few bees are milling about on the little platform. I must read up about the waggle-dance of orientation. It seems that bees have a fantastic amount to learn in just a few weeks of life. In those few weeks they are subject to disease. The Italian bee is robust, as its hooped yellow rugby jersey suggests, but still Luigi has dosed them against nosema. African bees are aggressive, he says, but they are never kept in domestic hives, although there is nothing wrong with their honey. It's first class, in fact. I must be on the lookout for African bees because they will rob a hive.

It is apparent that everything African – from over the mountains – must be feared. Africa contains unpredictability, a sort of innate anxiety; for those who live down here between the sea and the mountains, Africa is threatening. Where you see the shacks in the sand dunes, they see the advance guard of chaos. They imagine arms being chopped off, disease and cruel magic, the swollen faces of tyrants, but above all they see a strange and lethal lethargy, whose miasma will spread to consume vineyards, golf courses, schools, roads, hospitals, records offices, and even domestic bees. This may look like lethargy, but it is a natural phenomenon, a virus, that weakens everything it touches and reduces it to its basics. My mother feared it. Valerie fears it. Luigi fears it. Pennington fears it. The brown people fear it, and I see they are in a quandary here: they don't want Africa to overwhelm them, but they have no way to express this fervent desire that Africa should stay away, on the other side of the mountains. Alas, there is another natural law at work; because Africa is incapable of making and sustaining any form of wealth, order and decency, it heads straight for the money, the stability, the calm; and it will devour them. This is what they believe in their hearts, that Africa is a plague. It troubles them.

I have more personal concerns. I am concerned about Valerie; there's a certain crackpot haste about her. She's got it all worked out; she will cut down on her cetacean work, to help me organise the tea room and farm shop (featuring wild flower honey), and she will employ all the builders and artisans I need to produce my Arcadia ... and so on. At the same time, she will continue to provide the sexual and domestic comforts. She's not so precipitate as to suggest where this could all lead, but it's not hard to guess. On the face of it, it's quite an attractive proposition. She certainly has a sexual talent. She dies a few little deaths in the act. Last night, although I was reminded of the displaced Shawn by a mobile of seagulls and some romper-suit pyjamas lying in the bathroom, she produced the full range of her skills. Scented with chilli and prawn carapace and Portuguese wine, we were able for the first time to see each other. I was pleased

I'd become brown over the last few weeks. Taking off your clothes like this is a nervous moment, but her lean insistent body attached itself with gusto to mine. She was determined to show me the whole unencumbered repertoire. After all, she said, you are limited by a car.

I was grateful and exhausted, but unable to sleep. She lay as still as a dead person, needing support at every juncture of her body and the bed. I lay rigid, unwilling to accept the proffered embrace of the bed. She woke up once and asked me why I was awake. I said I was thinking of my mother, which was only partly true.

'Shame,' she said, sympathetically, before falling asleep again.

Actually what I was thinking of was people asleep. Of Ulla and how lying awake in her small flat I had once heard the clip-clop of horses' hooves on the road outside; and I was thinking of Daisy and her family in their smoke-grained sand-blasted shack; and I was thinking of Piet hunkered in his tea chest, and I was thinking of my mother, hoping to hear soon the bee music which would suggest that she had flown to join the number of the stars, despite the rough treatment which Piet had accorded her remains.

I was thinking night thoughts, which are always starker and less tractable than day thoughts.

I also saw what I already knew, that there is no simple life. My projects for the farm, my *grands projets*, would need much more money than I had. In the night I saw trouble ahead. My idea of a baboon buddy movie didn't seem so hot either. Why are our shafts of doubt tipped with poison at night, and why do we look disparagingly on our optimistic, daytime, gullible-bumpkin selves? No doubt it's a simple matter of diminished blood supply or hormones taking a rest, but this is not so reassuring either. Which chemicals are the true ones? Which state of mind accurately reflects the facts?

But now the sun is dulling the earth and browning the grass

and irradiating the mountains and causing the old diseased grapevine near the house to produce grapes the colour of lemonade. Most of the grapes are covered with a fungus, but still I am able to find the odd beauty, which reminds me of the grapes from the farm stall that stood near the end of the road where we used to live. These are the grapes that Carrie used for her jelly. I don't know why, but it seemed to me they were grapes with a secret, and I connived with them. I must have been an odd child. I take some of the mildewed grapes to Piet. His long, hairy arm, with the bare skin near the elbows, comes through the mesh to receive them. Carefully he picks out and discards the mouldy debilitated grapes and then he eats the rest appreciatively.

'Come, Piet, come and see the bees.'

I open the cage door, but he is unwilling to move out until I put the chain on him. Now he comes out warily, with his defensive pimp's walk. I call it an orchard, but in reality it is a graveyard of stunted apricot, apple, pear and peach trees, all of which will have to be grubbed out. Here too there is diseased and shrivelled fruit. I show Piet the beehives; we listen to the bee music which is building in confidence. From outside the house I hear the hooter of a car. It's Pennington.

'Jesus, what's that?'

'It's Piet.'

'Don't let it come near me.'

'He likes big people. Are you here as a customer for our legendary cakes, or do you have something to tell me?'

'I've had a fax from Albuquerque.'

'Good.'

'Not so good. Can you put this monster away before we talk?'

He shows me the fax. The University has had my father's manuscript appraised by the Acquisitions Committee. They are no longer proposing to buy it. It seems, they write, that it is substantially based on the work of an amateur zoologist, one Simon P. Bekker, who lived in a place called Noupoort. There he made observations and recorded data about baboons, and there he advanced his theories about the social life of baboons.

'It appears that your father acquired his manuscript after the success of his book on termite behaviour. Mr Bekker was an invalid, with a drug habit. Under the circumstances we are declining to purchase this manuscript, as it is our policy only to acquire original manuscripts for the David E. Buckmaster Collection. Certainly, interesting though it is, this manuscript does not qualify.'

Pennington is disappointed: he was in line for a commission, but more important, I think, he would have liked to be dealing with the bigger world beyond this one. His horizons are expanding; mine are contracting.

Bekker, he says, was a doctor, a poet and an occasional journalist writing in Afrikaans. He was probably homosexual, and after serving in the Medical Corps during the war, he holed up with a friend in a remote corner of the Cape Province and studied baboons. He had taken morphine in a hospital in Cairo after being wounded at El Alamein, and he continued the habit. He ended his days as a beggar, standing at crossroads in Johannesburg, alongside blind and disfigured black men from the townships. Two or three times he had been rescued and put in a home for Afrikaans senior citizens – after all it wasn't right for white people to beg – but he always escaped. Pennington tells me, too, that just before he died, aged ninety, Nelson Mandela had written him a letter saying that he had read his poetry while in prison. He had been given the volume *I walked by the Limpopo under the Moon* by a warder. It was in all the papers.

'Genius PR,' says Pennington.

We are sitting on the stoep, drinking tea.

'How's Valerie?'

'We went out to dinner last night.'

'Big fat, luscious, LM prawns, I hear. Famous for putting lead in the pencil.'

'Please.'

'Seriously, though, Peggy tells me Valerie says you are a bit of a bok.'

'A bok?'

But I know what he means: a goat, a stud, a bit of a lad.

Pennington has more papers for me to sign. When he has gone, taking with him his golf club bonhomie (tightly confined today in his office clothes), I wonder why my father would have acquired the manuscript. Had he dried up? Had he planned to publish it after Bekker died? It seems Bekker outlived him by ten years. Or maybe he wanted Bekker's work to be known to the world and had offered to get it published, with a foreword by himself?

Also I wonder exactly what Valerie said to Peggy. Valerie has a tendency to make the world in her own image. Her intense carnality has been attributed to me. Her lightly downed upper lip issuing tiny ecstatic droplets of moisture, her mouth twisting, motile, responding to some independent currents, her eyes first mydriatic then almost inverted so that I see the boiled egg whites of them, her deep gasps as if from a cave – none of these things it seemed could be attributed to me particularly. In fact, as she slept so contentedly – why should I dwell on this? – I wondered how many other men had set off this chain of reaction. In this way I see that a gap is already opening between us. It's my experience that there is a gap between men and women, an existential gap, sometimes narrow, sometimes wider. Of course I don't say such things in public, not out of hypocrisy, but out of a desire to lessen the sorrow of experience.

I walk down to listen to my bees again. Witbooi appears, as if he has been waiting for me in the shade of the old tractor lean-to. He wants to show me that he has already moved the ducks on and pick-axed the pond which lies in fragments, each fragment thickly coated in a duck-green slime. I praise him and we walk down to the beehives together. We pause to listen.

'They singing,' he says.

And indeed from the beehives there arises a deep, officious hymn, the socialist-realist anthem of their pygmy world.

20

Today we are moving the tea room into an outbuilding. The outbuildings are an unplanned museum of farm history. Expressive junk fills them, but there is one room with beautiful latticed floors and the remains of stalls. It has been cleared out and a sign has been painted: *Old Dairy, Teas and Farm Produce*. Actually even my rudimentary maths could demonstrate that the teas are a dead loss. A few walkers, a few lovers, a few elderly people with their own sandwiches, pass this way, but certainly selling tea and instant coffee and hundreds-and-thousands cakes is never going to pay for the renovations of the dairy, if it is a dairy. Nobody, not even Witbooi, can remember such a thing. Piet has been removed from view to a spacious run which encloses half of a large tree. And up there on a branch I have had a shelf and a small but solid house built. Piet is not aware of the Swiss Family Robinson appeal, but I take pleasure in his new quarters. He has become more confident, even a little demanding. The farm children are no longer allowed to tease him.

We have cleared the main rooms of the house and soon I'll be able to sleep here. The floors have all been exposed and polished so that the wide yellowish planks have returned to the house what I think is its Dutch character; I am thinking of the Utrecht School of painters. The new fruit trees are in, with the vines coming later. The duck pond and all the coloured benches and the breeze-block locomotive and the barrels have gone. As she promised, Valerie has supplied artisans – painters, gardeners, plasterers. Re-thatching will start soon. Valerie has also been able to find honey and biscuits which look suitably bucolic; we have labelled them with a woodblock print of the house. In place of the biscuit tin, we now have a small computerised till which takes care of the money. We have added carrot cake and death-by-chocolate to our range. Valerie has introduced me to her bank, and I have taken a loan to pay for some of the improvements. Soon I will be able to sell my mother's cottage and repay the loan with plenty to spare.

To tell the truth, it's not very demanding work for me. There are lots of willing people available, all at low rates of pay. I am a Louis XIV. In my Trianon I give orders: trees are moved, landscapes improved, carpenters create piles of sawdust. I see now why the rich love decorators and architects and properties: it is to be a Sun King watching the planet functionaries whiz about.

I have time for Piet. He has learned to travel in the car, sitting looking out of the window with tolerance and dignity. Sometimes, very early, we go down to the beach. He picks among the shells and gasping, stranded fish among the kelp. He does it with the seriousness of a French housewife at the market. When I run, he bounds along. If I surf, I chain him to a post that must once have held a lifebelt. He watches me anxiously, pacing about at the end of his chain. He loves best the mountain. There I let him roam freely; so far he has always come back. When he returns from walking, he scratches my head gently and I pick through the fur of his neck for ticks. His eyes lose their focus.

Twice I've taken Daisy and Zwelakhe to the hospital. The doctors want to make sure that he is taking the pills. He sits absolutely still as they draw blood. I don't know what Daisy thinks is going on, but there is something very dramatic about drawing off blood and releasing it into a phial. Perhaps she thinks that Zwelakhe has too much blood. She hasn't asked for anything, but I give her money and stop at the shops on the outskirts of the town. It's a basic place, old tin-roofed buildings, selling to the poor. I notice, discreetly, that she has bought a bag of maize meal, three oranges and some long-life milk. Valerie thinks I shouldn't have become involved: it's never ending. I don't remind her that she spends a lot of time involved with whales, none of which demonstrates gratitude for being re-floated or disentangled from nets. Nor do the whales appreciate all the goodwill which Valerie is directing their way. But I see that she thinks that nothing can be done about the migrant people, in fact I will be encouraging them when they find out that free food is available, whereas it may be possible to save the Southern Right Whale for posterity to enjoy. I take it she is not thinking of the Japanese.

Although I don't discuss this with Valerie, I see what my boyhood hero, Camus, was getting at: you are involved and you can't avoid it. At the same time you should not subscribe to any ideology, which is more dangerous than the plague. Anyway, the fairly modest amount I am paying for the drugs is nothing compared to what I am laying out on the house. Valerie believes that the way forward for the country is not through individual humanitarian acts, but through economic development which creates employment. I am doing my best; nobody could expect more.

Of course I am the person who should have done more. Eleanor believed that I was too eager to impress; in this eagerness I neglected what was important. When Matt died it was made abundantly clear that she was right. I have never allowed myself to blame her. She was there and she had the nebuliser and the drugs and the hospital's number to hand. The hospital was only a few minutes away. I was unable to question her: the man in the dock had better accept his guilt. But now, freed, I am beginning to wonder if her anger – duly sanctified – had an element of guilt. When you get right down to it, what was I doing with Ulla that most people – I'm not excepting women – wouldn't have, given the opportunity?

There is an imperative, sometimes subsumed by sex, to fight a rearguard action against mortality. When it presents itself, most people take it. Marvell had it right: *the grave is a fine and private place, but none, I think, do there embrace.* This is the adulterer's rationale, written three hundred and fifty years ago and as true today as it was then.

The sun, the thalassotherapy of the pounding waves, the bustle of construction and creation, the perky little fruit trees, the foraging bees – now right at home – the amber grain of the old wooden planks, the stooks of thatch piled ready behind the house, even Roos's loopy relation with a divining rod, pacing the property in search of minerals, the soft-spoken contentment of the Rhode Island Reds as they spread out into the orchard, the incessant inane liquid burbling of the turtle doves, the smells of vanilla, chocolate and sugar heating to make Bessie's icing: all these things are proof against my former cold and murky life. That life has gone back into the mists. England is a place that has never existed; I imagined it from oddments of books and films and myths. My new happiness is only slightly marred by remembering what Wittgenstein said: *nothing is as difficult as not deceiving yourself.* And Valerie sometimes reproves me, but in a kindly fashion as though she is cajoling a stranded dolphin (Whale Watch also looks out for dolphins) back into deep water. I haven't told her yet about Matt. I fear that she will see it as an opportunity to gain some purchase on my soul. For the moment I am only offering my body, a humble enough exchange.

As the sun sets I feel a particular ecstasy. Sunsets have been trivialised by films and commercials: they have become a sort of full stop, a cheap dose of exoticism, easily filmed on a telephoto lens. What happens here as the sun sets is richer and more personal. The air itself begins to thicken and the sun plays on the mountains behind the house. Sometimes it causes them to glow purple, sometimes to blush pink; then here below there is a quick, quivering dusk and we, all of us, take stock.

Night rushes in. The sky above the mountains is suffused with colour moving deliberately like a wine stain spreading through a tablecloth. Sometimes the clouds are caught from below in a pale yellow: they float like small boats of butter in the sky. Here it is easy to believe in the idea of the sublime; I have been set free: the sunsets, the warm scents, the peace, however illusory, of the old house, all require me to take stock and rejoice. I rest my bare feet on the low wall of the stoep, drink a beer straight from the bottle, and wave farewell to not-so-jolly old England.

I am a man of property. Even the sun seems to belong to me. As far as I can see it hasn't struck another house in the world.

Piet seems to suffer from anxiety as dark approaches. My father has written, plagiarising the drug addict Simon P. Bekker, that baboons display 'hesperidean gloom'. Apparently just before bedtime on the sleeping cliffs, baboons become silent and thoughtful. My father, or Bekker, attributes this to the phyletic memory, the inherited memory. Whatever the truth, Piet certainly frets. He sits very still for minutes and then suddenly runs for his box.

Late in the night I may have anxieties about the nature of this enterprise, but I think that these are anxieties about the whole human enterprise, which rests, I have discovered, on very flimsy supports, like Scandanavian modern furniture.

When I think of my former life, I see it as Dickens saw his, taking place beneath a grey canopy without a tear in it: *with never a rent*. Of course I know that this is not based on meteorological fact: sometimes speeding around London as a messenger I rejoiced in clear autumn air or sharp spring days and long evenings scented by mown grass from the parks. But now I dread that lowering gloom, slick wet streets, the shaven-headed plump complacent men with their white-ant look, the weeping, sullen bricks and concrete, the jostling lumpy children at bus stops, the indifferent deep shuddering river, the buses fogged with human damp, the ducks gagging on the soggy white bread floating in the pond in the park where we couriers – bike-boys, greasers – used to meet.

Because, like Piet, the dread lies deep in my memory, although hovering rather ambiguously between the conscious and the unconscious.

Valerie has found a four-poster bed which she believes will go nicely with the main bedroom. It's not an original, but made of old stink-wood. She wants me to come with her to look at it; she warns, it's not cheap. It's in the nearby university town of thatched and whitewashed buildings, oak-shaded streets and antique shops. Valerie comes to get me in her tomato-coloured Mazda. She finds my mother's old Escort embarrassing, although her excuse is that it's not reliable. I have been sitting with Piet near the stream, and watching with pride my stripy dago bees landing to take on water. There is one muddy spot they favour. Also I have been on the lookout for African bees. I put Piet away sometime before she arrives, because she thinks my relationship with him is *helluva creepy*. She is wearing very tight pink pedal-pushers, which show her brown calves and her neat hips off. In the bright sun I can see the endearing down on her face. She has taken half a day off from the wine estate for the task of showing me the Chartres of beds, which she came across purely by chance when she went to the flicks with Peggy. Peggy thought it would be just perfect. She doesn't normally agree with Peggy's taste – Peggy is a lot older – but this time she has to admit that Peggy has hit the nail on the tail.

Valerie kisses me as we get into the car. She smokes and her breath is tobacco-scented, which I think of as womanly. My mother used to smoke Wills Gold Flake, and Ulla smoked

Marlboro Lights. As we set off I wonder if Valerie thinks that she is staking a claim to a permanent berth with this bed. A four-poster suggests a kind of romantic abandon. It also hints at Lord (and Lady) of the manor pretensions.

Valerie is keen to point out the sights of the little town as we enter past the original wine-press. The main street is a succession of low houses, neatly thatched, with Dutch-paned windows and gables, huge oak trees, and small tin-roofed cottages opening right on to the street behind an irrigation ditch. It's obvious that the Dutch who settled here three hundred and fifty years ago – same dates as Marvell's coy mistress – were anxious to create something closed and finite and domestic, looking inwards rather than out to the frightening emptiness beyond: not a solid building until Cairo. Just before we turn off the main street, she points to the Theological College where she says half the prime ministers trained. God vouchsafed to them an understanding of the black man. And that's where the shit hit the fan, right here, she concludes sadly. If I will excuse her French.

The shop where the four-poster is housed – it's the prize exhibit – sells African art, pots, beads, and masks, and a few old wagon chests, as well as some local pottery. On the walls are roughly woven hangings, depicting African scenes and African animals done in an abstract style which is hopelessly dated. Provincial. (I must curb these judgements.)

The bed itself looks as though it could be launched, for example by the Swiss Family Robinson, from a desert island in a bid to get home. I say I'll think about it and I offer to buy Valerie a plant-holder of intricately shaped wire for the wall of her flat, but she refuses grimly and we file silently out of the shop. Later I try to explain that it's not that I don't like the bed, it's just that I'm not sure until the room is painted and so on . . .

'You think I'll come and jump straight in, don't you?'

'No, no. It's not that. I just want to see how it will look.'

'Are you sure that's what you mean?'

'Sure. Absolutely sure.'

But of course she is right. I don't want her to extend her proprietorial rights into my bedroom, and the giant bed – taller than the shacks in the dunes – is an invitation to connubiality. At the same time I see that she is hurt; she has tested the wind and finds that it is blowing in the wrong direction. Anyway – we are walking silently towards the wine museum – I'm not such a great catch. She is pretty, lively, boldly dressed and in her thirties. She doesn't want to hang about. I have told her about Eleanor, and now she uses this privileged information: 'Your wife, Helena, was right.'

'Eleanor.'

'Eleanor. Your wife Eleanor was right. Your mind is not on the ball. What's with that smelly baboon and the bees and your mother's shit car? I'm offering to help you make the place nice, and I am also helping you with the business side. Oh, thanks very much, Valerie. Jolly good,' (she attempts an English accent) 'but when it comes to the important things we aren't quite good enough. Oh, I know, you used to make films and you used to know important people, so you say. Let me tell you, we here know a lot more about life. We have lived through it. While you've been toasting muffins with the church clock pointing to half past four, or whatever, we've been in the real world. No, we whiteys have been the scum of the earth, our feet on black people's necks – so you think. Well let me tell you, some of us have risked our own necks in more ways than you can imagine. And I'm not just a bunny-hugger by the way. You think because you were sitting on your arse in Europe, somehow you're better than us.' (Her arm sweeps around to include the town, the few people in the streets, the mountain, and the receding antique shop.) 'All I wanted was to help you turn that place into a home, but you thought, no, shit, this doll is after my money, she wants to move in, the bed is just the beginning. If you think you're going to use me any longer, you've got another think coming.'

She is crying as we walk beneath the oaks; I marvel at her perceptiveness and also I feel a heaviness of heart, that I should have been the cause of her misery. I imagined that I had put the talent to cause unhappiness behind me. I offer to go back to the shop.

'Too late,' she says, 'too fucking late.'

Tears are caught on both sides of her nose, detained briefly by the down. They prevent me from answering. I could, for instance, ask why her husband left her, and I could explain that I am fond of Piet and that Piet is in some way a line to my father, and that I feel a duty to drive my mother's car for a while. I could tell her that I had been taking seawater treatment to cure delusions of singularity. But I don't, because it would be more difficult to answer her deepest suspicions about the Trojan Horse nature of the bed.

I do say one thing: 'Believe me, I don't think I'm too good for you.'

'Too right,' she says, 'soutpiel.'

We skip the wine museum and she drives me home in silence. After she has gone I consider the options. It's an old dilemma, one of the oldest.

The roof is half off. The thatchers are ripping it away and throwing it to the ground. Small animals are trying to make their escape, as their habitat is destroyed. The leader of the thatchers is an old man, whose face is as lined and crumpled as parchment. (I am thinking of the Dead Sea Scrolls in Jerusalem.) His eyes have lids like rolled-up manuscripts, so that the irises, flecked with brown and green chips, are barely visible. To me he looks like a Hottentot, the people who linger on only in their persistent genes. He tells me that he thatched the house thirty years ago. Maybe that was the last time. It certainly looks like it. He picks up a piece of the discarded thatch to show me that it is wet and rotten. The new thatch will all be in place in a week. For now the house is desolate, as though it has been ravaged. In the old dairy the new shelves are up, and Lena and Bessie are stocking them with honey, biscuits, chutney, home-made jam – not from our home – and dried sausage, supplied by Roos. The tables now have checked cloths and the two girls wear print skirts with white blouses and aprons. Valerie wanted them to wear the Victorian caps. Lena and Bessie are happy, it seems, although I am uneasy about the costume: it reminds me of the slave woman who dresses Scarlett O'Hara, with rolling of the eyes.

The seabirds are arrowing homewards. The sea itself is orderly and the sand where the water rests on it is gilded and burnished by the setting sun. I run along the water's edge. Valerie's unhappiness has blunted the pleasure: I dread a return of heaviness to my life. Also, I rang Pennington to ask what *soutpiel* means; he said someone with one foot in Europe, one foot here, and his cock in the water. A saltcock.

The fuzzy lights on the lower levels of the mountain are visible in the biscuit twilight as I enter the water. I catch a wave easily – they are strong but benign, rolling resolutely to the beach – and then another. The water always feels warmer after the sun has set, warmer and more viscous. I emerge from the waves a better man, towel myself, and sit at the water's edge. There are always a few birds which have underestimated the length of the return journey, and fly fast and anxiously. Fishing boats are returning to port down beneath the mountain, and their riding lights dip below the invisible waves, so that what you see is a dance, the rise and fall of a carousel. I remember going to the Easter Fair on Hampstead Heath with Matt: we walked up from the Vale of Health, and we could hear the strangled music and then see the mysterious muffled lights before we could make out the Camelot Carousel and the Roller Ghoster. And I explained to Matt – as fathers do – that there had been fairs here for hundreds of years. The rights were enshrined. I wasn't sure how many hundreds of years, but it seemed to me important to convey the idea of rights, sanctioned by custom and practice, to a small boy. It's part of the old England which I'd read about, of brave foresters and honest yeomen and sturdy farmers. All gone, except for their tattooed descendants, the fairground barkers. Matt had given a good impression of being interested in immemorial rights. My one-time employer, Simon Chiswick, had a fondness for the rights of Englishmen. In his vision of history, the English were paragons because of their ancient freedoms. These freedoms, I was to learn, were of the negative sort, freedom from immigration being the most important.

As I am sitting here, the children approach me.

'You come,' says Thandi.

'What's wrong?'

'You come.'

I follow them up the beach and over the first ridge of sand dunes. There is a fire outside their shack, and an old drawing-room chair is placed by it. I sit down. Daisy appears from the shack smiling. She pours me a cup of very sweet, milky tea, and kneels beside me on a woven mat placed on the sand. The firelight picks out the small scars on her cheeks. The little boy, Zwelakhe, stands beside me. I pick him up and place him on my knee, where he sits very still, scented with wood smoke.

To aid remembrance, small boys have a convenient hand-hold, just where their chicken ribs join the softness of their stomachs.

21

When I came back from beach, Valerie was waiting for me at the house. She was sitting on the verandah in my deckchair, under the wrecked thatch.

'I've come to say sorry.'

'No need.'

'You smell of smoke.'

'I've been on the beach.'

'No, really, I lost it there for a while. I don't want to give you a sob story, but it's hard sometimes with the job and my daughter . . .'

'Please, you don't have to apologise. A lot of what you said about me was true.'

'I shouldn't of mentioned your wife. I'm sorry. Will you forgive me?'

'Of course.'

I perch on the wall. We sit silent, and into the silence the crickets rush, abhorring an auditory vacuum.

'Anton Pennington said you were wanting to know what a soutpiel is.'

'Now I know.'

'It was a stupid thing to say. I didn't mean to hurt you.'

'Actually it's a pretty good description. Do you want a glass of wine?'

'Why not? Shawn's with her granny. I'm footloose and fancy-free tonight.'

I looked at her under the one naked and insect-besieged light-bulb; the desperation was coming through, like the ribs of a ship breaking up in heavy surf.

*   *   *

Up in the mountains, I've heard, there is a very small village which is set against a deep and almost impenetrable fault in the rocks. In this ravine which runs deep into the mountains, a troop of baboons have lived undisturbed for years as the town is almost abandoned. It was in this remote place that Simon P. Bekker made his study, which found its way into my father's possession. Piet is sitting gravely in the front seat as we leave the tarred road and set off up into the mountains. The landscape is suddenly harsh, as though what was below in the valley – wheat-fields, cows, orchards of apples – was a fanciful illustration from a child's book. Up here the rocks lie on the landscape like tortoises. The surface of the road is itself mainly rock or pulverised rock. The road ahead flattens and enters a narrow gorge. Off to the right, some way below, is a stream. The water is the colour of whisky. We follow this narrow gorge for a few miles in deep shade, and then the valley opens again. I can see castles of rock above, the spiny aloes silhouetted on them. From here they look like snipers. The change of scenery has not affected Piet, as far as I can tell. He treats it all with pharaohic indifference. My plan is to take him as close as I can to the baboons. It may be possible to release him one day.

The village consists of six tin-roofed houses baking on a spot where the valley flattens out. Some of the roofs have caved in and windows are hanging loose. There are a few chickens scratching around. One house sells drinks and postcards to the visitors who come to see the baboons and explore the mountains. An elderly woman comes shuffling from this house; she is wearing a floral housecoat and slippers, and on her head is a tightly wound cloth. Piet turns his languid, haughty gaze on her. I'm not sure she can see that well, because she does not react. Her face is pale and covered in large brown spots, and her features seem to be bunching in the middle of her head, as if the forces of isolation are causing them to huddle together. I ask her where the baboons are. Not so far. They are always waiting for visitors, although it is forbidden to feed them. She points out the Bekker house, which only has three walls standing.

I park out of the way and take Piet from the car on his chain, and we walk up towards the ravine which runs thick and tangled between cliffs of rock. We climb a few hundred yards up the gorge. The air in the ravine is much cooler, and ferns grow in crevices and around the rocks. There is a picnic table beside a stream, and we sit there. Soon the baboons begin to scream and bark. Piet leaps on to the table, and bares his teeth, and raises his eyebrows to reveal the pale patches. Now he begins to pant and grunt. Before we can retreat, two huge baboons rush towards us screaming. Piet screams too. I shout at the menacing baboons, and try to lead Piet away, but suddenly he jumps off the table, wrenching the chain from my hand, and runs towards some trees with the big baboons in pursuit. I have caused anarchy in the animal kingdom. I run after them. The rest of the troop is approaching, but they seem to be spectators rather than participants. I see small dark amused faces: other baboons simply foraging, uninterested.

Piet is hampered by the chain as he tries to escape, but these baboons are battle hardened. They circle Piet, screaming, as he tries to find a way out. Now the two baboons dance, panting and grunting, waiting for Piet to turn his back. I run, panting myself, just as one of the baboons gets hold of Piet and bites him. For a moment they roll around. As the second baboon closes, I rush them, screaming. For a moment the attackers pause and Piet escapes, bounding towards me. I hold his chain firmly and we retreat, menaced by the baboons all the way to the car park. Piet utters threats of his own, but they are not convincing.

The woman comes forward. When she sees Piet she says, 'Sir mustn't steal the baboons.'

'No, it's my baboon.'

'Oh sorry, sir.'

'That's fine, we must go.'

'Come again, sir.'

In the car, Piet sits trembling and panting, blood running down his neck. As we drive home – it's at least two hours – I wonder if in some way I am accursed. I seem, without intending it, destined to cause pain and chaos. Piet is bleeding and whimpering; soon he climbs into the back and lies down, covering his head. My judgement is poor. It's obvious now with the casualty bleeding on the back seat that wild baboons are never going to welcome Piet into their society with baboon blandishments. My father wrote that baboons dealt very harshly with newcomers, although it was sometimes reported – by whom? – that outsiders were accepted in a troop after a troubled initiation.

And the information which my father had so cheaply retailed was gathered back there in that deep, dark ravine. I wish now that I'd asked the old woman if she had ever known Bekker. From my father's writing, his description of the ravine and so on, it seems that he may have visited Bekker here. She may have met my father. After a while we pause by the roadside. Piet drinks a fruit juice, then he stands and puts his arm around me. The bleeding has stopped. I stroke his head and his eyes frost over.

The road leads back through farmlands, but these farmlands seem barely to have been begun. Whole mountainsides and fields are unploughed. In Europe every arable inch is worked. Here the human enterprise looks tentative; the landscape is not yet fully under control. Its wildness speaks to me, although I'm not sure what it is saying; now that I'm a landowner in a minor way, I will begin to tune in to these messages. And perhaps – finding without seeking – I will discover what the nature of the human enterprise consists of. In the process my judgement will improve – attuning itself to natural facts.

When Valerie asked me what I was doing with a smelly baboon, my answer could have been along these lines: a baboon's life may be a lesser, more restricted life – I doubt for example that the sleeping Piet is pondering baboon consciousness – but I believe that my feelings for Piet and his for me are not entirely meaningless. For instance, Valerie, I rushed to Piet's aid without pausing to weigh the dangers. Now I think the dangers were enormous. Piet and I were no match for the baboon warriors. We are soft, domestic and in need of comforts (Piet loves the sugary peach rolls), but the experience of danger, the yellowed canines and the psychotic screaming and barking, has excited my thoughts. War correspondents come back from the front charged with a sense that their priorities – as if one has them – have been rearranged. And maybe that is what I am looking for, some seismic change, some toppling of the mental hierarchies, some distant music. And I see now that my father too was always on alert.

Even the unfolding landscape is full of, as yet unrecorded, significance. Here is an apple farm, acres of trees running up hill and down dale, and here is a small railway siding littered with apple boxes, and here is a dam of metallic, bottomless, bird-free water, and here is a group of squatters, inexplicably building shacks at the foot of a mountain pass which rises up through iron-blue crags where trailers of mist move restlessly just below the highest outcrops.

Paradise. A slize of parrots' eyes. When the hurricane struck the Turks and Caicos and destroyed the beach and overturned the sales office and flattened the marketing suite and flooded the golf course, extending the range of the caymans by several hundreds of watery yards, I was pleased.

In a hurricane-free part of the island, the marketing director and I haggled over money. He wasn't prepared to pay me for my pre-hurricane work. Andrew, the actor, stood just out of range of our discussions, giving me what he took to be encouraging signals, his eyebrows contracting fiercely, and his jaw clenching determinedly. The Dutchman said that the office in Miami had closed his account and that my fee, and Andrew's, were only payable on completion. An act of God had destroyed the Paradise Club, and if I'd looked at my contract, I would have seen that acts of God were excluded. The rain that followed the hurricane, somewhat anticlimactic, whipped the hotel as we drank our rum punches. The marketing director said that he too was not being paid – 'Bollocks,' Andrew mouthed – we were all in the same boat. Suddenly Andrew rushed him and pushed him over some rattan tables on to the floor, to the sound of breaking glass and splintering cane.

'You bastard, you bastard, you fucking crook.'

Andrew was exhausted by this burst of violence, and slumped in an intact chair, while I hauled the marketing director to his feet and made an attempt to pick up broken glass, as if children in bare feet might appear at any second. In the end I got a thousand dollars in expenses, and the suit. Andrew was threatened with an assault charge and fled, penniless, in his own clothes. He had heard that the Turks and Caicos police regarded the judicial process, which was supposed to follow arrest, as a waste of resources. Before he left on an island hopper, Andrew said he would never forgive me; but actors can't afford hard and fast attitudes. Also they take comfort in grand gestures, and I treated him to a long and drunken lunch of expiation in London. How we laughed about the dissemination of the alligators, and the demolition of the show house, and the disappearance of the imported white sand, and most of all about the upending of Boudewijn van Aswegen. At the time, Andrew had been terrified of rough treatment, but now amongst the pristine napery and comforting, complacent English burble, we recalled 'the slize of parrots' eyes', and 'Robert Trent Jones designed Championship Golf Course', and the 'Cloob Conzept', and then

Andrew said, 'Free welcome alligator served on arrival at the Hawaiian-themed Tiki reception area,' and I began to laugh uncontrollably, sobbing silently into my napkin.

But I know that the original idea of paradise, as an area enclosed against the world, is a persistent one.

And now I'm returning to my own slice of paradise, roofless for the moment, and my beehives and fruit trees and contented, inoffensive hens. I lead the battered Piet to his cage. He climbs the tree slowly and sits on his platform. His eyes are wary, I think.

The bees are humming, the fruit trees are producing fat buds, and the hens are ranging happily with the sole purpose of producing perfect eggs. And up in the mountain my mother's ashes are taking the injunction of the funeral service literally: dust to dust, ashes to ashes. The stunned hot plangent day; the waves of heat bouncing off the mountain where the ashes lie scattered by a furry hand, the weight in the air, all seem to be directed to me, to sharpen my perceptions and in particular to remind me where my vanities got me. I can't say that the message is that I overreached myself – landscape doesn't deal in specifics – but the crude message is one of place. And I understand it.

The bees are fanning the hive to keep it cool. There is a faint fluttering sound, tiny fans performing a symphony. I am longing to don my bee suit and remove the honey. When I was a boy I kept silkworms. Later I bought some for Matt. There was a mulberry tree near his school, hanging over the sidewalk, and each day we would pick a few leaves, more on Fridays, for the worms. As a boy I couldn't quite believe that it was possible to unwind the cocoons and make suits and fabrics. Nor could Matt, and I have the same feelings about my bees. Is it truly possible that we will have our own honey produced by these little creatures?

Eleanor, I am sure, has a mulberry tree in the Cotswolds. It will be large and splayed, like a favourite horse or dog, possibly held up on stilts to emphasise its antiquity, and in that way to congratulate its owners, the Filkin-Halberts, on their good taste. Eleanor believed that she had taste, an inherited thing, Lamarckian even, that was of course denied to me. But I got the idea pretty quickly: it wasn't taste so much as a code, easily broken. I was in thrall in my own way to Englishness: for example the worn flagstones and fleeting hopeful faces and the creaking bicycles of Oxford, and the enormous, weeping anonymity of London and its mysterious river; and many small matters which included beggars with optimistic dogs, the scent of hops spilling from pubs and the faded velvet of theatre curtains.

It's easy to see that what I loved, what I love now, is the product of my early reading done not so far from here beneath the mountain, where the termites were conscientiously tunnelling under our lawn and my father was thinking of the grand designs and simplified layman's laws of the universe. For myself, I have the feeling that these laws are a form of litany, a reassurance in the face of the indifference that we perceive.

Here in my private paradise, I am trying to eliminate worldly anxieties, although there are indications that having money may bring its own troubles: *how to make a small fortune: start with a big one*. My small fortune is already under siege.

On my way to the sea for my ritual immersion, my own *mikva*, I see the sign to the wine estate where Valerie works, and I drive in to say hello and to demonstrate that there are no hard feelings. The old house was once the country residence of the first Dutch governor, or perhaps of his brother. The drive is long, through a grove of huge oaks. I get glimpses of the house, low and white with massive trees in front of it, trees so big and ancient that they seem to have strayed from the vegetable into the mineral world. In the shop by the car park I see that we have some way to go with our biscuits and honey. This is the Harrods of farm shops. The place has racks of wine and cards and souvenirs and baskets of fruits and is delightfully scented with lavender and freshly baked bread. I ask one of the staff where Valerie is, and she tells me she is having tea by the Lady Buxton tea garden. I walk down a lavender-fringed path, past the library and the rose garden. Sitting at a small table on a terrace is Valerie. Next to her on a cast-iron bench is Anton Pennington. It's too late to halt, as Pennington has seen me. He stands up and calls me over. Valerie looks around startled. In a film this look would demand a close-up, just to make sure that the audience gets the significance. So far I don't know what it signifies.

'We were just talking about you,' says Pennington affably. 'Come, sit down, they have the best malva pudding in the world.'

He orders tea and cake for me.

'I just came round to see you in your natural habitat,' I say. 'I don't want to disturb you.'

'No problem. We were only talking about my payments.'

'Or non-payments,' says Pennington, 'to be more exact.'

'My ex-husband has left the country without paying Shawn's money in.'

The garden is dense with the scents of roses; they commingle promiscuously. I hear my father's voice: *like a tart's parlour*. My mind has become easily infiltrated, and I take this as a sign that I am bringing down the defensive barriers that went up when Matt died.

'Anyway, we are more or less finished. Here is your malva pudding, enjoy. I've got to get back to the office. I'll leave you love birds in peace.'

His big wrecked face is sweating slightly. He hoists his jacket on to his broad shoulders: there is some resistance. The old sportsman ambles off. He's a little crocked, but still he walks with a kind of exaggerated looseness as if he was warming up to go on to the field of play. He swings one arm around and does a little jig. He is ready for any sporting eventuality.

'Does he often come out here to see you?'

'Only when it's urgent. He's trying to freeze some of my husband's assets, and I had to sign the papers.'

The air is stifling.

'I just wondered.'

'Do you think he's after my body?' she says.

'He would be a fool if he wasn't.'

'You smooth-talking bastard,' she says. 'I'm glad you came.'

'I'm sorry about the payments.'

'Ag, shit happens.'

'Do you want to come round when you've finished?'

'I can't tonight. There's no one to look after Shawn. Also I feel a little bit down, I would be no fun, you know what I'm saying. It's not a great thought, that the father of your child has abandoned her. I mean what am I going to tell her? Listen, I've got to go back to the shop to cash up.'

'I'm going to walk around and then go down to the beach.'

'You like a little dip. In fact I think you may be obsessed.'

The skin of her face as she smiles is stretched tight. She has just reached the age when the inherited characteristics begin to be obvious. I, for instance, found some years ago that my nose, once straight and inoffensive, had begun to become quite assertive, broadening at the bridge like my father's. Perhaps Valerie is destined to have that pained-skull look that some older women acquire, as though, defying the familiar laws of biology, their skin seems to shrink. Still, I am glad to see a little of her jauntiness returning.

There are sweet crumbs of cake on my plate. The gables of the house are decorated with vine leaves. As I stand up sparrows and finches fall on the crumbs.

And it occurs to me that Matt would be seventeen now if he had lived. I am fated to remember the boy with milk teeth, with his soft, questing hand sliding into mine. I would have liked to have seen how he turned out. Even with my new buoyancy of spirit, I feel a certain drag. Yes, I want to get down to the beach. I find that I am looking forward not just to the waves, but the little faces which appear over the sand dunes.

Zwelakhe duly arrives with the other children, although the drugs – he has to take fifty pills a day – are causing him drowsiness and diarrhoea. He walks into the shallows with me and I hold his hand. I don't suppose he knows the truth.

The young doctor thinks that the protase inhibitors could prolong his life for many years. 'Maybe, but don't quote me, I'm only an intern, long enough for them to find a cure.'

He's a good lad, accepting the white man's burden with grace. He's built for it, with surplus sturdiness and carrying capacity, which are denied to the brown people around him.

22

It's my first night in the house. The floorboards are handsome and waxed. The walls are as white as those of a Greek monk's cell. Some lengths of Somali cloth are doing well as curtains. I have a paraffin lamp, because Roos's brother has cut the main supply while excavating for minerals. No one is answering the phone at the power company. My money has allowed the Roos family to hire a drilling machine which is pecking away at the field near the dam. Roos's brother's divining rod has suggested to him that it is the most likely spot to find valuable, but unspecified, minerals. Underneath the sand his sensitive sinews have detected something solid. So far no luck, but for a week they have been drilling away. The generator is noisy and smells of diesel.

The bed is from my mother's cottage. It is her deathbed. The candlewick bedspread, the lamplit simplicity, appeal to me. The new roof is on, and from my room I can look straight up at the underside of the thatch. The whole house once had moulded tin ceilings, but I am happy with this safari-lodge look. There is a smell of creosote from the new roof timbers.

I have bought an old typewriter down in the village, and I have used it to write up my baboon idea. It has taken a while to remember how to fit the ribbon and correcting tape but I like the end product: the pages are textured, almost Braille, and the ink and the ribbon produce low-technology smudges. The pages look as though they are despatches from the front, and in a sense they are.

Today the treatment has gone off to my former agent, to be lost in a pile of hopeful nonsense.

Apart from the nuisance value of Roos's deluded brother who has taken to sitting by the dam on a chair to watch the drill rig at work, the place is tranquil. Roos's brother's sole task is to make sure the expensive rig is giving full value: it is well known that without supervision nothing would be done. He sits with a fixed, but ultimately vacant look. I wander over to talk to him, to find out how much longer this drilling will go on. Pennington guesses that Roos's people will soon give up.

They are a small, wrinkled, wiry family. Theunis Roos looks as though the lines and upheavals on his face are a congenital feature; like the contours of a cauliflower or like the surface of the brain, there is no other imaginable arrangement. In its folds and valleys, dark specks are embedded, so that in a sense – and very appropriately for a diviner – his face looks like a well-used chart.

'How's it going?' I ask him.

'Ag, no, not so bad.'

'Have you found anything yet?'

'We must send the samples away for analysis.'

'What are you looking for?'

'There can be lots of things.'

He has an old Thermos flask and some sandwiches. He offers me a meat-paste sandwich, which I refuse.

'The thing is, we are trying to get more visitors to the new shop and tea room and obviously if they have to pass all this, it puts them off.'

'Ja, I can see that can be a problem, but Tienie wants to go on. Maybe you must speak with her.'

The drill rig is a crude thing, mounted on the back of a truck: a few piles of white muddy waste are being shovelled on to the back of a small pick-up to be taken away, and three barrels of diesel stand near the rig. Two sombre coloured men in blue overalls operate the machinery. The drill itself is guided into the hole each time it has disgorged some more mud, with an abrupt clanking of levers and a wild rattling of chains.

* * *

Zwelakhe has to spend the day at the hospital in Cape Town, having his blood plasma assessed by a specialist, to see if the dosage of the inhibiting drugs is correct. I drive him and Daisy along the highway past miles of shacks. The wind is propelling plastic bags from the region of the dunes towards the highway. Some soar like the spirits of the dead, others run and lurch along the ground before snagging in a fence. As a result the fence looks as though dying birds are impaled there. It looks like a notice board containing the names of the disappeared. It looks like an advertisement for despair.

Daisy sits in the back with Zwelakhe. When I look in the mirror I see that they are huddled together, two people in a lifeboat. From them comes a smoky, musky smell, which is a proper human odour. Hundreds of generations for thousands of years have smelled like this, but I feel a certain resentment, not because I mind driving them about or paying for treatment, but because I want to . . . What is it exactly? I don't want to place myself in their story. I don't want to exercise dominion in their lives or make any judgements. I don't want to assume that their lives are hopeless. Camus criticised Sartre, saying that it is a mistake to believe that because life is wretched, it is tragic. Nor do I want to gain any kind of moral or personal advantage from the wretchedness of others. Maybe that's it. I'm not sure. My own moral ambivalences disqualify me anyway.

The mountain which stood over my childhood slides closer, this extraordinary arbitrary mountain beached on the sand flats, its granite cliffs as blue and smoky as slow-burning coal.

I leave Daisy and Zwelakhe at the hospital – the usual confusions – and drive over the mountain pass above the town in search of a small beach where we used to picnic as children. The sea laps this side of the mountain directly. It contains underwater currents from the Antarctic and I remember that the water is numbingly cold, although from up here it looks tropically inviting, as unreal as a travel brochure. There are now villas where once there were nothing but a few wooden bungalows, but I find the start of the path to the beach. I place my bush hat on my head and walk down through giant boulders and a small forest of succulents and wind-weary bushes, hopping with small birds. Suddenly the tunnel opens. The beach is below. It is deserted, except for a film crew working at the far end. It is easy to see why they would choose this beach: the waves break close to the shore, the sea is cerulean and the sand is white. It looks from this distance as though they are making a commercial; a young man and a young woman walk hand-in-hand at the water's edge, before being recalled to have their hair ordered. After a few minutes they walk through the water again.

In the Turks and Caicos I had seen stout newlyweds on honeymoon packages walking hand-in-hand in water as if this was an obligatory part of the experience: the connubial wade in the sight of palm trees, clutching a rum punch, fully inclusive. The Paradise Club was proposing honeymoon suites, *ateliers* (there were no ordinary rooms, only ateliers). Complimentary sparkling wine was to be included in every atelier. Andrew, the actor, drank the prop wine, warm, in his room, just after the hurricane struck. He could see that we wouldn't be needing it when the show atelier was demolished by a flying palm tree.

I settle myself in the sand and shut my eyes.

Now the film crew are walking along the beach, everyone carrying something: metal boxes, reflectors, camera equipment, awkward tripods and bags of all sorts. As she passes between me and the handsome water, I see Ulla. Ulla is carrying a make-up bag. She is still clad in oddments.

'Ulla. Ulla!'

She is startled as I approach in my bush hat.

'Good God. What are you doing here?'

'I live here now. Out of town. And you?'

'I do make-up these days. My tits weren't bringing in the money.'

She laughs and kisses me.

'You look well,' she says, 'so thin.'

'Thank you, I've been running. And you look just the same.'

In some outward respect she has changed, but the essential person is still there, although faintly blurred.

'No need to lie, James, it's great to see you. Can we have dinner? We go back in a few days.'

'Not tonight. I have to get someone from the hospital. Tomorrow?'

'Okay. I must go. We're doing a sunset shot somewhere else. What do I know? I just put on the slap.'

'Ulla, I was thinking about those little golden hairs on your tummy only a few days ago.'

'Don't say that.'

'Why?'

'It's painful.'

'Ulla, do you remember your little flat behind Sainsbury's?'

'A dump.'

'To me it's been sanctified by memory.'

'You always said lovely odd things. What was the name of that film we worked on?'

'I can't say it out loud. That's too painful.'

'Suzi something.'

'Are you still married?'

'No. I've been unlucky in love. I should have accepted your offer.'

'Did I offer?'

'You did. I've got to go. They're halfway to the car park.'

'I'll come with you. Here, give me the bag. God it's heavy.'

We walk up through the tunnel of vegetation. She holds my arm. We are serenaded by small birds. She has a slightly stolid look now, and her eyes are wary. But it requires no effort of the imagination to see the blithe, beautiful girl.

I arrange to pick her up from her hotel tomorrow. She climbs into a minibus with the other film folk, and I wave her goodbye. As I walk to my mother's car, I think that she has forgotten that Matt died while I was in her bed. I understand that other people's tragedies soon fade from the memory. She has forgotten my lost son. I had forgotten Sephos, who drowned. And my mother has excised him from her photograph album: clearly memory contains an element of will. Ulla thinks she remembers my offering to marry her. As I drive beside the wild crashing sea, I see that memory is a reordering of the present: it can cast a shadow forwards.

Zwelakhe and Daisy are waiting for me. They sit without impatience, close together in a corridor. I watch them for a moment, as Daisy wipes the boy's face with her sleeve. She smiles shyly, and the marks on her cheeks close. I have been asked to pick up some papers at the reception before we leave. It takes some time to find these papers which I am to deliver to the rugby-playing doctor.

The traffic is heavy. Taxi vans and pick-ups and buses are all fighting crazily for the road, as the inhabitants of the sand flats make their way home. What's the rush? First I drop the papers at the local hospital and then I take Zwelakhe and Daisy to the car park. As they walk along the beach, they are quickly consumed by the deepening evening and the thick wind off the sea. I have one last glimpse of them, rising into the sand dunes, the small boy holding the woman's hand, clinging to what is left to him. I am, of course, disturbed by seeing Ulla and as I walk along the beach towards the lights, I can't stop (I don't try) the tears from rising. They swell and rest, teetering, their surface tension preventing them from overflowing.

Valerie's car is parked outside the house. She comes from the verandah to meet me.

'I hope you don't mind. I brought some crayfish and some wine for us.'

She has laid the table and now she lights a candle. She is freshly dressed. Two large crayfish lie on plates. They are like lobsters without the big front claws. It's a mystery how they compete for the territory, an imperative which my father claimed is everything to survival. Perhaps they employ psychological warfare.

In many societies it is considered poor manners to be too direct, but in ours people proclaim their directness: *I'm afraid I say what's on my mind. Really I'm too honest, I can't hide my feelings. I can't pretend. I just come right out with it.*

Valerie wants to discuss where I think this is going. She can't wait until the carapaces are cleared away; the plates look like a war zone. It means a lot to her, and she was touched that I had come to ask her out and sorry that she was so low. She says she is also sorry if she was rude. Her main concern is Shawn. It's just not fair that he has deserted his daughter. Why, why? We are smeared and perfumed with crayfish and mayonnaise now. I make a show of biting the legs and drawing out the white, sweet, seawatery flesh, so as not to have to answer. Valerie says that her husband, Grant, was weak. Fine until the first crisis, then he was always running away. I feel a tinge of sympathy for Grant: he liked good news; he liked praise. Unfortunately, he couldn't hold down a job. He blamed the new government, but it was him. It was always his fault. That's why she started working. And then he became resentful when she was promoted. So he was always looking out for women he could impress. He was quite a bullshitter. He could charm the birds from the trees. Is that the expression? Anyway he went off last year to PE to work with sharks. On a tourist boat. That lasted about five minutes, then he was in Durban helping set up a restaurant. At least he was when she last heard from him. Now he's off. He hasn't seen Shawn for three months. Is that too much to expect that he should keep in touch?

'So I'm not asking for any commitment, or anything, I just want to know how you feel about me? I'm only asking because

I feel that I'm getting in too deep. And I have to think about Shawn. She comes first.'

'Valerie, let me say this. Your story is commonplace, even banal. What happens between men and women, how they see each other and apportion blame, and how they believe that the other is diminishing them deliberately, and how they feel jealousy and hide behind big statements of principle, and how they make accommodations with life and with failure and with disillusionment, can be seen from a certain perspective as being preordained. Like ants, like bees, people have allotted roles. What you are saying about the conflicting pulls of maternity, the insecurity of being a single mother, the unreliability of men, the cruelty of human beings to each other, the innocence of children, none of this is news. In fact the reverse would be news: the constancy of men, the selflessness of human beings, the joy of marriage, et cetera, et cetera. What you are saying is more or less the mantra of women, matched only by the muttering of men. And the reason for this is that we have been taught to believe that life equals some form of self-fulfilment; there is no such thing, only moments of happiness.'

I don't say any of this. Instead I say, 'Where is Shawn tonight?'

'She is staying with her grandmother by Wit Els.'

'Do you want to stay here?'

We sit for a moment in the crayfish-strewn half light, caught up in our lives.

'Yes,' she says.

Later in the night I tell her that I'm proposing to have Zwelakhe and his aunt and the baby and the little girl come and live out here.

'What a circus,' she says.

But sleep already has her captive. I am left to guess what she means.

I slip out (why should I be furtive in my own house?) to see Piet. He is in his new house, but when I call he comes out and climbs calmly down to see me. I stretch my hand through the mesh and scratch the hollow behind his ears. He presses his head against the wire. He grunts and smacks his lips. It's a rubbery, domestic noise.

'Once I believed in art, Piet. The redemptive power of art.'

Piet smacks his lips again. I now realise it is the sound of plimsolls on a cement floor.

23

Although it is too soon to remove honey, I dress in the bee clothes, including the veiled hat and gauntlets, and I light the pellet in the bee smoker. I puff the smoke – it smells like incense – into the hive. The bees soon become confused. Many of the long-range foragers have become pedestrians, wandering in and out of the hive, drugged. The bee music subsides. And now I feel confident of opening the hive without provoking a bee-riot. A few bees land on my clothes, looking for a way in. The bare frames that we placed there a few weeks ago are now encrusted with honeycomb and filling up with honey. The worker bees are fanning the honey to keep it cool, although some are simply standing stunned by the smoke. Despite the incense, the perfume of honey is strong and I imagine I can detect the scent of the wild flowers around the farm. *Et in Arcadia ego.*

Zwelakhe watches me from a distance. In the few days since the family moved in he has taken to following me or Witbooi around. Daisy helps the two girls, Bessie and Lena. She works willingly and sometimes I hear the three of them gossiping. A small room behind the sheds has been cleared of junk for Daisy and her family, and we have found two beds and a cot for the baby. I wonder if Zwelakhe and Daisy and Thandi think this place is beautiful, with its old oak trees, fields and stream. Here the wind passes us by and the turtle doves never tire.

Zwelakhe loves to look at Piet. Whenever he sees Piet he laughs. Something about Piet – perhaps his earnest near human-ness – sets him off. It's good to hear a little boy laugh, but his laughter is also unsettling. I have had to restrain him from throwing stones at Piet with his thin, ravaged arm. After I have removed the bee-garb, he tugs at my hand, leading me to Piet's cage. Piet won't come down to face Zwelakhe's hoots of derision. He hunches and turns away.

The Roos team is packing up. For the first time in more than a week the smell of diesel fumes is absent. The drill is being folded and lowered on to the back of a truck. Theunis Roos has taken his patio chair and his green Thermos flask. The waste has more or less been removed. The ducks are swimming around on the dam again. Ducks have more options than chickens, and a palpable sense of freedom when they paddle out on to the water. The dam, my dam, is fringed with bulrushes on one side and in the deep valley beneath it arum and canna lilies flower. Over at the small white houses the children play.

Witbooi tells me that one of the women who lives there has a sister working at the hospital who says that the Xhosa children are sick. They have told their children to stay away. I explain to Witbooi that Zwelakhe has a virus, but that you can't catch it. Will you tell them? He agrees, but his agreement is purely diplomatic.

Ulla and I dined overlooking a bay. She chose the restaurant. It was where film people went. During the European winter many commercials were filmed on the beaches and in the vineyards and upcountry on the savannahs, she said. She had been four or five times. It's a wonder to me that trivial people are transported all over the world in luxury, while serious people have to stay at home.

'Do you remember when I saw you in Julie's?'

'Oh, yes.'

'You were pregnant.'

'Yes.' She seems to have a moment's difficulty remembering. 'I lost it.'

'I'm sorry.'

'It was a blessing. Billy couldn't have handled domestic life.'

'What happened to him?'

'He was working in Yugoslavia on a film and he found himself a Serbian starlet.'

'Oh Jesus, I'm sorry.'

'Water under the bridge. How about you?'

I told her a version of my life. I explained that my father left me some money, and that I had bought a tumbledown farm. As I told her what had befallen me since we met in the brown candlelit wine-stained gloom, I recognised an inherited tendency to practise excision. For instance I didn't tell her about Valerie, nor Zwelakhe, nor Piet.

'Why did you run out so fast that day?' she asked.

'I thought I loved you. I couldn't bear to believe that you had shacked up with Billy.'

'You didn't love me. I know that. We were just caught up in something.'

I asked her to come and spend a few days somewhere along the coast when she was finished and she agreed. We walked on the beach below the restaurant after dinner, arm in arm, ourselves prone, it seemed, to believe in the romance of sand and sea. She felt more solid than the girl I had known, as though within her the matter had changed from something delicate to something durable. I allowed myself to think how it might be to sleep for years next to this more substantial person. We stopped at the gates of her hotel.

'Do you want to come in for a drink?'

'No thanks, I just want to get home.'

'Okay,' she said cheerfully, 'see you on Saturday.'

And it was true. I had a powerful urge to get home to my mother's bed in my own house. As I drove over the mountain and across the sand flats past the humped dark shacks, and then turned up towards the mountains, I believed that I would never leave Nooitgedacht again for any length of time. Who would have expected it? I laughed at my own joke; I was ecstatic. I lay down on the bed and looked up by the light of the lamp at the thick thatch. There was a muted scuttling up there, and outside the long open window the crickets and the bullfrogs were at it. They were pleased to see me safely home. As I turned to blow out the lantern, I caught a glimpse of my face in the mirror which, for the moment, stands against the wall next to the bed. I looked strangely at peace, I thought, although I acknowledged that the soft light of the hurricane lamp gave a phoney spiritual quality to everything it touched. As I fell asleep, I promised to speak honestly to Valerie, and I had a final thought about my baboon story, a brilliant idea, which I'd forgotten by morning.

It is morning. Almost morning. The sky is lurid, a trailer for the main event, the rising of the sun. I fetch Piet and we set off for the beach. The sea is the colour of pewter and the waves are small. Piet bounds along next to me; his style of running is not suited to the long haul and I have to stop frequently to allow him to root around in the mussel shells and kelp. I fasten his chain to a broken jetty and run into the water. The sun has just risen above the mountains to the east of the bay, and the water is changing texture fast, acquiring translucence as the sun hits it directly. I can see Piet pacing anxiously as I come out of the surf. He watches as I towel myself and dress. I hop up and down to get the water from my ears.

'Come, Piet.'

We jog and canter, each in his own way, back along the beach. On the way home I stop at a bakery and café, not far from Valerie's apartment block; they bake white buns there, which now lie on the counter exhaling yeast. In the car, Piet and I each have a bun for breakfast and he also has some peach roll. Just as I start the ignition, I see Pennington's car heading towards town from the direction of Valerie's apartment. I wave, but he doesn't see me. His large body appears to embrace the steering wheel. It seems likely that he has come from Valerie's flat although it is not yet seven o'clock in the morning.

I am in a generous mood. I have no claim on Valerie; in fact, I'm planning to renounce any she might imagine. Still I hope that she hasn't been carrying on with Pennington. I like him, but I have no wish to enter this kind of fleshly communion with him: only forty-eight hours ago she spent the night with me, although, on the scales of human deceit, this sort of thing wouldn't weigh very heavily. Yet I am disturbed: it's not prudishness, so much as snobbery. Surely she can't value this large, decrepit provincial sportsman as highly as me?

Piet and I drive home and by the time we swing through our gates – the pillars have been whitewashed and the word Nooitgedacht on each one has been neatly picked out in black paint by Witbooi – I am sure that there must be some other reason for Pennington's dawn excursion.

Down in the retirement village I am picking up some things from my mother's cottage. It is to be sold. As I stagger to the car with boxes of books, an old lady, so faded that she appears over-exposed by an unskilled photographer, speaks to me. Her voice is thin, but she has an unmistakable intensity. One arm is crippled.

'I just wanted to introduce myself. I am Nan O'Reardon and I often used to have tea with your mother.'

'Oh yes.'

'I am so sorry she has gone. We're all popping off here, of course.'

I look at her closely now, as if by concentrating I can drag her back from a limbo into this world. I have to make an effort to believe that she has children and grandchildren and a history of her own because there is something wraithlike about her.

'Your mother often spoke about you. She told me about your films.' (She pronounces the word 'fillims' in the Irish way.) 'I was a member of the Claremont Fillim Society for thirty years, and

I remember your fillim about the hospital and all that. It was a highly amusing and saucy fillim. Oh yes, your mother was very proud of you. She talked about you. She said you were a wonderful, affectionate child, always happy. Well, goodbye. Nice talking to you. I have to return this library book before twelve.'

She sets off on one of those pressing self-imposed tasks of old age, having delivered her speech. I can't remember who said that happiness is attributed by adults to children, and by children to adults, but I believe I was a happy child. And I am happy again.

With piles of books on the floor and the house still cool after the bull-frogged, cricket-shredded night, I sit down in the front room with the old typewriter.

Dear Norm,

I know I haven't exactly been a productive client for you over the years, but I also know that you will be taking my baboon treatment which I sent you a week ago seriously. Last night I went to bed and a brilliant idea struck me just as my eyes closed finally. When I woke up this morning, it had gone.

So could you hold on to the treatment for the moment? I will send it to you, revised, soon. Luckily I am happily busy with the little farm I have bought. (I mentioned this in my accompanying letter.)

It's a lovely place and I look forward to welcoming the frenzied, but orderly, posses of producers and investors you will be sending my way. I have a strange feeling about living here, however, that two countries are somehow occupying the same geographical space.

Best regards,

James,

PS This is sent by fax, so that it will overtake the treatment.

PPS For baboon, read ape/primate; we don't want to limit ourselves to the supply of trained baboons.

While I am sitting here in the *voorkamer*, once the tea room,

I write another letter, hammering away at the paper.

Dearest Valerie,

You asked me the other night where I thought this was going. It seems only fair to you to give you an honest answer, if indeed yours was an honest question, which I believe it was.

If you meant, do I see a long-term future for us together, I have to say, acknowledging my own precarious state of mind, that I can't imagine our future together.

Please understand that I am in a period of transition. I don't know what the outcome will be. For these incoherent reasons, I have written this bumbling letter.

Yours,

J

What I can't tell her is that I don't believe hers was an honest question. And I can't tell her that I've seen Pennington's car leaving her house at dawn. And that I am planning a trip with Ulla. Nor can I explain to her what I mean by a period of transition, because the more closely I examine my former life, the more unreal it appears. It's an unsettling realisation that your life has become a series of random events that have somehow lost their proper order and significance.

I see Andrew the actor with pond weed on his head; I see the alligator soup of the Paradise Club; I see Simon Chiswick declaiming *Henry V* on Rydal Fell, I see Matt's drained face at nursery school, I see the smug front doors of Chelsea, the cold indifferent river, the fat unruly schoolchildren, the rushing surface of the roads, the gobbets of semen between Ulla's breasts, the clatter of horses' hooves, the hieroglyphics of the criminally insane, the lost hedgerows of Kenwood, the thick historical layers of paint on window ledges, drunk girls in Soho, the clattering of celluloid in a camera; the bacon fug, stained hall carpets, damp unopened demands for money.

And so on; stretching back appearing to require some

understanding, but as susceptible to understanding as death. In this way life and death are the same. Neither has the faintest delineation of meaning.

Up in the mountain my mother's ashes have been scattered by a baboon, for instance.

24

The west coast was beaten by the wind. It had a crouched and wary look, empty, but inspiriting: stunned towns, ugly fishing ports and cheap holiday houses belonging to farmers, were all strung loosely along the non-stop beaches, which were taking a terrific pounding.

Ulla was a welcome emissary from a lost world. She had no idea where we were going, and little interest. I had a guidebook which spoke of whaling stations and carpets of spring flowers and Moravian missions. We missed them all, but rolled along happily in an immense landscape on whose bottom margin the seashore and the low olive hills had barely been scratched. Ulla had my mother's antique radio on, which played Afrikaans country music. She found it chic. She told me about her life: on one reading it could be seen as a string of disasters, but on another – hers – it was a very human life, lived as she put it, for the sake of it. What else can you do, really?

'That is your problem in a way,' she said, 'that you never quite lived in the moment. You wanted to have fun, but also you wondered if I made you look frivolous. You made that crap film, but all along you imagined that you were doing something artistic. That's why the film was such a disaster. It was just soft porn for morons. You couldn't turn it into Jean Paul Godard.'

'Jean Luc.'

'And you were pedantic. You were always wondering why I was wearing whatever it was I was wearing on that day. I tried to explain to you that I just grabbed anything that took my fancy, there was no plan. You also wondered why I didn't care who saw my knockers. I just didn't care, *e basta*. And I don't care now that I am a sort of ageing hippy on these film shoots, I get well paid, I travel all over the world, I stay in nice hotels and . . . the rest.'

She was about to tell me that she had plenty of sex, but decided to spare me.

She sat with her feet on the dashboard, as the bleached landscape came steadily towards us and then fled behind the car. We saw ostriches in fields and glimpses of distant furtive farms, with wind pumps and white houses. There were knots of brown people, on apparently hopeless journeys with donkeys. Every so often the road approached the coast and at one small town we turned off for lunch at a place recommended in the guidebook. On the sand dunes above the beach was an open-air restaurant, serving lobsters and mussels and huge fish. Ulla was enchanted. In her long skirt of light, North African material, and her loose Romany top and straw hat, she was an exotic amongst the diners in moustaches, Bri-Nylon shorts and trainers. But she was a benign and exotic presence attracting warmth and curiosity. I was of more native appearance in my bush hat and shirt with its many, useful pockets. Lunch lasted for three hours, broken by walks on the tumultuous beach while more sea creatures were cooked in cauldrons or grilled on spits.

As we drove away in my mother's stuttering car towards some purple-smudged mountains, Ulla leant over and breathed a warm, marine affection on me.

'That was perfect. Where is the magical mystery tour going now?'

'We're going to stay in those mountains. Do you see them?'

'I love them. Already.'

'You are a joy to travel with.'

'I'm eager to please.'

'Yes.'

There was a hint of lewdness. She hadn't lost the touching

habit which I now remembered vividly of suddenly blinking, as if startled. As idiosyncrasies go, it was a small thing but dear to me.

We were crossing a plain now; some crop had recently been taken from the empty prairies leaving only the whitening stubble. Everything here was bleached, except for the distant mountains which were bruise-coloured. Ulla turned the radio up and I tried to translate the words for her. The singer's name was Koos Kombuis, itself ironic. These Afrikaans country and rock songs were a deep well of significance. I was Jean François Chapillion uncovering the meaning of this musical Rosetta Stone. The songs drew up from the accumulation of nostalgia, regret and cynicism. From being the lords of creation, I explained to Ulla, the Afrikaners had become a minority, a band of gypsies with no title. Their history, which had been portrayed as heroic, now looked more like a history of atrocity. They had begun to see it themselves and their morale was poor.

'Low self-esteem,' said Ulla.

'You could put it like that.'

'Don't be irritated.'

'I'm not.'

'There was just a hint there.'

'Ulla, I've lost any sense I might have had of being superior to anybody. Here, somehow, I find my own vanities seem to be of a pygmy variety, dwarfed by the mineral and physical facts. Do you know what I'm saying?'

'Sort of.'

'I hardly know myself, but I feel since my mother died I am being merged with something fundamental. I swim, I walk, I'm rebuilding the house, I play golf with my lawyer. And I appear to be acquiring dependants. One of them is a baboon.'

She didn't seem surprised.

'How wonderful. A baboon.'

Just below the mountains was a small town on a river. We drove straight through, beneath towering Dutch Reformed steeples and broad streets where water was led in furrows to the gardens of the low houses. Already there were Cheddar-coloured lights shining in windows as we headed across a bridge and out of the town to a pass which ran boldly up the mountains. These mountains had suffered extreme forms of torture somewhere back in geological time. Huge boulders lay scattered around and the vegetation was appropriately disordered. The few tattered and beaten trees looked as though they had survived a pre-history shelling.

I said to Ulla that I thought I was achieving a communion with the landscape, but I didn't really know what that could mean. My mother has perhaps achieved this communion fully, with the intervention of Piet.

We found the turn-off to the lodge where we passed through gates and a wire-mesh fence, and then along a track for a few miles. A dam lay below; it was the colour of a blood orange in the dying light, and beside the dam was a collection of thatched cottages. In our cottage in front of the log fire – it was cool up here – Ulla told me more about her life. Her story was accompanied by the howl of jackals outside. She was the sort of woman who expected very little of men, so she was seldom disappointed. After Billy, she had lived for a few years with a man who sold vintage cars. And then she had moved herself to Los Angeles with an actor, who took a job in a soap; but it didn't work out because he was at the studio every day from five in the morning.

'Maybe it's me. I just seem to be missing some domestic gene. I get bored. I'm not looking for excitement particularly, it's just that I love the transience and the unexpected. I'm probably crackers.'

And the uncharitable might have thought that she was a little mad, as she lay in front of the fire, her beautiful goofy naive face smiling up at me, her hair a thicket of optimism.

'Let's do it now,' she said, 'it's hanging over us.'

Outside the jackals' howling became more insistent as if they had been sitting patiently through the supporting programme, and were ready for the feature film. I was thinking that in my childhood we went to see cartoons on Saturday mornings, followed by a cowboy film.

Ulla has gone back to her powdery, smudgy world. I miss her. At the airport she cried, but these were ambivalent tears, tears which indicated no particular emotion, but signalled a general and pleasurable turbulence. As I drove home past the endless shacks I envied her still undimmed blitheness. I told her that I had no plans to go back.

'Pity,' she said.

The tea room in the old dairy is doing steady business. Yesterday we had a busload of oldies coming up from the retirement village to buy jam and boast quietly about their past lives. Two men wandered amongst them, survivors, hopelessly outnumbered and curiously passive. The whole party sat down to tea and cakes, and Bessie and Lena were exhilarated and happy to collect the tips which clattered on to a saucer. There were plans to make this a regular outing.

I no longer allow anyone to go and look at Piet. I can't see him as an exhibit. A few baboons have twice come down from the high mountains, barking as we approach, but Piet shows no interest in their threats and alarm calls. I believe that my father was right when he said that baboons and humans could form friendships. I think that Piet sees himself as a friend, and regards the wild baboons as alien.

I am sitting at the loud typewriter, working on the baboon script, when Valerie arrives. She comes straight to the point: 'How's your precarious state of mind?' she asks. Her face is set for trouble.

'Hello. I'm fine.'

'And how was your trip? Nice trip?'

'Yes, thanks.'

'Was she impressed by our lovely country?'

'Who are you talking about?'

'Is her name Ulla?'

'Oh, Ulla. She's a very old friend.'

'Oh, Ulla. Who conveniently appeared one day, and then you wrote me that pompous letter.'

'I met her in Cape Town. It was pure chance.'

'A likely story. And all the time you were keeping me dangling on a string.'

'I wasn't keeping you dangling on a string. You came to ask me specifically where our relationship was going and I tried to explain honestly my position.'

'Nothing to do with the Norwegian nympho, I suppose.'

'How do you know about Ulla anyway?'

'Anton told me.'

'I told Anton where I was going and with whom, an old friend, so that he could call me in an emergency, and I suppose he told you for a laugh.'

'I notice you didn't tell me where you were going. Anton told me because he's concerned about me and doesn't want to see me get hurt.'

'I'm not sure why he would have told you at all, but he shouldn't have. In my experience the reasons people give are not always their real ones.'

'Now, as well as being a famous stud, you're a psychiatrist too. Listen, you may have forgotten, but here out in the sticks, we say what we think. And I think you are a prick. Goodbye. I won't be sourcing jam and honey by the way. Soutpiel.'

These kinds of conversation have a way of becoming basic very quickly, as though the emotions involved turn rancid at the first suspicion of betrayal. Vile words are spoken in haste. She rushes to her Mazda and drives away.

To calm myself, I walk down to the beehives. Little Zwelakhe appears, and I hold his hand. The bees are busy, as always, and the music from deep in the hive is resonant, as if it is coming from a well. Zwelakhe wants me to take him to see Piet but

I shake my head firmly.

'No. Aai.'

I take him instead to the tea room where Daisy and Bessie and Lena are clearing up and restocking the shelves after a rush of oldies. I wonder if they have heard Valerie shouting at me.

Just as I am starting to type in the cool interior, Pennington arrives.

'Look, I'm sorry to disturb you. Your phone is still off. I've got some bad news. I'm one hundred and ten per cent sure we can get round the problem, but it may cost us.'

'By us, you mean me?'

'Ja. I'm afraid I do.'

Roos and his brother, in their search for diamonds or oil, have discovered kaolinite which produces kaolin used in diarrhoea medicine and in the making of fine china. Kaolinite is messy stuff. Roos is actively trying to sell the rights to a big company. Of course there are environmental laws and Pennington believes he could block exploitation for years. So Roos would probably sell the rights to us, particularly if Pennington blinds him with legal words.

'You told me they wouldn't find anything,' I say.

'How was I supposed to know that they would find a treatment for the runs, right here, where your Muscovy ducks are dib-dabbing about? Anyway, they're disappointed. They were hoping for King Solomon's Mines.'

Luckily it isn't a huge deposit, as far as he can tell. He's already got to someone at the Assay Office and he knows Roos will sell out. I remind him that some of the money from the sale of my mother's cottage is already owed to Valerie's bank. We agree on an amount to offer for the rights. I sign some papers requesting an injunction. An injunction will frighten the Roos family, who despite the good wishes they directed to me for a happy life at Nooitgedacht now want to bury the place in a fine, white powder.

* * *

When he's gone I try to finish writing the treatment. It's clear I'm going to need money. In the morning I'll take the treatment down to the print shop, which lies between Morkel's Garage and Pickin' a Chickin.

I write: 'The baboon (or other ape/primate) sees that it can escape. It hesitates. It sees that its buddy, the agent, is wounded. It sees that Asberger is coming to finish him off. The audience waits agonised. The baboon (or other primate) must act now. In these moments we wonder which choice the baboon will make. Will it attack Asberger, setting off the bomb attached to its back, or will it run? Just as the suspense becomes unbearable, a shot rings out. Asberger falls dead, killed by his colleague who has discovered the truth at last, that Asberger is the traitor to the agency and a murderer into the bargain.'

As Andrew the actor once said about Suzi Crispin, 'It's not Shakespeare.' Although Shakespeare often piled up the corpses in the denouement; in *Macbeth* the stage is littered with them. It's easy to write about corpses, but for me the sight of the three corpses I have seen, of Sephos, of my son and of my mother, has eaten my soul away. I have nothing to spare for Valerie, pathetic as it was to see her retreating to her tomato-soup car, her back contorted, trotting with every other step.

I read through my treatment again. No, no, this is rubbish. Absolute crap. I am plagued by the forgotten idea. I tear it up.

Piet greets me with coquettish eyes. His delicate black hand with the very distinct, short fingers comes through the mesh and I place a pecan in it. He eats the nut deliberately, suggesting he can take it or leave it. Luigi of *Luigi's Bees* arrives to help with the honey extraction. I have all my kit laid out, eager to take part. Although Valerie has jumped ship, I have the bottles and labels ready. *Nooitgedacht Wild Flower Honey* will be just that. We don our uniforms. Luigi wears less protection;

as he says, he has built up an immunity. He explains to me
how we will do it: we stun the bees with bee smoke, lift out the
frames, place the frames and cones in the plastic buckets we
are carrying, and return to the kitchen where we will extract
the honey. The honey can then be heated, which he favours,
or left natural. It can be bottled with a little honeycomb in
it or without. He will help me get started. It's all part of
the personal service of *Luigi's Bees*, established 1969. This
bee talk is soothing. The prospect of honey, genuinely home
produced, is entrancing: 'How blessed are they who receive
from bounteous earth a simple life.'

We walk down to the orchard together. I am so encum-
bered I move as stiffly as an astronaut. But when we get
to the beehives we find that they have been pushed over
in the night: their neat, clapboard layers are scattered, and
the honeycombs have been broken. Confused bees are crawl-
ing over the honey as if in search of clues. Unknown creatures have broken the combs and dragged them away. Luigi
is angry.

'Who did this? Who could do this? No, man, no, this is kak.
This is shit.'

He inspects the lowest reaches of the hives, where the
queens live.

'Your queens have gone. They've swarmed.'

The confused bees are the drones, unable to fly. In our
bee outfits we stagger foolishly back to the house. Lena and
Bessie and Daisy, who are standing by to help with the honey
bottling, are mute and frightened. Perhaps they already knew
of the attack. Luigi promises to bring me a new starter pack
of bees, although it's late in the season. I say I'll think about
it. I walk with him to his van.

'I'm sorry, man. These people, Jesus, these people. For five
thousand years we've been keeping bees. I don't know. What
do they want?'

I can think of many answers to his question, but he doesn't

require answers. He sees only barbarians at the gate threat-ening his little stripy-dago-bees, who encompass the best of the classical age, right up to the Renaissance and everything, except possibly Mussolini, since.

Witbooi comes to see me. He is holding his hat in his hands.

'Who did this, Witbooi?'

He tells me it was probably a ratel, a kind of badger. Or baboon bandits. He says *bobbejaan bandiete*. It is a strange phrase.

'They likes the honey,' he says in English. 'Sir, the people ask me to tell you they doesn't want the Xhosa children here. They must go away. They doesn't want to get sick also.'

I wonder if he is inviting me to make a connection between the bee vandalism and this pronouncement.

'Witbooi, the child may be sick, but you can't catch this sickness. So tell your people that they must understand this. The Xhosa children won't be going, you understand?'

I find myself speaking with a certain harshness in my voice, a peremptoriness, as if I am responding to a call of the blood. Witbooi shakes his head sadly but obdurately. I have a sickening urge to hit him.

'I don't want to hear any more of this, you understand?'

'I unnerstan sir.'

He places his hat on his head and walks away. His head is bent low. He is weighed down. I believe I know exactly what he is thinking: that with my futile gestures I am insulting him and his people who have lived here since before time. I decide that I must make some restitution to the farm people. I will electrify and improve their cottages without waiting for the grants which Pennington says are available.

Daisy and her family are going on a visit to the squatter camp. First we drop Zwelakhe at the hospital; the fat sister takes him to her bosom where he reposes content for a moment. Then we drive out to the sand dunes.

'Happy, Daisy?'

'Happy, seh.'

I watch the little party set off. Daisy is wearing new shoes which sink into the sand as she carries the baby.

'Goodbye,' says Thandi.

Her corn rows have been freshly arranged. Perhaps I have cut Daisy and the children off from their own lives. I have understood for some time that how we see landscapes is the product of conditioning. These windswept sand dunes and the flimsy shacks built of industrial and agricultural leftovers may be as attractive to them as the soft Cotswold hills and their luminous stone are to the Filkin-Halberts. But the child is ill and needs his medicines and regular food and a bed to sleep in. Nor has Daisy complained.

As I run on the beach to clear my mind of these uninvited worries, the classical bees, Witbooi's deep grievance, the question of Zwelakhe's future, I feel that the wind is cooler than it has been. It stands to reason: the honey season is coming to an end, the clouds are more dense, the wind is turning to the north. But also I see that you are never going to be free of the world, not before death. My mother in her last weeks was not peaceful or resigned. She was planning a drinks party, she wanted to renew her lapsed membership at the club. She was snipping up her pictures. She was concealing my legacy from me.

Although the air is cooler, the water appears to be warmer. Perhaps since the wind veered from the south, the deep Antarctic currents have slowed, or perhaps it's just the diminished contrast. The waves are violent: they start with promise but they fall suddenly from a height. I don't care. I spend an hour or more being battered and scarred. As a wave collapses I roll into a ball. Once my head hits the shingle produced by these disturbed waves, and my forehead is grazed. But there is a joy in that instant when the wave is about to fold in a crashing torrent, and, with the aid of my little hand flippers, I am poised, my head poking optimistically out of the top of the wave, ready for Armageddon. Each time I survive, sometimes after being submerged for thirty or forty seconds, and rise up to the foaming surface and strike out again. I can't quite eliminate troubling thoughts, but still I emerge from the water treatment calm and fatalistic. What I said to Ulla, whose worn tenderness has lingered since she left, about aligning myself with the mineral and geological facts, seems truthful although I know it is irrational.

My fourth game of golf, and I am getting worse. The early insouciance has gone. Now I am hampered by knowledge. I fiddle with the grip and I adjust my feet.

After the first, disastrous hole, Pennington, less genial today, his mind burdened, says, 'Listen, I want to talk to you. The bank has been making enquiries. Apparently they have received some information about you.'

'What information?'

'It's about the money you borrowed from them.'

'That was against the sale of the cottage.'

'Yes, and Valerie's guarantee.'

'Valerie never guaranteed anything. She just offered to introduce me to her bank.'

'She vouched for you. She said she'd known you for some time. Now she's told them that you twisted her arm and that she hardly knows you. It's been on her conscience.'

'Oh Jesus.'

'It's not for me to say, but I don't think you have been totally on the level with her.'

'You're right. It's not for you to say, and while we're at it perhaps you could tell me why your car was leaving her flat at six-thirty in the morning when your receptionist told me you were on business in Port Elizabeth. Maybe you should go and explain that to the bank. And by the way, thanks for the clubs and the free golf lessons, but I've decided to give up golf. And as for the mineral rights, tell Roos I never want to see him or his brother on my property again.'

'Hold on. Hold on a moment. It's not that simple.'

It's a short walk back to the clubhouse. We're only on the second hole, which Pennington has told me is called Delville Wood, commemorating a First World War battle. And indeed there are some trees on one side of the fairway, gum trees, which are shedding their bark in reams of parchment. I have tried to overcome the prejudice induced by my mother against these trees, but it hasn't entirely gone. They're useless trees, unfit even for compost, unfit for civilised life. In the locker room as I remove the hired shoes with their silly spikes, and as I change my guinea-fowl crested shirt for my khakis, I feel a certain sympathy for Pennington.

'Hold on. Hold on a moment,' he said, just before I walked away leaving him with two bags of clubs. His big, sporting face was in motion, but the words that his face was seeking to form didn't emerge. He was standing there, an iron club in his hands, in his fine golf raiment, stranded like one of the whales down on the beach. Anyway, I don't really care that he has been carrying on with Valerie. I only spoke to his secretary out of curiosity, as part of my undeclared task of understanding the human project. Also I am aware – I have been for some time – that in this important field of human endeavour, the sexual, there is no end to the ingenuity and duplicity of those caught up in its excitements and torments. Nor are their private mental states susceptible to understanding. I can only hope that my outburst will persuade Valerie to stop making mischief with the bank. I've already committed most of the loan to the improvements, and no doubt the Roos family and the diarrhoea medicine are not going to go away. But still, as I drive in fits and starts through the club's gates for the last time, I take comfort from the knowledge that I have not taken refuge from the facts. I see that I no longer have the exemption from the facts of life that I used to imagine had been granted to me.

Zwelakhe has had some unpleasant tests and painful injections. So we stop off at the bakery on our way home and I buy a bag of doughnuts for the children. The sight of the little boy happily covering his tortured face with particles of sugar and blobs of unnaturally coloured strawberry jam causes me deep feelings of a mixed kind. Naturally, I think of my lost Matt and I remember the custard doughnuts from Patisserie Valerie which were his favourite, but also I think, like the other Valerie, that I'm getting in too deep. It's clear that there is no easy end to this. As Pennington, the sexual voyager, had warned me.

Daisy is smiling now, as she tries to wipe Zwelakhe's face, and Thandi is hiding her mouth and giggling.

'Don't worry,' I say, 'don't worry, it's fine.'

I grab a doughnut and stuff it in my mouth and show solidarity. Look, sugar and jam are no respecters of rank. I have a curious thought: what if, smeared and sprinkled, we were turning into the gates of The Old Rectory, Middle Turkdean, instead of the gates of Nooitgedacht? And what if Piet was sitting next to me? That would scare the amiable Labrador shitless. *We were just passing and we popped in to get the name of your lovely children's clothes supplier. Our children need some new togs. Is it Tom and Dilly? Daisy & Tom. What a coincidence. This is Daisy and these are our children Zwelakhe and Thandi. I'm afraid I don't allow them to watch television, it's such rubbish these days. Perhaps they would all like to take the baboon for a walk. He's been cooped up in the car for hours. No, we don't need the loo, we'll just piss in the garden, like ninety per cent of the world's population.*

Daisy and the children don't know if I'm laughing or crying

as I stop the car in the deep evening shadows of the oak trees, but then neither do I.

Piet and I walk down to the stream. He is always anxious – the hesperidean gloom – as night closes. I stroke the side of his neck to reassure him. In a pool under the bank, small fish are rising as hatching insects fall on to the ginger-ale surface of the water. The turtle doves are still; but now I can hear an owl and the frogs are competing loudly. Piet may feel gloom, but I feel a sort of ecstasy as the last light of the day rests on the top of the mountains above us, so that way up there it will be full daylight for a few more minutes, while down here we are in mounting darkness.

Although it is not cold, I light a fire in the open Dutch fireplace which we have exposed in the voorkamer, and I marvel at the neat pile of logs that Witbooi has placed on the hearth, and I rejoice in the way the fire trembles and feints on the rough white walls, which are still bare. The electricity has not yet been reconnected.

I have a post box in the town, set into a wall of pale bricks in a blank room next to the post office. It is a wonder to me that post is delivered at all. Ulla has written: her handwriting is familiar, curlicued, heavily stressed at important points, and sprayed with exclamation marks. She is looking forward to coming to stay, as we agreed, at Easter, but she would understand if I had changed my mind. She gives me a charmingly disordered account of the jobs she has done and places she has been since she saw me. She adds, as if in an afterthought, 'I think I could love you, again.' It is difficult to know how seriously she means this; it could just be a strong form of endearment.

There is also a letter from Pennington, resigning as my attorney, and detailing the state of our affairs. There are some enquiries about my resident status, which he is forwarding. He details also the money he is holding and the money I owe. He concludes by saying, 'I await your instructions for the satisfactory and prompt settling of these accounts.' The legal shutters are down. There is no mention of the human heart, whose accounts, of course, can never be settled. Also, he has withdrawn his sponsorship of my membership for the golf club as he believes I would understand that it is not appropriate at this time to forward my name to the committee.

Does he want me to give up wearing the noble guinea fowl on my breast? I'll do it gladly.

I go to see Roos at his butcher's shop. He receives me in the back office, after wiping his hands on his apron. I explain to him that Pennington is not acting for me any longer. I'm arranging to hire – I say – an international commercial lawyer. I understand that there are environmental and other laws which could delay any agreement for years. We should work together. These big companies are very devious. They will cheat us. We will end up with nothing.

'They are controlled by Jews,' he says.

It's well known around here that Jews are much more adept at commerce. They'll make monkeys of our attorneys. When you're dealing with the big boys, you have to fight fire with fire. We don't want to look as though we were hatched out from under a turkey, I add, remembering an old Boer saying.

25

Two days later I received a letter from Consolidated Mining. It turns out that I was the only one who was hatched out from under a turkey. Roos had sold the rights weeks before to a consortium, which included the hayseed attorneys employed by him and some local businessmen – golfers and expert alfresco grillers of Roos's famous sausages. They, in turn, had sold an option to a mining company, which had solid connections with the provincial government, who were understandably keen to create local employment, not least to provide a decent future for the migrants who lived in the sand dunes.

All I had to do was to allow access. It could be enforced without my consent. I guessed that they were bluffing.

My father once worked for this newspaper, although the offices have expanded into the next building as well. The library is in the older part. The more recent cuttings have been recorded on microfiche. Earlier cuttings are pasted on to card and filed in the mahogany sliding drawers. I look through them briefly: all the follies and madness and lies of the last one hundred and twenty years are preserved here. I wish I had more time. But I must find out about the mining company and turn to the microfiche. An elderly man wearing a white Muslim skullcap on his fine grey hair helps me with the machine.

'Begyours, sir,' he says as I have the first cutting in focus, 'I saw your name in the book. Are you any relation of AC?'

'Yes,' I say, 'he was my father.'

'He was a fine gentleman, sir. It's a pleasure to meet his son. I was a junior messenger when he was a junior reporter. He became very, very famous. He wrote King's English. It's not the same no more. I am retired now. I just do this job on Wednesdays and Fridays.'

I love the way he speaks, with that curious Cape sing-song which we once, in our foolishness, thought was comical. More and more I am susceptible to lurches of emotion, brought on by unregarded sounds, scents and phrases. We talk about my father and his colleagues. It was an age of innocence. (In retrospect all ages acquire innocence; it can't be possible that innocence is shed generation by generation, relentlessly.) His name is Ahmed Staggie, and I note it with delight. He is seventy-nine, the age my father would have been. He asks after my mother, who he remembers as a beautiful young woman. I tell him she has died recently, and he raises his hands up to his face for a moment.

'Shame. Would you like some tea, sir?'

He says this as though he is offering an antidote to grief.

Later, as I am reading about the mining company's adventures, Ahmed Staggie comes to me with a clipping, pasted on to yellowing paper.

'We were very proud of you, sir. I wish your father had been here still.'

He hands me the paper.

White Lightning
Cape Town boy fastest in world

In Mozambique yesterday a Cape Town schoolboy recorded the fastest time ever recorded for the 100 metres by someone under eighteen years of age.

There is a picture of me. My fair hair is standing up. I have my hands on my hips. My chest in the athletics strip looks thin. I don't tell Staggie that this white boy had been exploring Africa the night before. In fact, as I see myself, so young and skinny, I am wondering if the tropical heat hadn't affected the stopwatches.

My mother's car moves slowly on the homeward journey. I fear that it is going to come to a stop, but it keeps going towards the mountains, which are buried in cloud today. The bay is dark.

The files show that Consolidated Mining have been involved in many legal battles, and won them all. Questions have been raised about corruption, but the public good has always been cited, with success. I can't win.

I swing through the gates and park under the trees. There is nobody about. The old dairy is empty. I call out but there is no response. I go to Piet's cage. He is sitting in his box. He will not come down. There is blood on the ground, terrible amounts of it, on which a crust has formed in places. This is now being invaded by ants; columns of black and brown ants, which are – as we know – well-organised creatures.

Something appalling has happened.

It takes some time to find out what it is, from the police, from Lena and Bessie, and from Witbooi. The baboon has torn Zwelakhe's right arm off, and the boy has bled to death. Zwelakhe – Witbooi says – was trying to give the baboon some nuts.

26

It's cold. The rain is moving from the north in ranks, driven by the wind.

I have loaded up the old car with blankets, ground sheets, a tarpaulin and food. The windscreen wipers don't work well, but still we leave the gates of Nooitgedacht steadily and resolutely. From the farm cottages smoke rises to be doused immediately by the rain. The water is puddling on the track, and I wonder how the ants are doing.

We skirt the town; a few people huddle outside the shops under the extended tin roofs, but otherwise the rain has killed all hope. From the car park in the sand dunes I trudge down the beach carrying a huge load on my back. I am like the Jewish peddlers who used to roam the countryside. My father, of course, has written about them. Some went on to found immense mining houses. Perhaps even Consolidated Mining, who are taking control of my farm with unstoppable energy. The test drilling has produced a fine white powder, which is now, under the influence of the rain, coating the house and orchard and the Old Dairy with what looks like make-up.

The grey waves are huge. The wind is holding them back so that they rise and fall sharply, their crests dispersed by the wind. Gulls cry in their cold-hearted fashion. Here on shore the rain and the mist are so low that the tops of the sand dunes are obscured, but out to sea, some miles away, a filtered light is striking the water, forming a silver island within the bay. The water there reminds me – uninvited thoughts have been assailing me over the past, desolate weeks – of the dimpled silver teapot my mother produced on special occasions. Where the sun strikes the sea it is exactly the colour of silver after it has been cleaned, but not yet polished. It has a sort of muted brilliance, full of promise.

I climb up the dunes from the beach, until I can see Daisy's shack. I wait for a few minutes. There is no activity, but wisps of smoke rise from it in a doomed ascent. I approach, bowed under my load of domestic comforts.

'Daisy?'

There is a pause. Water is running off my bush hat and on to the linen suit, which I have donned. The handover seemed to me to demand some formality: trade goods, barter, peace. The hardboard door, attached by wire hinges, is pulled aside, and Thandi's face appears. Her hair is disordered; the corn rows are coming apart; *sportive woods run wild*, I murmur to myself.

'Thandi, hello.'

She goes back in. Daisy comes to the door.

'Daisy, I brought some things for you and the children.'

She opens the hardboard door fully so that I can enter, stooping low, almost crouching. The older woman is there too, and the baby is in the cot from the farm. I lay out my goods on the floor.

'Thank you seh,' says Daisy, quietly.

'No, no. I am so sorry about Zwelakhe.'

She doesn't look at me, and the little girl stays close to the older woman. Daisy pours me some tea as I sit on a white patio chair. The fire in the corner makes the air in the main room thick and pungent. My eyes are running. The older woman busies herself with the supplies, putting the food into fruit boxes behind what must once have been a plastic tablecloth, decorated with intertwined sunflowers, which remind me of the promiscuous parrot motif of the Paradise Club. *A slize of parrots' eyes*, I say, in a Dutch accent.

As the older woman lifts the tablecloth, I see a sparse larder behind, a few tins neatly arranged, a bag of sugar, some maize meal and a tomato. In a metal basin is some part of an animal. I give Daisy the money. It should be enough to keep her and the two children for a year or more. She takes the wad, held by a rubber band, without looking at it and puts it in the pocket of her housecoat. She doesn't thank me.

'I am going away,' I say. 'Overseas.'

I point in the direction of the turbulent ocean. The older woman speaks to Thandi who goes out into the rain. Now we are sitting, silent. The fire spits into the dense air.

'Daisy, can you tell me what happened to Zwelakhe?'

She doesn't answer.

'Did Witbooi take him to the baboon?'

But she doesn't speak.

'Daisy, baboons love small children.'

Now a man comes into the shack. He has a plastic bag over his head and shoulders, and he is wearing a torn track suit top in green, which reads *Castle Triangular Series*. He shakes my hand in a three-part action. He is drunk; already the shack reeks with the smell of fermenting grain.

'Who are you?'

'I am the father of Zwelakhe.'

I look at Daisy for confirmation, but she stares downwards.

'We have suffered a big loss,' he says.

His eyes are yellowing.

'I have given Daisy some money.'

'Not only Daisy has suffered. I am the father.'

'I must go now.'

I stand up, but he does not move from the doorway. He is small, but I have to stoop. He is still holding the black plastic bag over his shoulders.

'If you want to come over and see me to talk, come to the farm. Goodbye, Daisy.'

He moves out of the way at the last moment. Thandi is standing in the rain outside.

'Goodbye, Thandi.'

'Goodbye.'

But now the man has come out of the shack. He grabs me by the arm, just above the elbow. I feel the blood stir; he has gone too far: he is a black man.

'Let go of my arm, please.'

'We have suffered. We are suffering.'

We are about to suffer. We shall suffer. We shall have suffered. We shall have been suffering. We should have suffered, conjunctive. We should have been suffering.

'Let go.'

Now two other men appear from the dunes. They are very young. One is a boy of about fifteen, who is holding a heavy stick with a knob at one end, rounded like the ball held by the claw of my mother's drinks cupboard.

I wrench my arm free.

'I am going home now. I will be there at my house if you want to talk. I can help you.'

We stand for a moment in the rain. Thandi is crying. The boy suddenly hits me on the ridiculous bush hat with the stick and I fall. When I get up they are standing over me. Daisy comes out of the shack and shouts at the first man, who speaks to her harshly and raises his arm. She goes back inside.

I run for the beach. I am hampered by the wet suit, but my legs are full of power, the power of flight, for which I have been training ever since that tropical night thirty years ago in Mozambique.

I rise up over the sand dunes and then down through a valley. The rain has made the running easier by crusting the sand. I am flying. Up and down one more sand dune and I am on the beach. The water's edge is firm. I leap over kelp and stranded blowfish and mussel shells. They will never catch me. My legs are pumped full of emergency supplies of blood. But then I see a group of four men coming down the beach towards me, the fugitive. They are sharing a piece of sheeting against the rain. The boy, followed by the other two, is closing. I slow to a walk, hoping to make a break for it, but the boy shouts at the men, and they fan out so that I am driven towards the sea. As they come closer, I sprint for the water.

Because of the coolness of the rain-drenched air, the sea feels warm. I run up to my waist and then dive into a breaker. As I emerge from this mountain of water, another huge wave follows and tumbles me over, so that I am rolled towards the beach again, where the seven men are wading. I duck under another wave which contains ropes of kelp torn from their moorings, and I begin to swim out towards the Georgian silver sunlight in the bay, which is intermittently visible as I rise to the top of the enormous waves. As each wave breaks, the north wind sends a flying curtain of spray back towards the open sea. I look back and see the men still standing on the beach. Perhaps they think they have killed the golden goose with their impetuosity. I don't know. I'll never know.

I am beyond the breakers now, swimming steadily, breast-stroke. My plan is to swim far out of sight and wait until night falls, perhaps an hour away, and then to come ashore in the dark. I turn towards the beach, but the waves are so high that I cannot see the beach itself, only the sand dunes behind. I keep swimming. Out in the bay the sunlight now extends from the sea to the mountains beyond, so that they are glowing, although back at the shore, far away beyond the breakers, the sky is thick and dark. The luminous mountains are draped in the lightest imaginable purple, a floating, trailing cassock of vapour.

It is hard work swimming into the swell, but the wind is propelling me onwards and I keep going steadily – I have a rhythm – swimming out to where my father nearly caught the biggest Red Steenbras ever seen, swimming out into the bay, towards the dull silver ahead, and the luminous mountains to the south.

Dear Norm,

I have now remembered my brilliant idea. (My fax of two or three weeks ago.) Baboons love small children. They have a well-documented tendency to try to protect them. My father wrote about one such incident.

I now see that what was missing from my film treatment, *Surfing with Baboons* (working title), was something less conventional. So here is what I propose: Trying to force the hero to surrender, the opposition kidnaps his small child from the home of his estranged wife. They are holding the child in an anonymous apartment building. The hero discovers the location, but cannot gain access. Instead, he reaches an apartment two floors below, and the baboon climbs up the outside of the building to rescue the child. (Obviously we will need a previous scene which involves the baboon and the child meeting.) The tension and the pathos of the baboon climbing down clutching a two-year-old to its chest will be very, very powerful. (Shades of King Kong, non?) Needs work, but what do you think? I am excited. At the moment my phone line is down. There has been a small fire. I am proposing to come home soon.

Yrs

James

I find, swimming along towards the sunlight, that my mind is free. I think that I must speak to Valerie, and make my peace with her. I must wish her good luck with Pennington who has left his wife and moved into Oahu Court. I guess that Pennington was trying to resolve a tricky problem by introducing me to Valerie. I will establish contact with him and ask him to handle the sale to the mining company, which is offering me a graded series of threats if I try to hold out. (Although I have no evidence to blame them for the fire in the Old Dairy.) And I need Pennington to keep the bank at bay and pay off various people in local government and the farm-workers' union. I have no one else to turn to. I will apologise to Pennington for my harsh words. I will plead jealousy, which will exonerate me, because human weakness is universally understood, even exalted.

I swim now, surprised at my own strength. It seems that I can't stop. Maybe death is a journey, after all, and this is the first leg. This is training, the endless water without boundaries or landmarks a presentiment of what it will be like to die. Of course a fish or a dolphin or a Right Whale could read these marks in the ocean, but to a solitary swimmer they are not apparent. Now, I laugh, remembering that whale navigation isn't all that terrific either. *We know bugger-all about whales.* Maybe the whales, subject to the phyletic memory, are keen to join their mammalian relatives on shore, while I am obeying the imperative to join the dead: Matt and my mother and Zwelakhe.

The mountains have become dark shapes, the shreds of their episcopal vestments suddenly lost. The sea ahead, the direction in which I am headed, is dulling, as if someone – perhaps our cook, Carrie – is breathing on the silverware.

Now I could safely head for land. My pursuers will have gone home. Still I swim on. My arms are heavy but I have achieved an understanding with the sea; each rise on the swell and fall on the other side seems to propel me onwards, away from Africa.

Dear Ma,
    You were right. You used to say that they would drive us into the sea.

I must have been in the water a few hours, because the sea is now dark. Wine dark. The water begins to throb; it is the noise of a boat's engine, and then I hear voices, shouting. I see the side of the boat: on it is a pictogram of a whale spouting and the words *Whale Watch*. I am fully aware of being hauled from the water, and conscious that in my sodden suit, with the torn pocket, I look ridiculous.

Valerie was on the boat which picked me up. It was returning from a sighting of a pod of whales, with healthy young, rounding the point, going who knows where.

27

Piet sits regally in the passenger seat. It's not yet dawn, but the sky out to the east, beyond the bay, is glowing in preparation. Yellow clouds like bunting run along the ridge of the mountains. In the last few weeks, the air has become ever colder and the clouds over the mountains more dense. I don't go to the beach any more. In fact, I have left the farm only once in the last ten days.

We rise up into the mountains, leaving the bay behind. We are headed for Noupoort, the village of the baboons. The clouds have come down and we are in a thick wet mist, so that all sense of place is lost. At times I am not sure if we're going up or down. Rows of trees, a squatter camp, a few farm buildings, pass by the window but too briefly and indistinctly to place them in the landscape. They have the quality of those dreams in which you never quite get the point of what's going on. Piet, unperturbed, dozes. He is a baboon pasha. Who knows what luxurious dreams he has? I stroke his hand, and his fingers close for a moment on mine.

It's been a week now. Lena and Bessie and Witbooi have gone. There is still some muted life down at the cottages, but the children hide when I pass. Yesterday I had to turn away a party of the elderly who came for tea as arranged. I gave them each a jar of counterfeit Nooitgedacht Honey in recompense. They commiserated with me on the unreliability of staff in these parts. Mice have begun to forage boldly in the shell of the Old Dairy. They have nibbled the sacks of flour so that small pale pyramids are forming on the floor. These mice are boldly striped, cheery, Wind in the Willows creatures.

I have been down at the police station. I have told the sergeant that I think they should be investigating the possibility that Zwelakhe was deliberately placed in the cage with the baboon. I have asked to see the statements which describe the circumstances of his death, the witness statements, but none is available. I am, instead, being prosecuted under health and safety regulations and also under the Dangerous Animals Act. Pennington is going to buy them off. He is dealing with the sale of the farm: the mining company is buying it at a greatly reduced price.

In hospital, where I was kept overnight, I discovered that I had swum just a mile, almost into the mouth of the little port, where Whale Watch has its headquarters and Valerie has her flat. Valerie has been to see me, to explain that she and Anton had genuinely been trying to break it off. Also, a date has been fixed by the police for a vet to come to the farm to destroy Piet.

I try to take comfort from the fact that young male baboons are usually accepted into a strange troop after a period of violent subjugation by the dominant males. But I am not sure how reliable my father's information is. Piet must take his chances. We have no other option.

The mist clears as we descend into the valley of the apple trees, and closes again as we begin to rise towards the second ring of mountains which enfold the baboon village. If I hadn't been this way before in sunlight, I would not have turned up the rock-strewn road into the thick mist. The drive between the narrow cliffs is disorienting. It takes an hour to cover the last ten miles beneath the wet rock walls. Suddenly the road widens and we have arrived. The first cottage is only just visible. There is no sign of the old woman who is the guardian of the place. I back up to the start of the nature trail and listen for the baboons. But the air itself is too wet to carry sound and even the insects are silent. I have a roll of dried peaches, so big that it could almost be a prayer mat. Piet is reluctant to leave the car – perhaps it's just the wet – but I coax him out with the peach roll. I break off a piece and give it to him. He eats it quickly. He has had no food for twelve hours. I undo his collar and then I throw the rest of the roll into the thicket. As he bounds off to find it, I run for the car, start it up and drive off into the mist as fast as I can in these difficult conditions.

After half an hour, I turn back. It's a tricky manoeuvre in the narrow pass. Just before I arrive back at the village, I see Piet sitting on a rock near the road. He is bleeding from the head and back. One of his orange eyes is missing. This side of his face is deeply gashed and his lip has been severed so that it hangs in flaps.

'Come, Piet, come, my boy.'

He walks towards me. One of his hind legs is dragging. He whimpers and puts his arms around me.

'Poor boy. Come, Piet.'

I take Roos's cattle gun from the car. Piet stands shivering as I shoot him in the head on the blind side. I heave his beloved body with difficulty down the rocky slope towards the river. The mist and the scrub take it.

If I could speak I would say that I too, like so many of my countrymen, am a murderer, but the limits of my language have met the limits of my world.

London

A motorcycle messenger – his name is James Kronk, forty-seven years old – sits in a park finishing his sandwich. Today he is eating a chicken tikka sandwich. More often he opts for a bacon roll.

The spring weather is encouraging the dark London clay to produce daffodils and crocuses. The daffodils are plump, on the point of flowering. The crocuses are white and purple, and subject to daily desecration by dogs. Also there are mushrooms beneath the trees; they are ink caps, small ragged soft consumptive mushrooms, which grow in nervous clumps. The ducks, always on the scrounge, waddle from the pond to see if there's anything going.

Kronk often has his break here. He used to read, now he simply stares, but with no indication of boredom. He spends as many as twelve hours a day roaring around London on his Suzuki Bandit. Themes preoccupy him. For instance this morning he picked up from an office near the Dickens House in Doughty Street and delivered to a lawyer near the Old Curiosity Shop. And soon after he delivered a tape to an address next to the cottage where Dickens's mistress once lived in Islington. It was a Dickens morning.

He would have liked to have seen the state of the roads in Dickens's time: horse manure, cobbles, perhaps even mud. He spends a good part of the day looking down at the surface of the road and this is one of the reasons that he seldom falls off. He looks at the road, and he looks at the wheels of the vehicles ahead of him, to get an early warning of what they are intending. He also looks out for white lines, holes in the road and slicks of diesel. All of these can be dangerous.

Another theme is industrial buildings. Two days ago he spent almost the whole day between loft apartments, design studios, and canal-side conversions, all located in former industrial buildings. He has noticed that these buildings house a certain kind of person, a person who thinks that the big open spaces and cast-iron window frames and bare bricks and a view of mercantile water are an expression of their own openness. And indeed the receptionists in these places are more friendly and cheerful. If he needs a pee, they barely hesitate before pointing the way, even though his leathers, his visor and his tabard – *City Flyers* – are usually filthy.

A couple of weeks ago Kronk had a delivery to the Zoological Society in Regent's Park. He asked politely if he could go and see the baboons for a few minutes, through the back door of the offices, but they told him that Solly Zuckerman's baboons were removed years ago. He wanted to explain that he had had a baboon himself once, but he couldn't find suitable words. Later that day he found himself, uncannily, at Windsor Safari park. The day had a distinctly zoological leaning.

Another of his recent themes was academic. He swept around a corner in Bloomsbury past the curiously alert stone lions at the back door of the British Museum, through a road layout which demanded that he lean right and then left sharply, before rounding the square to stop at one of those university houses with large, white, paper Japanese lanterns visible from the street. Cheap and effective lighting. Classics. Here he picked up a padded envelope which had to be in Oxford by noon. It was a thesis. He particularly noted Dillon's, the Senate House, the Royal Academy of Dramatic Art, and the medical school of St Mary's, Paddington, having just passed one street north of Queen's College, Harley Street. In Oxford he dropped the package at St John's College and stopped off to buy a Trinity College – his old college – tie. He was served with impeccable courtesy, although his face was grimy. The tie is dark blue, with diagonal stripes of a brighter blue.

Almost every day he is able to trace a romantic theme. There is a house near Harrods where he used to see a girl called Jenny in a tiny flat on the top floor, and in Chelsea just off the King's Road is a basement flat where he had a girlfriend called Jill, and behind the Sainsbury's in Cromwell Road he knew a girl called Ulla. And others. Quite a few. He was something of a bok in his youth.

Now Kronk has finished his sandwich. He walks a few yards to the bin. Not everybody bothers. He throws away the plastic triangle in which the sandwich came. He avoids looking into the bin. From the top-box on his bike, he removes a small can of enamel paint and a fine brush which he picked up earlier in D'Arblay Street. He begins to paint on the petrol tank. He thinks the white paint looks good against the racing green.

Just then the park keeper appears. His eye-sockets are deep and dark. One day his eyes will be so far inside his head that he will have difficulty with lateral vision. He is carrying a motor-driven strimmer.

'Time goes quick, dunnit?' he says.

He says this as if he has only just noticed and wants confirmation. Kronk nods.

Over near the swings, only one of which is still attached, the park keeper starts the motor by tugging violently on a cord.

Kronk's walkie-talkie, attached to his jacket, blares: ''Allo. You got two personal messages. One's from a Ulla who wants to see yer, and the other's from a Norman, who says they like it but they prefer a chimpanzee to a baboon. I fink that's it. Fuck me, you're a quiet one. That's it. Over.'

'Okay.'

Kronk continues to paint. It takes him some time to get it right. He still has the far side of the tank to do. Some of the other riders have started to paint their call signs on their bikes:

TommyMiddlefinger; *Skidmarks*; *EatMyDust*; *OrganDonor* and so on; scatological, demotic, humorous.

Kronk's call sign is more lyrical, and possibly more evocative: *White Lightning*.

Acknowledgements

For my information on baboons, I am indebted to Barbara Smut's *Sex and Friendship in Baboons* and I have referred to Solly Zuckermann's works. I have also read Eugene Marais's books on baboons and Leon Rousseau's account of his life, *The Dark Stream*. My own father did write a book called *Animal Chatter*, which I remember with great affection.

My interest in baboons was sparked in Botswana a few years ago, when a baboon fell out of a tree and landed, mortally wounded, beside me.

I would like to acknowledge the unfailing support of Roland Philipps, my editor over a number of years. Sometimes the literary life can seem hard and lonely and not a little obsessive; Roland has always been to hand. My agent, Michael Sissons, equally, has helped me immeasurably.

Sceptre
21 Classics for the 21st Century

GHOSTWRITTEN
David Mitchell
'Remarkable' *Observer*

CARTER BEATS THE DEVIL
Glen David Gold
'Electrifying' *Independent*

SCHINDLER'S ARK
Thomas Keneally
'Extraordinary' Graham Greene

THE LONG FIRM
Jake Arnott
'Truly fascinating' *Guardian*

BARCELONA PLATES
Alexei Sayle
'Terribly funny' Douglas Adams

THE MYSTERIES OF PITTSBURGH
Michael Chabon
'Astonishing'
New York Times Book Review

THE SOLDIER'S RETURN
Melvyn Bragg
'His masterpiece' *Sunday Times*

NATHANIEL'S NUTMEG
Giles Milton
'Magnificent' *Independent on Sunday*

LE TESTAMENT FRANCAIS
Andreï Makine
'Superb' *Scotsman*

WHITE LIGHTNING
Justin Cartwright
'Hauntingly brilliant'
Independent on Sunday

WHAT I LOVED
Siri Hustvedt
'Breathtaking' *Independent*

AUGUSTUS
Allan Massie
'A great achievement' *Scotsman*

COLD MOUNTAIN
Charles Frazier
'Magnificent' *Observer*

McCARTHY'S BAR
Pete McCarthy
'Hilarious' *Sunday Times*

HEAVIER THAN HEAVEN
Charles R. Cross
'A joy to read' *Observer*

DOCHERTY
William McIlvanney
'Intense, witty and beautifully wrought'
Telegraph

COLOUR
Victoria Finlay
'A delight' *Sunday Telegraph*

FRED & EDIE
Jill Dawson
'Triumphantly good' *Sunday Times*

PETER COOK: A BIOGRAPHY
Harry Thompson
'Unputdownable' *Guardian*

RESTORATION
Rose Tremain
'A tour de force'
New Statesman

INGENIOUS PAIN
Andrew Miller
'Astoundingly good' *The Times*